# Here's Where She Meets Prince Charming

## KRISTIN WRIGHT

OWL HOLLOW PRESS

Owl Hollow Press, LLC, Springville, UT 84663



Here's Where She Meets Prince Charming




Library of Congress Cataloging-in-Publication Data
Here's Where She Meets Prince Charming / K. Wright.
— First edition.

Summary:
Seventeen-year-old Natalie has it all: stellar grades, a passion for theater, and a good shot at a swimming scholarship at her dream college. Her only problems are socially—the tall and buoyant body that benefits her in the pool has only ever intimidated boys at school. But when the enigmatic new kid shows up, their connection is instant, and he is a mystery Natalie is determined to crack.

ISBN 978-1-958109-58-8 (paperback)
ISBN 978-1-958109-59-5 (e-book)

*To my parents, who gave me the great gift of books.*

# One

*M*y name will be in the top spot.

*My name will be in the top spot.*

*Please let this "manifest" thing not be total BS.*

Mrs. Murchison always taped the final cast list to the auditorium door at seven a.m. the day after callbacks. Emails would be later. Anticipation made my head buzz: I'd read lots of other cast lists in high school, but this was my last chance to see my name as the lead part in the spring musical. And I deserved to get it. I'd never sung better in my life. Ten feet of faded hallway linoleum stretched between me and the list.

I halted, suddenly certain my name would not be in the top spot.

Like a bad omen, Max Finney stood between me and the list. A sour taste rose in my throat. What the hell was Finney doing in the same area code as a theater cast list? I would have liked to do my celebrating—or crying—alone. Instead, I'd have to spar with the guy whose first language was Insult.

Arriving students crisscrossed the hall, yelling morning greetings. For half a second, I thought about melting into the coat-shucking crowd and looking at the list later, but I was cursed with curiosity, and I couldn't stand to be derailed by douchelords. Finney peered at the sheet of paper. Why would he care?

"Hey, Tree Trunks," he greeted me. "I would say you look lovely this morning, but you know." He squared himself between me and the list. To read it, I'd have to get within a foot of him and read it over his head. I most definitely was not going to do that.

Ugh. Max Finney was one of those guys who compensated for lack of height with weightlifting and snark-rage. We'd met in seventh grade. I was six inches taller then: already five foot eight at twelve years old. "Tremayne?" Max had said, after the teacher said my last name and turned her back. "More like Tree Trunks—check out the size of those thighs."

He and his buddies had snorted with pleasure at his astonishing cleverness throughout the class. It stuck for a while, though Finney was the only one of that original crew who still called me that infantile name.

"You got the teapot part," he said, finally moving to the side. "Good thing. That costume should be big enough even you can fit in it."

The teapot. I didn't get the lead. No pretty dress. No opening number. No kiss at the end. No last curtain call in this, my last play in high school. I kept my face neutral, knowing Finney wouldn't see the gut-kick of disappointment unless I let him.

Not that the teapot was a surprise, deep down. I'd tried to convince myself this time would be different, but nope. I always got the part of the old lady, the one whose hair had to be sprayed silver. I leaned closer to check. There it was: "Mrs. Potts: Natalie Tremayne."

I tried to tell myself Mrs. Potts was better than not being on the list at all.

It didn't work.

Amelia Buchanan's name was in the top spot. She got Belle, the part I'd really wanted. Of course. Amelia had yards of shining chestnut hair and a killer body. She'd had the lead last year in *The Music Man* as well—despite having a reedy singing voice and a tendency to say her lines without inflection. Amelia and I didn't run in the same circles outside the theater clique, but we got along fine within it. It wasn't her fault she'd gotten the part.

Finney hung around, leaning against the cinderblock wall to watch my reaction for some emotion he could spin into pain.

I stayed on the offense, refusing to let him. "Is that Axe I smell? And why are you here, anyway?"

"Try not to faint from excitement," he said, giving me his professional smirk. "I got the clock part. So we'll get to hang all semester. It's your dream come true, Tree Trunks."

"You're going to be Cogsworth?" How had I missed it? I checked the list again. He wasn't lying. Shit. "You? In a play? Don't they take away your future frat privileges for that?"

"My parents and Mrs. Stick-Up-Her-Ass got together and said Duke wouldn't take me if I didn't 'broaden my resume.' Besides, Amelia is in it. I hear she's lonely after she and Carranza split. And Amelia Fuck-Can doesn't stay lonely for long."

Nice. Finney amazed me with his ability to cram maximum offensiveness into minimal wordage. Mrs. Stick-Up-Her-Ass would be Mrs. Stevenson-Cash, the school's college counselor.

Amelia, even if single, would not be making any beelines for a guy who twisted her name into something that gross.

"Um, yeah, I admire your optimism," I said, raising one eyebrow.

"Whatever, Fat Girl." He stalked away, taking his overpowering pine forest smell with him.

I pushed away the uninspired insult and decided his retreat meant I'd won.

Alone, I checked the cast list again to see who'd be playing Chip, the little teacup who was supposed to be my son. Tyler Donaldson. I didn't recognize that name. He must be from the middle school. My brother might know him. Mrs. Murchison liked casting younger kids to play the children in our musicals—added "verisimilitude," she said, and also created kind of a farm team of kids who'd then be more interested in being in theater when they reached high school.

One more glance. The Beast/Prince: Campbell Adams.

Campbell Adams?

Oh, God, it wasn't Noah. Noah Jones had played the lead sophomore year and junior year and had condescended to disclose his plans for how he'd play the Beast as noble and kind of constipated. Noah lived for theater. He enjoyed using giant words and giant gestures and planned to go to some conservatory for college next year—or straight to New York City if he didn't get in. Where was Noah's name? He'd been cast as the candlestick. He'd get to sing "Be Our Guest," but he wouldn't get to kiss the girl. Not that that part would bother Noah in the slightest. Campbell would bother him, though.

Campbell transferred to our school a year and a half ago, for our junior year. Nobody knew anything about him, except that he swam on the school team with me and had supposedly gone to some private school near here before. He stayed quiet and kept to himself. Smoking hot, taller even than me, and into theater apparently. That was everything I knew. Campbell'd always seemed nice to me, when he spoke at all.

I'd stood here too long, reading my name over and over. Shifting my backpack off my shoulders and onto one elbow, I whirled around and met a wall. I caught a whiff of clean laundry and men's shaving cream and found my nose an inch away from the hollow of a male throat. Campbell Adams, the inscrutable Beast himself, stood there peering over my head at the list. Not many people could see over my head. I jumped backwards against the actual wall, losing my grip on the backpack.

"Oh, excuse me," I said, though he was the one who'd boxed me in. "I didn't know you were there."

"I'm sorry," he said, keeping a careful distance between us. I'd literally bounced off his noticeably muscled chest. Heat flooded me as I realized I'd been staring at that impressive part of his anatomy for too long. I moved my gaze up to his face and scrambled for something to say.

"Congratulations," I said, dodging to the side and scooping up the backpack. "You got the lead!" I had no idea he'd tried out for the Beast. He'd make a good one. Definitely mysterious. He could more than pass for a handsome prince. He'd be way more brooding than Noah, whose out-there personality and commanding voice dominated every room he entered. Also, I'd seen Noah's Beast-as-constipated face. It was… perhaps not the right acting choice.

"Uh. I see. That's good, I guess." Campbell moved closer after I got out of his way, to read the list. He glanced at me. "Congrats to you, too. I heard your audition. You should have gotten Belle."

"Thanks, but whatever. Girls like me never get the lead."

"What do you mean?" he asked, eyebrows drawn together.

"You know, because—" His face stayed blank and mystified. Wow, very polite. Somebody raised him well. "Oh, nothing. Anyway." I stared at him, my curiosity at the breaking point. "You didn't try out last year. For *The Music Man*. I didn't know you…" He hadn't come anywhere near the musical last year, not even to work backstage. I, of course, had played the old lady with sprayed gray hair and an Irish accent.

"Right. I didn't. Try out, that is. Last year." He closed his mouth, apparently finished talking.

I could move a conversation, but not without any help. "So, I'll see you tomorrow night at rehearsal?"

"Tomorrow? Yeah. I guess so. If…" He'd finished reading the list but didn't move.

"If? Mrs. Murchison isn't big on 'if.' She's going to expect you to be at all the rehearsals."

"Right. So, see you."

"Later."

He remained motionless, offering no more conversation but not doing the normal things to make clear the interaction was over. I waited a few seconds, but he didn't say anything more. I inched toward the stream of passing students. Two sophomores from the swim team yelled my name and I grabbed the excuse to move.

"So. See you," I said, giving him a stupid little wave and diving into the river of bodies.

God, how awkward. I hated awkward. I yanked up my unbalanced backpack and threaded my way to the language hall. Campbell had an odd effect on me. Off the top of my head, I couldn't think of any other recent time I'd had trouble thinking of something to say.

On a whim, I stopped by Mrs. M's classroom. She sat at her desk, scanning what looked like Facebook on her iPad.

"Hey, Mrs. M."

"Good morning, Natalie. I assume you saw the cast list?"

"Yeah. That's actually why I stopped by." Dammit, I'd worked hard for that part. I worked hard for everything, and most of the time, it paid off. I wanted her to tell me why I didn't get Belle, and I needed it to be based on something I could control. Something fair. "Was there something wrong with my audition for Belle? Did I not sing it well enough?" I asked.

Mrs. M's mouth worked a bit as she struggled for an answer. My chest deflated. It would not be something I could control. "I thought you were perfect for Mrs. Potts. You'll blow them away when you sing the title song."

"Right, but Amelia had the lead last year."

"I've always seen you more as a character actress, Natalie. And of course, Amelia looks just like the Disney cartoon. She and Campbell look so beautiful together—him so fair and her so dark."

Noah and I would have been an even bigger contrast, given that I was blonde and he was Black, but okay. I understood what she was saying. "It doesn't have anything to do with the fact that I'm five-ten? And not skinny like Amelia?" Proving my acting skills, I got that all out with the perfect tone of polite curiosity.

Her inability to meet my eyes gave her away. I'd lost the part because I was tall and had a layer of swimmer's fat. She didn't work hard to hide it. "You're not a classic ingénue, no. You have a maturity about you. A physical maturity, even. No one else can play the adults like you. You're one of the most talented actresses I've ever had at this school."

Hurt made my throat tight. Talent's great, but beauty is better. Nice lesson, Mrs. M. I couldn't leave it alone. I poked my own bruise. "So, if I lost, say, thirty pounds? Would I be an ingénue if I were thin?"

She fiddled with the papers on her desk, clearly desperate for me to leave. "Well, dear, you'd still be so tall, even then.

You are majestic. Statuesque. There's nothing diffident or shy about you. You're a warrior queen."

A warrior queen. That might be great for a superhero from DC or Marvel or even a streaming drama about cutthroat lawyers, but in high school, warrior queens ranked well below homecoming queens. While I'd never fixated on homecoming queen as a personal goal, it's not much fun to be reminded just how far out of reach it always was.

The first bell rang. I gave her what little smile I had left. "Great. See you, Mrs. M."

AFTER SCHOOL THAT AFTERNOON, my mom caught me with one hand in the kitchen pantry, reaching for the Cheez-It box while I scrolled my phone.

"Natalie, how many times have we discussed this?" she asked, dumping her purse and keys on the table. "Wait 'til after dinner. You don't need to eat so much processed food."

Again with the weight. If it weren't for the adults around me, I'd be fine with my body, but God, it never stopped.

I towered over my mom: all my height came from my dad. She kept to low-carb salads with the all-encompassing focus of a movie blockbuster supervillain, but never exercised at all. I, on the other hand, spent an hour at the school's swimming pool every morning before eight a.m. My muscles have muscles. I got the school record in the fifty backstroke as a sophomore. My grades were good enough to get me into lots of colleges, but not good enough for a free ride to take me out-of-state. Swimming, on the other hand, could be my ticket to cover the tuition. Coach had already introduced me to a couple of people.

"So I ask again, Mom. Why do you buy the processed food if you don't want me to eat it?"

She dropped her gaze and her hand fluttered, straightening her sweater hem. She had the willpower to ignore the cookies and the Goldfish and the peanut butter crackers, but she wasn't without sympathy. "Your dad and brother like it. What can I do?"

"You don't fuss at Ethan for eating Cheez-Its."

"Ethan is a bottomless pit. And underweight. I still have to buy him adjustable waist pants, and he's in seventh grade."

"Nice double standard, Mom." I got a handful of Cheez-Its out of the package and stuffed three in my mouth, making sure she watched me crunch them.

"I just worry about you, honey. That's all."

"You worry I'm too fat. Well, get in line," I said with more heat than she deserved, letting her have it for Mrs. Murchison and Finney as well.

"No, that's not… it's just that…" She closed her mouth, the apology already written across her face.

"I know, Mom." My mom and I were once really close. I remembered trailing her as she worked in the kitchen, getting little squeezes every now and then, the feeling of safety in her orbit. Sometimes I hated that I could still read her mind. Knowing what thoughts were in her head made me want to return the hurt in kind. "You don't want to have to watch me swim looking like a Beluga whale. Don't worry. Come stand next to me. Think how skinny you'll seem by comparison."

"Natalie. That's enough. I'm not going to let you talk to me that way."

"On a happier note, I got a part. Mrs. Potts. She's the teapot."

Sunshine and relief broke over her face. Watching her shift from chagrin to anger to mom-rooting in less than thirty seconds reminded me of the man behind the curtain in Oz. We'd done that one when I was a freshman. I played Auntie Em.

"Congratulations! Is that the part you wanted?"

*No.* "Yep. It's a good one. And I get to sing the title song solo."

"You'll be amazing at that, honey. Your dad and…"

A text came in. Marisa. Saved by the bell. Er, the ding. Or whatever.

"Thanks, Mom. I have homework. See you." I rounded the corner scrolling my phone. Marisa and I had known each other long enough for shorthand.

Her text read: CAMPBELL ADAMS?

I hit FaceTime as I took the stairs two at a time. Marisa picked up as soon as the call connected.

"Bruh." Marisa's very traditional mother hated how often she used the word "bruh." "That is not a gender-neutral term, sweetie," she'd say. Her mother's disapproval only meant Marisa used it twice as often, calling everyone from me to her new puppy Bruh. The dog thought his name was Bruh. It probably would be.

"Yep. Campbell Adams." I shut my bedroom door and sprawled on my bed.

"Noah threw a massive fit in Physics fifth period when somebody asked him about it. He slammed his book shut and said he'd heard Mrs. Murchison had been bribed." Marisa rolled her eyes. Her mother and Noah's mother were best friends and had shipped them for years until it became more than apparent the match was destined to fail.

"Did he? It'll be good for him to have to watch somebody else take a curtain call after him."

"Oh, Noah will watch, all right. Campbell is supernova hot. Noah keeps a mental Hot List of every guy in the building. I think he even put teachers on it." She used the hand not holding the phone to pile her dark hair on her head in ever-fancier top knots.

"You never know. Maybe Noah will get lucky."

Marisa snorted. "You don't think Campbell is gay, do you?"

"You don't?" I didn't bother to hide my shock. Adrian Barrett, who swam the backstroke like me, told me Campbell was gay back when he first joined the swim team. I'd never questioned it. I figured they shared a locker room.

"No way."

For the second time today, I struggled for words. "Come on, Riss. Adrian told me that. Ages ago. And besides. He's never dated anyone. Never looks at girls in swimsuits at practice, even though Annika Anderson chases him to the locker room."

"Uh, I'm telling you he's not gay. Did I see Max Finney's name on the cast list?"

"Yeah. I asked him about that. He was clear on his reasons: mainly to get with Amelia. As if. What I can't figure out is why Campbell auditioned. He wasn't in the play last year."

"Maybe Campbell wants to get with Amelia too. Bruh. It's possible."

"No way. Adrian swore he was gay. Why would he make that up? Maybe it's Noah he's after." Might be. Noah was very good-looking. And single, last I'd heard.

"Adrian's probably jealous." Marisa laughed as she lost her grip on her phone, so I got a good view of her dresser. Neat, as always. Marisa's mom still cleaned her room once a week.

"Anyway. I wonder if he can sing." If Campbell Adams was not gay, I would have to seriously adjust my thinking. He was beautiful. I'd been acting totally normal around a beautiful guy because I'd thought he was gay. If I'd known, I would have… what? Who was I kidding? I had no idea how to attract a guy.

"He must be able to sing. It's a musical, right?" Marisa asked.

"It is. He'll have to open his mouth. I don't think in a year and a half I've ever heard the guy say more than three words put together." I scanned my memory: Campbell, walking alone through the halls. Campbell, silently lining up for the blocks at swim practice. Campbell, never raising his hand in the class we'd had together last year. Then it hit me.

"Until today."

# Two

I arrived early and staked out my corner in the auditorium seats. We hung out in these seats, in the front, stage left, at every one of Mrs. Murchison's three-hour rehearsals. I'd never minded the long rehearsal time; it was great for studying when I wasn't needed onstage. I had four AP classes, and our class rank wasn't determined until the end of the school year. My GPA was still a work in progress, which meant my backpack gave even my backstroke-honed shoulder muscles a workout.

"Your parents must be so proud of how hard you work, Natalie," Mrs. Murchison said as she bustled around, scripts in hand. This first rehearsal would be music-free, so Arnold, the first-name-only musician who somehow made a career out of playing the piano for the musical and for Mrs. Murchison's choir classes, wouldn't be making an appearance today.

"Haven't asked them, Mrs. M. But thanks." I had no idea if I made my parents proud. To the extent I could appreciate their position at all, it was more that they weren't pissed off. I'd seen pissed off before—the time I got a B- on the reconstruct-a-chicken-skeleton group project in biology in tenth grade, and the time I skipped swim practice when Marisa couldn't stop crying after Drew Asquith posted the thing about "boobless stick figures". I hated to admit how hard I worked to keep them from having anything to criticize.

"Do you know yet where you're going to college?"

"Um." It was January. The final decisions didn't come until April. Mrs. M should know that—she'd been teaching since before I was born. "Not yet. I've been admitted to a couple of schools, but I don't hear from Berkeley or UVA until April."

"Oh, right. Right. Listen, Natalie, I'd love it if you'd do me a favor. The music teachers at our elementary schools have asked our cast to present scenes to their children at school, in costume, as we get closer. Can I put you down?"

Oh, hell. Me in a teapot costume singing at my old elementary school? Embarrassing, but whatever. It was theater. I'd signed on. "Um, okay, I guess."

"They're hoping to film it and use it for the promotional video for the school system."

Even worse. Immortalized as a teapot and shown in the video everyone watched at every major event in the school district, like graduation and freshman orientation. Even for someone with my Teflon personality, that would be mortifying as hell. Maybe I could figure out a way to get out of it later.

At that moment, Mrs. M lost her train of thought amid the noisy arrival of Noah Jones, who threw back the auditorium doors and stood in the doorway, framed and posed for notice.

"I'm ready! Let's do this!" Noah's voice rumbled deep and resonant. His voice surprised me every time, because though his perfect dark skin and striking eyes went with it, his average-to-skinny frame did not. He sang beautifully and had been a front and center in the choir for all four years.

"Don't know if you've noticed or not, Noah, but you and I are the only ones here, besides the underclassmen, of course." I gestured in their general direction. They'd be playing the pitchfork townspeople and the "Be Our Guest" plates and silverware. Their group had gathered nervously on the edge of the stage, feet dangling into the empty orchestra pit. Their leader, Amber Glass, had settled naturally into her position of authority based on her casting, as a sophomore, as the sexy broom with a line or two. She studied hard for her real-life role as the future Amelia Buchanan.

"Nonsense," Noah said, stepping out of his doorway picture frame to admit Amelia and Max Finney. Finney followed Amelia too close and only barely kept his tongue inside his mouth and his panting silent. She swept in before him as if his admiration were her due. "All we're missing now is our Prince Charming."

If Noah was trying to hide his jealousy and resentment, he had not succeeded. Then again, I'd known Noah since we were in children's theater together. His emotions had no insulation: always out front and loud and proud. He used the dramatic emphasis to cover a fair bit of struggle to find a place to belong. Because I knew that about him—not many people did—I could tolerate his quirks and occasional verbal woundings. Usually.

Mrs. M checked her watch. She hated tardiness.

"God. Give him a chance, Noah. He might be amazing," Amelia said, arranging herself so as to display her endlessly long legs on the stairs at the side of the stage and fluffing her masses of brown hair. "So. What's the tea? Where's he been all this time?"

"Not here. He's never auditioned before," I said.

"It's bizarre, is what it is. Sus," Noah said. "When was the last time a first-timer got a lead? Never happened." He gestured at the underclassmen. "Most of them have paid more dues than Prince Charming."

"There's no law that you have to pay dues in the chorus first," I said, without knowing why. Like Noah, I'd paid my dues—in the chorus—and had lost out on the part I'd wanted. He was correct: it was odd for a lead to go to someone who hadn't participated enthusiastically for years.

"Whatever. As if I'd have wasted time doing this bullshit before now," Finney said.

Noah, Amelia, and I stared at him. Finney had gotten a sizable part as a first-time auditioner too. If anything was suspicious about the cast list, that was. Maybe Finney had been telling the truth and the guidance department had intervened to help his college chances. His parents were rich. It was possible. Had Campbell struck a deal?

Finney preened with Amelia's eyes on him. She looked away. "Who knows anything about Campbell?" asked Amelia.

Everyone shrugged or looked at the floor.

"Doesn't say much," I offered. "Actually, he doesn't say anything. He's on the swim team."

"Oooh. I might have to come to one of those games, then," Amelia said. Amelia had previously confined herself to attending her ex-boyfriend's lacrosse games and those of his buddies on the football team.

"Meets. They're called meets." Could she be any more obvious?

"Whatever. Do they wear those little Speedos?"

Yes to the Speedos, but not the little ones. And yes, she could be more obvious, and she'd managed it. Finney cleared the thunderous expression off his face before anyone saw it but me.

Okay. Amelia would be glad to see Campbell arrive. Everyone else would be ready to have his head on a pike at first sight. I resolved to be friendly. He'd need it.

"Well, we can't wait forever for Campbell," Mrs. M said from the stage, checking her watch and counting heads. "I was going to do the read-through, but we have everyone here for Noah and Max's introduction scene. We'll have to get on stage and start blocking it out instead."

I wasn't necessary for that part. Amelia, Noah, and Finney, along with the bit-part underclassmen, went on stage to get organized. Mrs. M went into her pointing and yelling routine. This would take a long time. I pulled out my AP Physics binder and got comfortable.

The auditorium door opened softly. The bedlam on the stage covered the noise completely, and Campbell rushed in, stuffing his phone into his heavy backpack. He threw himself into the seat on the other side of the one taken by my backpack. "Am I late?"

"Yep. You'll want to watch that. Mrs. M is hardcore." She'd be pissed about having to skip the read-through. He'd already started off on the wrong foot. No reason to tell him—he already looked frazzled enough.

"Is she? Well, I'll try to be on time. Do I need to be up there?"

"No. The Beast isn't in this scene. Or very many of the big crowd scenes."

"Good. I need to catch my breath." He stretched out his long legs, almost reaching the seat in front of him. His jeans fit him well.

"Why? What were you doing that made you so late?"

"Just… stuff."

I hated it when people kept things from me. I had a lot of faults, but nosiness had gotten me in more trouble than the others. Until five seconds ago, I didn't care what made Campbell Adams late. Now it was the foremost question in my mind. I examined the evidence. His face glowed red, and his over-long golden-brown hair was slightly wet but combed, as if he'd recently showered.

"Where've you been? Swimming?"

"No. Job."

"What kind of—"

"Shh. We don't want to distract anybody," he said, gesturing at the stage, where Amelia stood watching us, her head cocked, hip out, twirling the end of a hank of hair around her finger. Mrs. M had to call her name twice to pull her back in.

"Right." I watched him pull binders from his backpack. AP Physics. Huh. I didn't know he took AP. He wasn't in any of my AP classes. He opened the binder and became instantly absorbed. I went back to mine.

Physics held my attention about four and a half minutes before I had to glance over. A lock of drying hair fell over his forehead, and from the sides, his darker lashes were so long that I couldn't imagine how he blinked without getting them tangled. I'd never noticed before. Campbell might be the best-looking guy in the school.

Still, there was some kind of… impenetrable shell around him. An exoskeleton of aloneness or separation or something. He never talked to anyone and cut off any conversation anyone tried to start. I'd tried, at the beginning of last school year. Junior year he'd been in my Shakespeare class. Nothing. One-word answers. Headphones whenever possible. He treated everyone the same: polite remove. Over the last eighteen months, we'd all given up. He'd kept his head down and his mouth shut, and we'd let him. Only now, since he'd put himself out there as the lead in the play, had anyone noticed him again.

As I stared without thinking, he looked up. A hint of a smile curved his lips before he caught himself acting like a human. He shifted in his seat and looked back down at his book, twisting away slightly. I didn't let up staring, hoping he'd look up again.

Mrs. M dismissed Amelia while she continued working on placement with the underclassmen. Amelia made a beeline for Campbell and sat down in the seat next to him. Almost instantly, he twisted away from her, back in my direction.

"Campbell, right? I'm Amelia. I've seen you at school, of course, but I don't think we've ever had the chance to talk."

I allowed myself a slight roll of the eyes. She'd never spoken to him because up until two weeks ago, she'd been the girlfriend of Joe Carranza, king of lacrosse and the richest asshole in a public school that had more rich assholes than lots of private schools. Campbell would have been wallpaper to her.

"Nice to meet you." His smile was brief and the minimum required, and then he turned back to his work, ending the conversation before its birth.

Undaunted, she leaned in closer. "We'll totally have to get to know each other better. We wouldn't want the onstage chemistry to be… awkward. We kiss at the end, you know."

He kept his eyes on his paper, but he bit the inside of his cheek. The cheek on my side. "Ah. Right. Yeah."

Amelia blinked. She would be totally unused to this lack of enthusiasm. She'd done the whole beautiful-girl thing all her life. Her mom had her in pageants until she realized it was tacky long after reality shows made the pageant moms look like rednecks. Amelia had been on the homecoming court every year, had been the star of a few local TV and print ads, and basically believed that her marketable skill was beauty. In my ugliest moods, I imagined her life topping out in a Hooters by the interstate.

Which was not only ugly but unfair. Amelia wasn't evil. She'd been raised to believe that she had only fabulous beauty to offer the world and that the guy she dated defined her worth. That wasn't her fault. Off the top of my head, I could think of ten less beautiful girls at our school who treated people a lot worse than Amelia Buchanan did, even so.

Most guys parted like the Red Sea when she walked into a room. Here sat Campbell, inches away from Amelia Buchanan's magnetic pull, as unaffected as if she were his mother, staring at a physics worksheet.

Marisa was full of crap. He had to be gay, or at least ace. Amelia had essentially offered herself up like a not-very-virginal sacrifice for a little extra-extra-curricular kissing practice, and nothing. No reaction. Nobody ignored Amelia. I glanced at the stage. Now it was Noah who watched as Mrs. M tried fruitlessly to get his attention.

Not that I really thought Noah would make any overt moves without good reason. Noah had been out and proud since eighth grade but tended to keep his dating life far away from our still relatively conservative high school. This was Virginia, after all, but in this major university town, we lived where the red state and the blue state turned purple. Noah might not be a stellar student, but he wasn't dumb.

Amelia hadn't given up. She leaned on the armrest between her and Campbell and tried another tactic. "So, Natalie, how's the swimming going?"

I gave her my candy-store sweet smile, the one I reserved for ladies at church. "You know what they say. 'Just keep swimming.'"

Campbell's lips twitched at that. I was sure of it. Amelia saw it too, and she redoubled her efforts. "You're on the swim team, right, Campbell?"

"Yes."

She waited. He didn't elaborate.

"What… um, what do you do on the swim team?"

Campbell looked up at her blankly. The obvious answer to that hung in the air, and I choked back a giggle. "I think she wants to know what strokes you swim."

"Free."

Now it was Amelia's turn to look blank.

"Freestyle," I translated. "You know, the crawl?" I mimed the motions.

Her face cleared. "Oh, right. Ugh. Y'all have to get up super early for practice, don't you?"

Nothing from Campbell. He waited for me to do the talking.

Fine. "Yeah. Practice is before school."

Huh. I had no idea Amelia sucked this bad at conversation. I guess she'd never had to learn. I'd help her out a little. Might be fun to see what Campbell would do.

"Amelia, what other extracurriculars do you do? Is this it?"

"Oh, no. I have the prom-planning committee. And student government. And I do some modeling." She gave Campbell a glance to see if he'd caught that. No reaction. He was a damn robot. "And I've danced Clara in the regional *Nutcracker* three years running. I also compete for the hunt club. Equestrian, you know." She flipped her hair in an expert manner while also managing to throw her boobs into sharp relief.

Interestingly, that move got a reaction. Campbell's face creased in consternation for a millisecond and then it was gone. What in the actual fuck? Amelia's boobs were un-ignorable. They were so spectacular even Noah sang the line from "America the Beautiful" about "purple mountain majesties" with a certain degree of respect when they caught his attention.

Finney and Noah came down and sat backwards in the seats in the row in front of us, excused while Mrs. M worked with the underclassmen, who were proving to be an unwieldy school of fish.

"What're y'all talking about?" asked Finney. He tended to double his Southern accent and deepen his voice when talking to girls. It came out sounding like a half-price Matthew McConaughey impression. Amelia didn't notice. Her eyes stayed on Campbell's face.

Now that he'd been surrounded, Campbell kind of shrank into his seat, a difficult feat for someone so large. He really didn't want all this attention.

"We were talking about my riding," Amelia said.

"Riding, huh? You like to ride?" asked Finney, odious suggestion dripping off every syllable. Amelia rolled her eyes but looked relieved to be back on her familiar pedestal.

"Careful, Max. Your tongue's hanging out and the floor's dirty. Don't think you want to lick that crap up," I said, gesturing down as Noah gagged theatrically.

"Sorry, Tree Trunks. I'm sure you're totally unacquainted with riding."

I rolled my eyes halfheartedly.

"Tree Trunks?" asked Campbell.

"Oh, Max has been teasing Natalie about that for years. You really need to come up with something more creative. It's totally old." Amelia, if possible, scooted in her seat a little closer to him. Finney scowled.

"But what does it mean?"

Dammit. He wasn't giving up. Fine. "It means, Campbell, that Max here assessed the size of my thighs back in middle school and determined that they resemble tree trunks. Isn't that right, Finney?"

Finney bit his lip. It's one thing to be a dick on general principles, and quite another to be called out for it in a group when, let's be honest, the nickname is cruel, and worse, stupid.

Campbell turned wide greenish-blue eyes my way. They distracted me for a second—dear God, the lashes on that boy—while I waited for him to drop his gaze to my lap to see if Finney's pronouncement was correct. He didn't. A range of expressions flashed there, most of which I couldn't interpret.

Then he focused on Finney and spoke slowly as if Finney had recently arrived from a non-English-speaking country. "You're kind of a tool, aren't you?"

The only sound was the shuffle of the underclassmen's feet on the stage.

Noah began slow clapping. Amelia's mouth opened in delighted surprise. Finney swallowed a huge ball of rage, saving it up for later. I'd need to make sure I wasn't around when it broke, though I felt bad for Finney's younger siblings if they were still awake when he got home.

I should have been delighted and appreciative, and I was. Those words even didn't cover it. I glanced at Campbell, who met my eyes. His expression was unruffled, but in his eyes lurked something protective, something caring, prepared to smack down any more tool-ishness. After a second or two, I caught myself staring and blinked, looking for escape. I piled my books on the floor by my seat and headed for the bathroom, the better to hide the source of the odd stinging at the corners of my eyes.

# Three

My parents aren't big on church, but my mom was raised to go every Sunday and we followed suit, me yawning, Ethan surreptitiously untucking his shirt when my parents weren't looking. I wasn't sure what I thought of God. I mean, I liked the idea of Someone up there watching over us, collecting all my dead pets and great-aunts so they'd be around to hang with if I got in a car wreck or something, but I never could figure out why He handed out what He handed out to each person.

Take right now. Marisa and I yawned as we changed out of our sweaters and leggings into our swimsuits for early morning practice in the stale-smelling locker room. We'd stripped off in locker rooms together for four years, and before that on our local swim teams, and before that at a thousand sleepovers at each other's houses, which meant we'd spent a lot of time in close non-sexual proximity with each other's virtually naked bodies.

Marisa had beautiful skin that stayed a perfect light tan color year-round, and those skinny legs with the thigh gap the jeans retailers and teen moviemakers would have us believe is totally standard for all women between twelve and sixty. Of course, thigh-gaps in nature go along with non-existent boobs, and Marisa was no exception, much to her loud and everlasting dismay. At the same time, she looked awesome in all her clothes and could eat whole Chipotle burritos without even so much as a temporary food baby.

She had no muscle tone and never developed any, despite swimming the same number of hours as me. Consequently, she swam her four events competently but never won any place ribbons. She hated that. Her dad hated it even more: he'd gone to our high school back in the eighties and had been a championship swimmer. It was a thing in their house.

We'd taken a lot of teasing over the years, because as best friends we couldn't have been more opposite physically. I stood as tall as the football team's quarterback. My shoulders were wide with muscle, the better to support my wingspan, and I had the layer of fat that made me more buoyant in the water. It puckered slightly where the spandex of my racing suit ended on my back. My thighs, to be fair to Finney, were hardly tiny, though they didn't jiggle and could probably kick some ass in a kick-fight. If there were such a thing as a kick-fight. They did kick a lot of ass in the pool and might be more than adequate to get me into a good college.

"Tell me again what he said to Finney." Marisa had already hung on every word of the rehearsal story from the night before but clearly hadn't let it go.

"You know what he said. I just can't figure out why he bothered. Finney's not a good enemy to have. He's sneaky as shit and guided by no moral code." I wrapped my long blonde hair into a tight bun to go under the swim cap. Marisa watched. She made no secret of coveting my hair, which was fine. I wanted her tan-able skin. We'd both have to live with the disappointment.

"Maybe Campbell doesn't know any of that. He's only been here a year and a half."

"Please. That's plenty of time to get to know Finney." I tossed my leggings in the locker without bothering to fold them.

"He's a lot bigger than Finney."

"True. Though I don't think that'll help much. Finney doesn't go in for brute strength."

Marisa pulled on her own swim cap. "Did you know Finney was in my homeroom in sixth grade? On the first day, someone bumped his elbow walking down the aisle and he burst into tears. Right out in the open where everyone could see him."

"Really? Finney?" I twisted and yanked and danced as I wiggled into my suit.

"Yeah. He actually was pretty nice those first few days of middle school. But Joe Carranza gave him so much shit for the crying he turned into an asshole overnight."

"Great. It's like Joe is patient zero in the Asshole Zombie epidemic. I can't see how Amelia can stand him."

"How was Campbell at rehearsal?" Marisa asked, changing the subject.

"I don't know how to describe him." I stood up and kicked the locker shut. "Like I said, it's like he's allergic to other people. No interest in any of us."

"He defended you."

"Um, Riss, he's been on the swim team for two seasons. He's never spoken to me before. He barely spoke to me last night. Don't get over-excited."

"Okay, okay." Marisa locked her locker.

"What's with all the sudden interest, anyway? You've been on the swim team with him for two seasons, too. And you have a boyfriend." Marisa and Ron had been going out for six months. He was a sweetie, slightly built, bespectacled, and devoted to her.

"But you don't. And you should. You'd look good together. Same amazing hair, both tall, et cetera."

"Yes, because all you need for a perfect relationship is to be physically similar. Everyone knows that." I snapped her shoulder strap against her back for sarcastic punctuation.

"Okay. I get it." She adjusted the hated rubber swim cap over her dark curls. "Whatever. He's hot. You ready?"

Outside the locker room the perfume of the indoor pool, chlorine and dank stale air, grew stronger. A lot of people say it stinks, but to me it smelled like satisfaction and future. The boys' locker room door on the other side of the pool opened to admit the last stragglers. Campbell towered over Luke and Adrian. Swimming in January was an inside sport, so nobody had much in the way of a tan, but the color of Campbell's face and neck differed noticeably from the rest of him. And while I was at it, I took a good long look at the rest of him.

As a rule, guys who swam had pretty good bodies. Swimming is a great full-body workout, though even Olympic swimmers usually have a softer physique than, say, a marathoner. Campbell had no faults. Not too thin, not too fat, tiny amount of golden chest hair, good posture, no gorilla arm overhang. The boys on our team revolted some years back against the tiny Speedos favored by gray-chest-hairs who were once hot and went for black suits similar to bike shorts that clung tight and left their chests bare. The look worked.

Dammit. I'd seen Campbell Adams in his swimsuit in this pool a hundred times before. Now Marisa had ruined all my peace of mind. With one sentence from her I took off down all kinds of ridiculous pathways where Campbell and I stood near each other, posing like a celebrity couple whose names get mashed together. I'd be wearing a fabulous dress that would show off my killer arms. I didn't have a date for prom yet.

Stop. Nothing had changed. Campbell had called a tool a tool. It wasn't a declaration of love, or even awareness that I existed. If anything, it proved awareness of Max Fucking Finney. After he said it, Mrs. Murchison had called us all up on stage and put us to work at the read-through. Conversation ended.

Coach Phillips blew his whistle, which meant lining up in our lanes for drill. Our pool had six lanes. The boys used three and the girls used the other three. We were divided into three tiers—fastest of each gender took the two middle lanes, the slowest on the outside. We practiced our starts by stroke and did laps for the first twenty minutes of practice. I swam in the middle lanes. Campbell lined up next to me but didn't speak. Some adrenaline-fueled urge to test myself, to compete even where it wasn't necessary, overcame me. I adjusted my goggles as he stretched his body in preparation for the dive and took the set position myself. When he took off, I did too.

We always started practice with the freestyle. I had a pretty good freestyle, though backstroke felt more natural for me. Campbell swam freestyle like a sea creature: muscles working so smoothly he created almost no splash. It was lovely to watch, especially from my underwater vantage point. I tried to keep up and lasted at his speed about two-thirds the length of the pool before the efficiency of his stroke, his height, and his power carried him past me. I let him go, admiring his kick, and allowed myself the enjoyment of the flip turn and the powerful push of my legs off the side.

On occasion I'd get all emotional if I took time to dwell on what swimming meant to me. The water always held me up. It didn't change moods or let me get away with anything. In the water, power lit up my muscles. I could do anything there, and improvement came easy if I worked hard. During the break as we climbed out of the pool after the warm-up laps, I imagined I saw an expression on Campbell's face that mirrored those thoughts.

He caught me staring, but I couldn't tear my eyes away. What the hell was wrong with me? I shook my head, marveling at my own idiocy, and mopped my face. I'd always avoided these stupid crushes-based-on-wishes before. When we practiced our timed events after the water break, I punished myself by driving as hard or harder than I did in the meets, hard enough for Coach Phillips to tell me to save something for the weekend meet. Exhaustion gripped me when it came time to haul myself out of the pool, dripping.

"Natalie?"

I turned around from the chair where I'd draped my towel. Campbell stood there, towel around his wide shoulders, green-blue eyes serious.

"Good swimming."

Huh? Campbell Adams never spoke to anyone at swim practice.

"Right back at you."

He stood there, wordless, for another second or two. Marisa pulled the swim cap from her head and came over to stand beside me, her curiosity raging no doubt.

"Did you need something?" I asked. He was so much bigger than me. Rare for a high school boy: how had I missed it?

"No."

"Okay. Um. See you. At rehearsal, I guess."

Without another word, he pivoted toward the boys' locker room. Class started in forty minutes.

"That was weird," Marisa said, unnecessarily.

"Yeah."

"Huh."

"Huh, nothing. We knew he was weird." I realized I'd been staring at the locker room door, as if further communications would be written on it in glowing paint or something. I forced my eyes away.

"We knew he was silent weird, not come-up-to-talk-to-you weird. Sorry. I shouldn't have come over. Maybe he would have said something else."

"Something else weird, probably."

"Probably."

A TWITCHY CURIOSITY plagued me the rest of the day. Who the hell was Campbell Adams? How had a guy that beautiful and, well, enormous, walked our halls for eighteen months without speaking or disclosing the first clue about himself? I marveled again at the inside-out world of high school: where it didn't matter if you really were beautiful, witty, or smart and where it only mattered if the right people thought you were. In high school, perception was reality. The emperor wears no clothes in grades 9-12.

Once I spent a rainy afternoon with my mom's yearbook, judging the attractiveness of her senior class. Amid the ridiculous giant eighties hair, I spotted a girl named Kimberly who gave Bella Hadid a run for her gorgeous money and said so. My mom, surprised, said Kimberly had been gawky and unpopular and no one thought she was pretty at all. I googled her and she'd gone on to become a soap opera actress after a career in modeling.

Campbell had caught Amelia's eye, but she'd demonstrated a total inability to find out the good stuff. Natural nosiness gave me the advantage there.

Operation Who Is Campbell began now. I refused to ask myself why I needed to know.

I started after first period by locating his locker, hardly difficult sleuthing because the school alphabetized them. I lurked fifteen feet away as he opened it, exchanged books, and then banged it shut without speaking to Claire Agee, who checked her eyeliner at the locker next to his without glancing in his direction. Not a single clue. He had nothing taped inside the door. No pictures of girlfriends. No product logos. Nothing indicative of any personality at all.

Third period I had study hall with Coach Phillips. Normally I sat in the back with Noah and Annika, where Noah entertained us with scathing descriptions of everyone he'd ever met, but today I pointed at my bag, shrugged my shoulders as if weighted down by a crushing load of homework, and took a seat in the front row across from Coach. Once I had my books spread out convincingly and the whispering in the back corners had settled down into a drone, I caught Coach's eye.

Coach loved me. I'd never be rude to a teacher, but Coach took the time to talk to us about our lives and was the means to helping my Berkeley dream come true.

To get things rolling, I asked a question I already knew the answer to. "So, who's going to be swimming in the medley relay this weekend?"

He looked confused. "Well, you, and Annika, and Hayley…"

"Right. No, I meant for the boys."

The confusion continued its reign. I had to admit the question was out of character for me. I'd never shown a sliver of interest in the boys' side of the pool before, and besides, we'd swum several meets already. Though scheduled at the same time, the girls' meet and the boys' meet were separately scored. We didn't need the boys to have anything going on to be state champions ourselves.

"Uh, Adrian is doing the back, Sam has the breaststroke, Trace the fly, and Campbell has the freestyle. Same as last year. And last week, for that matter." He narrowed his eyes at me, lips pursed, while he tried to figure out what I was up to.

Hell with it. So he'd figure it out. Not like he'd announce my interest during the pre-meet pep talk. "I saw Campbell's freestyle this morning. Looked pretty good."

The divot between his eyebrows disappeared, to be replaced by a repressed smile. He might as well have said, "Aha!" He pretended we were having a serious conversation. "It does. I wish all my swimmers could swim that well with their head in the clouds like he does."

Gah! He was helping me with my ultimate goal.

"Head in the clouds?" I asked, shoving down my excitement and putting on my most casual interested expression, eyes wide, blinking in a "spill" kind of way.

"That boy's always thinking about something else. Don't think he gets much sleep. Asked him about it once—he said he had a lot of stuff going on in the evenings."

Campbell couldn't have meant the play. We'd only had the first rehearsal last night. He must have other "stuff" going on in the evenings. But what? A job?

"Well. I guess it's a good thing he can swim when he's tired." I tried to remember if I'd noticed any dark circles. Nope. As I pondered, a brilliant but reasonable question came to me. Oh my God, I was so good at this. "Did he swim for his old school? I don't remember him."

"I think he did. Saw it on his sheet when he tried out."

"Oh," I said, so casually flies could have been dropping off me dead, "what school did he used to go to?"

Caught. Dammit. Coach's mouth went into a well-worn sardonic position he used to convey knowledge that someone was trying to pull something. "Interested, huh? Answer is, I truly don't know. One of the private schools hereabouts. We don't swim in the same league. Can't remember the name of it."

He smiled now, the big kind with lots of teeth. "But good luck to you, finding out."

AT LUNCH, I recovered my contraband phone from my locker. Most people flouted the rule and hid them in their backpacks or pockets, but I'd always kept mine in my locker. Phones were the whole reason the school kept the lockers in use, even after Covid. I pulled up Safari, ignored the flow of bodies passing me, and had a list of private schools "hereabouts" in no time flat. Not that it helped much. Our county was full of horse estates and vineyards and other playgrounds of the rich, and that type liked their kids to go to private school. Combine that with a bunch of organic-everything university families, and the place was a breeding ground for expensive alternative educations. Before the bell rang for my next class, I had a list of local private schools with swim teams (seven) and had run a fruitless Google search for Campbell Adams at any of those schools. I ran out of time before I could do any more checking.

And besides, there was a way to find out what I wanted to know with much more speed and accuracy than Google.

Sixth period I had Physics with Kameron Moody, the queen of the tea. I'd been called nosy, but I couldn't begin to approach the NSA-data-collecting nosiness of Kameron Moody. Kameron chose her friends for their memories for detail and had once managed to locate and circulate a copy of the divorce complaint of our principal's wife, which alleged impotence and "mental abuse." She would know about Campbell. All I had to do was figure out how to ask her without causing her to direct the suction power of her info-gathering vacuum on me.

"Hey, Natalie." Kameron flopped into her seat and pulled her notebook out of her bag, stuffed full with all kinds of things that probably had nothing to do with academics.

"Hey, Kameron. Listen, do you know Campbell Adams?"

"I know who he is," she said, twisting her finger in her long red ringletty hair. I did an internal eye roll. Right. That was like Steph Curry saying he played a little basketball. "Why?"

"I don't really know him. Coach Phillips, you know, swim team? Coach was wondering where he swam before here. Asked me in study hall. You know, because he's a transfer. I didn't know, but I figured you would." Close enough to the truth.

She preened a little, blinking her white eyelashes with feigned reluctance. Nothing made her happier than to be at the center of information-sharing. "I think he went to St. Anselms. Fancy rich kid school. I heard he was a scholarship student there. I wonder if they cut off his scholarship and that's why he had to come to public school. Or…"

Kameron closed her mouth, watching the teacher get organized. We had one more minute before the bell. Whatever else she wanted to say must be juicy because she tried hard to pretend there was such a thing as discretion. I gripped the edge of my desk in frustration. I'd have to cut her a break before her head exploded from the unaccustomed secret-keeping pressure.

"Or what?"

"Well, I also heard there might have been some legal difficulties. In the court system. Apparently around the time he left St. Anselms, this girl he dated left for homeschooling. My dad is friends with someone whose kid goes there. I heard they got in some massive fight, and he hit her and her parents took her out while the charges were pending."

"He hit her?" Oh my God. A sick rush of horror raced through my stomach. Oh God. That's what I got for sticking my nose where it didn't belong. Knowledge I'd never wanted in a million years.

"That's what I heard. Supposedly their families kept it super quiet."

"As always, Kameron…"

The bell rang and Mr. Davidson brought his book down on his desk with a deafening crash to silence us.

"Your powers amaze and astonish. Thanks," I whispered. Kameron gave me a brief "it's nothing" wave.

I didn't hear a word Mr. Davidson said as I sat there, trying to imagine Campbell raising his hands to threaten some nameless high school sophomore. After the first blast of horror passed, I couldn't make the picture assemble itself. He was so quiet, so walled off. As I sat there, though, that quiet took on a malevolent quality. Maybe he'd been ordered not to have any contact with any of his peers because of the violence, but he had to go to school, so they'd worked it out somehow. Maybe Coach knew more than he let on and had bribed the court to suspend his assault sentence and let him swim for us so we could win the boys' medley relay.

*Maybe you should submit a fantasy story to the creative writing contest.*

There had to be more to the story. Campbell was, I assumed, seventeen or eighteen like the rest of the seniors. He'd been fifteen, sixteen at the most, when he finished his sophomore year at St. Anselms. Did people arrest fifteen-year-olds for domestic assault? I supposed they did, but more to the point, I just couldn't reconcile Campbell with violence. It didn't pass the sniff test. Wouldn't the school have known about the charges if there were any? Would they have let him enroll? Kameron hardly ever got any wires crossed, but this time she had to have gotten it wrong.

# Four

"Well, he's done it," my dad said, putting down his phone to crack eggs into a bowl in our kitchen on Saturday morning. My mom hated cooking—too much temptation—and my dad did it whenever enough of us were around to eat. On Saturdays he made what he called his Traditional English Breakfast—eggs and sausage with fried toast and grilled tomatoes. His parents still lived in Reading, near London. My dad had moved to the U.S. for college and stayed. My mom told us over and over how she'd fallen hard for his accent. Most of my friends backed her up. English accents didn't do it for me. Not at all. I associated them with Dad-ishness.

"Done what?" asked my mom, not looking up from the *Washington Post* in the adjacent family room. "And who has done it?"

"Larry Bryant. That's who."

I stretched my feet out onto the ottoman across from Mom. My dad sat on our county school board. This fact, and how some teachers acted around me because of it, embarrassed me. Dad's thing was programs for the gifted. That was his issue. No bias at all—both Ethan and I had been in the gifted programs since first grade. Dad wanted to see more "rigor" added to the curriculum. I prayed I would graduate before he was successful. Sucked to be Ethan, though.

"Larry Bryant? The pastor?"

Dad rinsed off his eggy hands at the sink and pointed at the phone, as if it would share the news for him. "Yes. Larry Bryant the pastor, at that enormous Love of Jesus church in that building that used to be the Circuit City near Staples. Always been more about rules than love, in my opinion. He's here in the local paper, announcing a run for my seat this fall. He's been interviewed, attacking me as 'lax' and saying that he is a stronger force for the moral education of the children in our schools. Abstinence. Sexual purity. That is his platform. Ridiculous. The train left that particular station some decades ago, but he's got a big pulpit. And, apparently, friends on the staff of the paper."

"Natalie, does your school hand out condoms?" asked my mom.

"Not that I know of." Oh God. They weren't going to interrogate me about my need or lack thereof for condoms, were they? Kill me now.

"They do not, for your information. This is still Central Virginia," pronounced Dad, with his professorial enunciation. He taught calculus at the university, which always surprised my friends, who thought he looked like a classics or literature professor. Many of his students went on to become high school math teachers. He knew an annoying amount about the high school climate. More than I did. I'd have preferred him to be a little less aware of what went on in my school.

"So what is Bryant's problem? He wants them to *not* give out condoms more emphatically?"

"He wants them to teach abstinence. Specifically, pointedly, and mandatorily, to every single ninth grader in the county."

"I guess he's never heard that some people discover their private parts earlier than that?" As soon as the words were out of my mouth, I regretted the opening I'd given them. Fortunately, they were both too wound up in politics mode to have paid any attention.

"Bryant has children, doesn't he?" Mom asked, folding the paper.

"Two. Two, I might add, who attend private school. As if a man with no children in the school system is in a good position to sit on the board that governs our public schools."

"Are his kids virgins?" I asked.

"That would be convenient, wouldn't it, if I could prove that they were not. I think it's likely, however, that they are. It says here that one is six and the other is eight." My dad had stirred the eggs, in his distraction, far past fluffy and into clunky. He dumped them into the pan and promptly forgot about them. I jumped up and went to go watch them. Better to eat clunky eggs than no eggs.

"So, what's the big deal, really?" I asked, keeping the eggs from burning while my dad dealt with the toast and griddle. "Won't all that make him easier to beat if he runs against you?"

"You'll have to read the article, Natalie, and see if you think he'll be easier to beat."

My mom had pulled it up and read it. She tossed her phone onto the sofa in disgust. "I see what you mean. He's implied that you—oh, look!" She snorted. "That our whole family is less moral and upstanding than he is."

"Ethan's twelve. How can he be immoral?" I asked, carefully leaving myself out of the hypothetical.

"Exactly. This is hardly a den of iniquity. Our family is just as moral and upstanding as his. The election isn't until November. That's an age. No one will remember this article by then." My dad, having recovered his equilibrium, took the spatula from me and resumed his breakfast mastery. I backed off, letting the master work.

"Can't you use the fact that his kids don't go to the public schools he wants to represent?" Mom asked, coming over to pinch off a piece of finished fried toast.

"He's gotten out in front of that. Told this reporter that he loved the public schools dearly, a proud product of them himself, he says, but that he couldn't justify putting his children into schools in the condition they're in. That I've let them get in. Can you imagine? He's defined the debate."

"Does he want to improve them?" I asked. What did they need that they didn't have? We had great amenities, all the sports teams, AP classes behind every rock, kids going off to the Ivy League every year.

"No. He wants smaller government and lower taxes—less money to the school system. His kids don't attend because he prefers for them to attend religious schools. He'd most likely cut the public school funding if he gets in. So, good chance his interest has nothing to do with kids and everything to do with taxes."

"Oh." All that seemed unlikely to me. The voters in this county—so dependent on the state's flagship university—were all about education. They'd smell that BS a mile away. But it had Dad upset.

"I know it seems stupid to you, Natalie. But apparently, we're to be scrutinized. Please keep your nose clean."

Affronted, I put my hands on my hips. "My nose is so squeaky clean that it glows. I could lead Santa's sleigh. What are you talking about?"

My mom put a hand on my arm. "He's only saying this spring won't be the time to skip on Senior Skip Day or participate in any ill-advised senior prank." She smiled mischievously. "Might want to wait on any public orgies until after the election."

"Mom!"

"Just kidding. And you knew it. You're a good kid, but now is definitely not the time to surprise us with some late-blooming rebel thing. And if Ethan ever gets out of bed, we'll be telling him the same thing, too."

Unbidden, Kameron's wild story about Campbell came to mind. I hadn't been able to confirm any criminal charges via Google. If anything Kameron had said was true, Campbell definitely fit the description of someone they'd prefer I not add to my friends right now.

LATER THAT NIGHT, Marisa and I lounged in the glassed-in den of Noah's family's upscale house, ignoring our red Solo cups. Marisa didn't care for alcohol, and my dad's words from this morning about keeping my nose clean stuck in my head. Noah had invited us, and about half the senior class, to this party earlier in the week as soon as he found out that his grandmother was in the hospital and his parents would be gone until they got her settled back in her house.

I'd been to parties like this dozens of times before—Noah had a sister living nearby who was old enough to buy us beer, and he never hesitated when his parents left him alone. His house, with its huge kitchen, massive family room TV, and open floor plan, screamed entertaining. I suspected his parents knew he did this and didn't care. Never before had I felt any urge to moderate my already-fairly-exemplary behavior, but my dad's worried face kept popping up in my head.

As always, I marveled that Noah was willing to expend the effort to clean up the house after one of these gatherings. Already, spilled beer made the floor in the kitchen sticky and gross, and people ate stuff directly out of the pantry, dropping crumbs everywhere. Much as I'd love the popularity boost that would come with hosting an illicit party, I had no inclination to stay up all night afterwards scrubbing scuff marks off the floor and dispelling the odor of cheap beer with enormous quantities of Febreze.

Annika from the swim team came over and sat with us. "Hey, Natalie. Saw Campbell Adams talking to you the other morning. Bizarre. I thought maybe he'd had his tongue cut out when he was a child."

"Seemed to be in fine working order to me."

"I'd like it to be in fine working order on me," Annika said with a wink. Someone called her name from across the room. She stood again and left.

I caught myself scanning the crowd for Campbell's height and gold-streaked hair, then shook my head at myself. Campbell never came to parties or socialized in any way. I'd be more likely to see my dad's prissy school-board opponent than Campbell here.

Even though I knew he'd never show, I let myself imagine it for a second. He'd come in, looking around for someone he knew. I'd stand up casually to make it easier to see me. He'd come over, grateful for a familiar face. We'd talk, maybe touch arms. I'd double over laughing at something he said, and then…

Noah threw himself down on the sectional beside me and let out a tortured sigh of dismay. "Don't tell me. You're overcome by the sadness of this crowd. Half of them are sophomores, and not the good-looking ones. Well, maybe that adorable blond one over there."

"You're just fishing, Noah. Fine. It's a great party. You've outdone yourself. You've got both Amelia and Joe here, and if you're lucky, they may get into a screaming match before long."

Marisa snorted. Noah glanced into the dimly lit kitchen, where Amelia stood with Amber Glass from the play. Amelia put her arm around Amber, who seemed upset about something. As we watched, Joe approached with his entourage of suck-ups. He stood, flexing his muscles, while waiting for Amelia to see him. One of his posse hit on Amber, separating her off from Amelia. She took notice of Joe and tossed her hair. Apparently they planned to make sure the other knew how indispensable and desirable each was. I hadn't heard who dumped who, and frankly, I didn't care. Last year, I would have cared. The fact took residence in my head and unsettled me. It made me feel like a boat untied from the dock, motor not yet started.

I shook it off and returned my attention to Noah, still clearly in need of propping up. I loved Noah, but he tired me out at times. He was a confusing mix of overconfidence and insecurity, and I had to wait for cues to know which side I was dealing with at any given moment. Sometimes if you grabbed hold of the wrong end, you got stung.

"What's up with you, anyway, Noah?" asked Marisa. "Anyone good here for you?"

"Alas. The pickings are slim at this school. I believe I've already picked all the fruit off the trees in my orchard." He wiggled his eyebrows, marring his overdone solemnity so that Marisa and I convulsed in giggles, his intent all along.

"Oh my God. Only you could get away with saying something like that," I said, gasping for breath.

He snorted, pleased at the praise. "You're right. Don't try that at home. I took a long look at our new Prince Charming, but more's the pity, he doesn't grow on my tree."

Marisa fell into renewed giggles. I sat up straighter, then caught myself. "What?"

Noah peered at me, coiled like a cat. I forgot he never missed clues like that. Shit.

"A-ha," he drawled. "At long last the Siberian tundra is unfreezing? I'm not the only one who noticed our fine specimen of manhood, apparently." He stretched his feet out onto the cushioned leather ottoman, satisfied the mouse was in his grasp.

"Wait," Marisa said, recovering herself. "So once and for all: Campbell is not gay?"

I elbowed her in the ribs.

Noah's beautiful white teeth showed—he was enjoying himself now. "Not."

"How do you know?"

Insulted, Noah glared at me. "You must be joking. Surely you realize the… *apples* around here are scarce enough that I could hardly allow myself to be careless enough to mistake a zucchini for one."

"A zucchini," Marisa said, engulfed once again in giggles. She worshipped Noah.

At this moment, I hated him for having me at his mercy. The best defense was a good offense. "You hit on him, didn't you?"

"I may have made a few inquiries."

"And?"

"And he informed me, very politely, that he wasn't interested in guys. I'd say that means that he is decisively not gay. Then he dashed off somewhere."

"Aw, Noah. I'm sorry." Marisa reached across me and patted his hand. Marisa was way too sweet to manage Noah, who was about as cuddly as a mountain lion, or to anticipate his swings.

"Don't be," he said. I realized where he was going almost at the same time as he put it into words and winced. "It'll make it far more pleasant to get him kicked out of the play. He never should have been cast. Some spectacular BS went on with that casting. And now I won't have to suffer a single minute of guilt."

"What are you planning?" I narrowed my eyes at him.

"I spoke to that toad, Max. He apparently dislikes Mr. Charming. Seems to believe that if it weren't for him, Amelia Buchanan would even now be writhing under his squat little body. While I seriously doubt that his belief is rational in the slightest," he said, inclining his head at the continuing dance of seduction Amelia and Joe performed in the kitchen, "it certainly won't hurt to have an ally in my undertaking. When I proposed as much, Max jumped at the chance."

"Don't be a dick, Noah," I warned, growing angry. "You auditioned for the part, and you lost out. Campbell got it, fair and square. The chips fell. Be gracious." Where the hell had this come from? Since when did I care about whether Noah planned to liquefy someone?

Noah snorted. "I prefer to think of it as returning the world to its normal axis." He reached over and patted Marisa's hand, and then mine, in a caricature of Marisa's earlier gesture. "It's nothing personal. He's a fine piece of ass. If you, my dear Amazonian Ice Queen, are interested, by all means take your shot. I wish you well. It might even be some consolation. But he should not have gotten my part."

# Five

AFTER SCHOOL ON MONDAY, I got stuck at the end of seventh period when my AP Lit teacher stopped me to say my paper on Flannery O'Connor didn't aim high enough. She gave me a chance to pull my grade up to an A with a revision, but it meant I rushed to my locker with extra homework. Already running late, I caught Campbell, loaded backpack slung over his shoulders, headed for the parking lot.

"Wait! Campbell!" He heard me and turned around, stepping away from the double doors so as not to impede the determined flow of bodies out. I skidded to a halt, closer to him than I'd intended to get, yet it would be way too awkward to move back.

"Hey, Natalie." Something in his expression relaxed, but not all of it. A kind of tenseness remained in the pinch of his eyes.

This close I had to look up at him, unusual for me. "Aren't you going to the rehearsal? You're not going home, are you?"

"What rehearsal?"

"You know, the extra singing one in the choir room? Mrs. M sent the text yesterday. It's right now and then we have the regular one on the stage at six like usual. Didn't you remember?"

"Uh. No. I forgot. And I... I can't make it to the singing one."

I stared at him like an idiot. "You can't make it?"

"No. Why? You think I need it?"

Oh, crap on a cracker, his smile. Was he flirting with me? I had trouble processing. It made me stammer. "You... no. You have a great voice. A natural. But Mrs. M..."

"I'll try to be there for the six o'clock one."

"You'll try? Campbell, it's important. You know Mrs. M will have your head, right?"

"I'll talk to her." Worry darkened his face.

"And you know that..." I hesitated, unsure whether to tell him about Noah's plans. I might still be able to talk Noah out of that. I glanced at him, trying to decide, and stopped short when I saw the look in his eyes. Human, interactive, different from the opaque mask he usually wore.

"What?"

God, his eyes, above his blue shirt, were so... I wanted so badly to push back the lock of hair that fell forward and tangled in his eyelashes. I reached for it before I could stop myself, then awkwardly pretended to rub my own nose. I shook my head. I'd lost my mind. "Nothing." I smiled at him as he kept checking the increasing flow of outgoing students. "I guess I'll see you at six. Just... don't be late."

He touched my shoulder lightly, then pulled his hand away. "I'll see you then." He disappeared out the door, racing toward the parking lot.

I hesitated by the door, watching my less-confused classmates talk and joke and rush off to other things to do.

What had just happened?

It had been a long time since a guy had touched me in anything other than jest or by accident. I'd kept my mouth carefully shut during that awkward conversation with my parents about condoms, but I'd seen the business end of one before. Once before, at a party after a swim meet last year. Gabriel was a year younger and just as inexperienced. The whole thing was totally devoid of any kind of feeling. A business transaction, mutually beneficial to divest us both of unwanted virginity. Not painful or awful, but… freakishly intimate for two people who didn't know each other all that well. Gabe and I still saw each other on the swim team, and he had a cute girlfriend named Caitlin who followed him around and held his hand every chance she got. He'd been kind.

There'd been nothing since then. No boyfriend. Most guys liked me and enjoyed my company, but high school guys weren't known for confidence, or early growth spurts, and way too many of them still had hairlines at or below my eye level. Although I'd have been okay with going out with a guy shorter than me, it seemed none of the guys felt the same. I worried that was a rationalization. What if none of them cared about my height and just didn't feel any attraction toward me at all?

And then here was Campbell, touching my shoulder for no reason. Already I'd attached way more importance to it than he could possibly have intended. No doubt he thought I was irrational to act like a rehearsal was so important that he couldn't miss it.

Which reminded me that I was now late for that exact rehearsal. I pivoted and rushed toward it.

MRS. M HADN'T BEEN HAPPY when Campbell hadn't come to the early rehearsal in the choir room, even though Noah, Amelia, and I did most of the singing in the show. Campbell's absence improved Noah's mood substantially, and he offered, like an overeager altar boy, to sing Campbell's part in the few songs he did have. Mrs. M allowed it, and Noah gave it everything he had. She made him understudy for the Beast for the duration of the rehearsal.

While we waited for Campbell in the auditorium at the second rehearsal, Noah grinned while Finney repeated the full "There once was a man from Nantucket" limerick as if he were the first person ever to appreciate its cleverness. Campbell arrived twenty minutes late. This time, Mrs. M took him aside and spoke to him for a few minutes. Noah broke into one of Campbell's songs. It got no reaction from Campbell but an approving smile from Mrs. Murchison.

"I'd be happy to be the understudy full-time, Mrs. M. You know, in case Campbell has car trouble—or whatever he had tonight—again. You know I always want to help in any way that I can," Noah said, fully involved in his portrayal of an earnest, freckle-faced, Depression-era sidekick.

"That's fine," Mrs. M said, patting her pockets for her glasses, which were on her head. She hadn't heard him, but Noah would take that as an official blessing on his new status as understudy. "Natalie was nice enough to volunteer for the elementary school outreach program. Do I have any others willing to put on a show for the children? And for the video—that's definitely a go now. Noah? Max?"

Everyone stared at her. Most of us would rather die. It was one thing to do the play on a stage. Pieces of the whole always seemed sillier without context. Singing and dancing as a teapot or a candlestick in front of a classroom of squirmy children while your old fourth-grade teacher stood by, smiling tolerantly, tested the limits for most high school students.

Noah found his hoodie zipper extremely interesting. Amelia stared unblinking at the floor.

Finney spoke up. "I'm busy that day, Mrs. M. So sorry." Under his breath, he added, "No fucking way. I wouldn't do that even for a week locked up with the entire Homecoming court. The naked Homecoming court."

Mrs. M gazed out into the sea of indifference and sighed. Eventually she found her glasses and moved off to work with the underclassmen on the pitchfork-waving townspeople scene. Noah, Finney, Campbell, and I did not appear in this scene. Campbell, clearly uncomfortable, opened his backpack and started unloading his stuff. Noah grinned at him, with Finney sitting alongside him, prepared in his troglodyte way to assist Noah in whatever way he could. Theater, at our school, caused the formation of some deeply unusual alliances. Outside this auditorium, Finney and Noah wouldn't speak to each other. Here, they were the best of buds.

I glared at Noah, making clear I knew what he was up to and didn't appreciate it. He shrugged as if he had no other choice open to him and continued to stare at Campbell without speaking. Minutes stretched. Campbell tried to pretend not to notice, keeping his eyes on his book, but he never turned the page.

I couldn't stand it. I put my books on the floor and stood, stretching. "Campbell, do you mind? There's something I need to talk to you about." Relief showed in his eyes, along with confusion, because really, what the hell could I have to talk to him about? Nevertheless, he stood and followed me to the back corner of the auditorium. Noah sat on the edge of the stage, never taking his eyes off us. I sat down. Nope. I wouldn't put it past Noah to be able to read lips. I stood up again, causing Campbell to do the same. As confused as he must have been, he didn't say a word. I knew Mrs. M liked for everyone to stay in the auditorium so we were available when she decided to change scenes, but the pitchfork one was complicated and would take time. We had a few minutes.

"Noah's going to keep on with his ludicrous first-grade staring contest if we stay in here. Let's go out into the lobby."

He nodded.

Outside, with a door between us and Noah's unblinking glare, we sat down on the benches that ran along the outside wall where people sat during intermissions.

"Okay," I began, somewhat breathless. "You should know that Noah wants your part, wanted your part before you got it, and he'll attempt to make your life pretty miserable if he doesn't get it."

"Why?"

"I don't know if you've noticed or not, but Noah dreams of a career on the stage."

"That's pretty unlikely."

I must have given some start of surprise because he laughed—actually laughed—and went on. "Oh, I don't mean Noah's not talented. He's got a great voice, and if anyone can make a candlestick believable, it's that guy. It's just unlikely overall, you know. Think of all the thousands and thousands of people who want to be movie stars or Emmy winners or whatever. It's like getting struck by lightning, don't you think?"

After this unusual speech, the longest ever heard by human ears out of Campbell Adams' mouth, I had no idea what to say. For a second or two, all I did was stare at him, grinning like an idiot, happy he spoke like other people.

"If nobody tried it, there'd be no movies," I said, unable to resist poking him even after such a rare opinion-offering. "No plays. No TV. It does happen to some people."

His eyes widened and he bit the inside of his cheek. "Sorry. Of course it does. Do you want to be an actress?"

I considered saying yes and watching the mortification spread, but in the end, Campbell was so alone and in the sights of attacks from so many directions I didn't have the heart to tease him. "No. You're absolutely right. The odds are terrible. I kind of hope Noah does make it, because he's not much of a student and he might end up serving fries or folding clothes at Target if he doesn't. But no. I want to be a geneticist."

Campbell's face relaxed into a smile. "Like DNA and cloning and stuff?"

"Yes to the DNA. But not for cloning or any weird science-fiction stuff. Not anymore, anyway." My mouth kept moving even as I marveled at what I was about to say to this virtual stranger. I dug my fingers into the carpet covering the bench but couldn't stop myself. "When I was little, I wanted to breed my own dragons."

Had I ever thought he was brooding? His face was as sunny and open as Noah had been pretending to be before. "I get that. I liked dragons, too. I'd still like to have a dragon."

We smiled at each other for a few seconds, while I wondered wildly what it would feel like to touch his face. His stubble, so light-colored as to be invisible, might still feel rough under the palm of my hand. I blinked, horrified at myself, and forced myself to sound at least ten percent rational. "Now I want to cure disease. I want to study why some people get Alzheimer's and some don't. I want to figure out what makes one cell mutate into cancer when ten million don't."

What was it about Campbell that made me want to say every uncool thing I'd ever thought?

"I want to be an engineer. Build bridges and improve transportation. Or I did…" He closed his mouth, his posture stiffening.

"Until?" The curiosity was killing me. At that moment I completely gave up on trying to restrain my obsession with him. I had to know everything. Now. Whatever he'd tell me, and what he wouldn't I'd track down to the ends of the earth.

"Until nothing. I… I'm still deciding."

"Where did you apply for college?"

He blinked. His clasped hands worked, and he widened his seat, spreading his knees until one came within inches of me. "So, tell me. Has Noah gone after anyone's part before?"

I raised my eyebrows, letting him know I'd noticed the subject change, but let it pass. For now. "No. He's never needed to. He's had the lead in every play after his freshman year. And even Noah knows freshmen have to pay their dues to get decent parts."

"Any advice?"

He wanted advice from me when that knee came so close to touching my leg. "Give it everything you've got. Flatter Mrs. M. She's a sucker for flattery."

"I'll give it a try. Everyone knows about my legendary charm," he said, making the facetiousness show. "Anything else?"

"Show up on time, every time. That's probably the main thing. To give your part away, Mrs. M would have to admit she was wrong, and from what I've seen so far, she wasn't wrong."

Oh God. That counted as flirtation, didn't it? It must have; he rewarded me with a blush.

"Showing up on time every time might be a problem." He glanced at the still-closed auditorium doors, as if Mrs. M would burst through them at any moment, angry we'd been gone too long.

"Why?"

"I have a job, and sometimes it runs over."

"Is that why you missed this afternoon?"

"Yeah."

"And you rush straight here, don't you?"

"Yeah."

"When do you eat dinner?"

"Later. At home."

He dropped the eye contact, lashes on his cheeks. Hiding something. What?

I stared at him a moment. Something had happened to change his mind about being an engineer, and what was with a job that killed any chance at eating dinner at a normal hour? Was he poor? No money for college? That alone would make him an oddity at this school.

Eighteen months he'd come here every day. Possibly no one had asked him anything about himself. Maybe he wanted to tell.

"Okay," I said, going for a calming tone. My mom had annoyed me for years by repeating her favorite saying: You catch more bees with lemonade. Or some crap like that. "Wait. If we're going to be friends"—his head came up—"then you'll have to get used to me. I ask questions."

"What if I don't feel like answering them?" he asked, a smile beginning that made me feel like I'd caught a bee. In my lungs.

"Then I'll ask a different one."

He shrugged, giving it his consent. "Go ahead. Give it your best shot."

Delight blossomed. I'd get to ask my questions, and somehow he'd turned it into a little game, a flirtatious game, even. "Okay. Full name and age."

"Seriously?"

"I never joke," I said, ten percent joking.

"Right. Campbell Joseph Adams. Age 17. I turn eighteen in April."

"You've got a month on me, then. My birthday is in May. How tall are you?"

His face split into a smile. "Why? Do you need me to reach something in a high cabinet?"

"No." I tried to stay businesslike. "How tall?"

"Six three. Since ninth grade."

"Do you have any brothers and sisters?"

"One sister, seven years older. She lives in North Carolina."

"Where did you live before you came here?"

"Same place as I do now. I changed schools, not houses."

"What do your parents do?"

"Nope."

Huh? How is that sensitive information? Whatever. Try another one. "Why did you change schools?"

"Next question," he said, his face implacable.

My eyes widened. "Seriously?"

"I never joke, either." He held a somber expression that might not have been entirely serious, but then again, he hadn't answered the question.

Whatever I'd planned to ask disappeared entirely from my mind. He'd shifted in his seat, and his knee accidentally touched mine. He pulled it away with reflexive politeness, but I'd been seized with determination. Hell. This was my senior year. I had four more months in this building. After that, all these people who seemed so vital to my existence for the last few years would disappear from my life, leaving behind only their faces in my yearbook. I'd be gone. I had nothing to lose and I didn't care what anyone thought of me anymore.

I moved my knee to touch his and left it there. I could have sworn he had a fever. Heat burned through the leg of my jeans. I wanted to touch him more. I had trouble keeping my hands still.

Color suffused his face, but he didn't move his knee. He met my eyes, something challenging in his gaze.

I liked nothing better than a challenge.

"I have a question for you." His eyes weren't really aqua. They were blue, with a yellow ring around the iris that made them change color, depending on the light. A little shiver started at the base of my spine.

"Yes?" I kept my knee where it was. Tension tightened his.

His hand flexed, hardly more than a twitch. "What are you doing?"

"Huh?" I widened my eyes and shook back my hair in a move copied directly from Amelia.

"With your knee."

Recklessness buzzed through my veins, slashing and burning my inhibitions. The empty lobby was silent except for the heating unit on the opposite wall. "Is it bothering you?"

We stared for a second or two, and as I watched, a muscle jumped in his cheek and the expression in his unusual eyes went from alert and playful to the same opacity I'd seen before. "No," he said, his voice a decibel above the hum of the heating system.

Drunk on my own daring, I scooted over even closer so that our thighs touched full length, while testing him by holding his gaze. Longing flashed there, widening his pupils. He swallowed,

Adam's apple moving. His hand brushed the top of my knee, making a sinuous "S." My breath caught.

He blinked and moved over on the bench to separate our legs. "Trust me; you don't want to go down that road."

With a little shock of horror, I remembered far too late what Kameron had said about Campbell being charged with violence against women. And he'd refused to tell me why he left St. Anselms, lending unintentional credence to her story.

Still. I watched him, took him in. The lines of his body remained calm, unthreatening. We had a cat once that did this pausing thing before she pounced. I'd watched her for years and learned the signs, and there was nothing of that banked aggression under Campbell's skin. If anything, I got the vibe that I was scaring him, not the other way around. Kameron hadn't heard the rumor firsthand. She had to be wrong.

He stood and extended an impersonal hand. I took it, keeping eye contact and refusing to let him embarrass me away. His skin was hot and a little damp.

"What if I do want to go down that road?" I asked, keeping my voice steadier than it should have been.

"You don't." He swallowed whatever he wanted to say, then looked away. "We'd better go back inside. Mrs. Murchison may need us by now. I can handle Noah. Thanks for telling me."

He held my hand for exactly four seconds too long before letting it go.

I spent the next school day wrestling with my own thoughts, trying to force them into some kind of order. Teachers stood in front of classrooms gesturing and writing on whiteboards. I wrote things down I didn't comprehend. People moved in and out of classrooms. Only my body was present.

I get that teenagers are supposed to be full of angst and drama and injustice and all that, but none of that had ever troubled me much. I enjoyed my life. I had good friends, success in the pool and in the classroom, a relatively easy path to college, and all the pieces in place to make the future I wanted a reality. Mom and I snapped at each other, but I had a home and food and love.

Swimming in angst and drama was not the kind of swimming I was used to.

I had to know what was going on with Campbell. Today. Right now. It suddenly seemed impossible to continue breathing if I didn't find out more, and here I sat, stuck like a prisoner in my seat for the forty-one excruciatingly long minutes left in seventh period. If I could make it, and I had doubts I could make it, I planned to jump in my crappy car—nothing is cooler than a handed-down former parent car—and follow Campbell straight to wherever he went. You don't want to tell me about your job, bro? Fine. Let's do this. I'd carefully noted the make and model of his car at the end of the rehearsal last night. He might even be anticipating it—I'd caught him staring at me, memorizing the silver color of the Ford truck he drove.

If I could confirm that Campbell wasn't a violent meth-cooking criminal, it might be time to admit to myself that I had a pretty major crush. Okay. I could admit that much now, at least, in my head, silently. I glanced over at Charlie Duncan and Marquez Vassal, who sat nearby, hoping neither could read my mind.

Thirty-seven more minutes.

I doodled a linking chain border on my folder.

Twenty-nine minutes.

I copied down meaningless words from the whiteboard in my notebook that I didn't read and could very well have been in Latin.

Eighteen minutes.

I pondered the poor handwriting of the person who'd written "School Sucks" on my desk.

Thirteen minutes.

I picked through a few split ends in my hair, pulling and breaking them off.

Six minutes.

After what seemed like at least seventeen more minutes, the final bell rang. I jumped up and pushed past Charlie, knocking his backpack off the desk. I ignored his muttered curse and dashed for the door. I'd planned ahead carefully. I loaded up my homework and my car keys after sixth period. I came up with a question, a stupid one, to ask Claire Agee, so that I'd have an excuse to be near Campbell at his locker. This morning I parked my car near his in the lot.

As it happened, I didn't have to ask Claire where she got the dotted shirt she'd worn yesterday, which was a relief since I didn't care, and because Claire would have gone on and on out of delight. Campbell slammed his locker as I rounded the corner. All I had to do was fall in step fifteen feet behind him and follow him out to the parking lot. He had earbuds in and didn't even notice me.

Thanking God my ancient Subaru station wagon, still decorated with the frolicking family stick figures on the back window—oh, yeah, I loved my mom-mobile—had started, I put on my sunglasses and pretended to check my phone as I waited for Campbell to pull out.

Distracted by a GIF, I almost missed him turn right, away from town and toward the more rural parts of the county. I didn't know this area well—none of my friends had ever lived on any of the farms or wineries out here. I followed his car around twisty roads, past ramshackle trailers next door to neat white farmhouses. The road began to climb as the fields grew large and manicured, the driveways stretched longer, and little signs with house names began to appear at the ends of them. This was the horse-y part of the county, where people built barns nicer than my house for their stables full of Arabians and… I stopped. I knew nothing about horses and couldn't come up with a second kind.

Did Campbell live here? He'd been a little cagey about where he lived, but surely if he did live in a house with a name, his parents would have enough money for college.

Without warning and not much responsible use of turn signals, Campbell turned left into the tree-lined driveway for an estate called Tir Na Nog. Nothing of the house was visible from the road, which meant big acreage. The discreet sign yelled Serious Money with small silver letters etched into a dark blue background. No cutesy pictures of a horse head on this sign.

No way could I just drive up there. People with signs like that had security cameras, alarm systems, and possibly booby traps. Across the road, the shoulder widened where someone had overbuilt the spot for the mail carrier's truck, creating room for at least three vehicles to pull off. It was well past mail time. I'd wait. We had rehearsal in a little over two hours. He'd have to pull back out of that driveway. Meanwhile, I decided to snoop some more and recovered my phone from the floorboard, where it had fallen.

For a second I worried that this far out into the country the signal might suck, then remembered that each of these properties sold for well over a million dollars. If we had decent coverage nowhere else in the county, we'd have it here.

I Googled the address. Nothing of interest. No owner's name came up. I went to the county's website and ran the address through their real estate information system. Tir Na Nog, it appeared, was a 127-acre parcel with a pond, a 5000-square-foot house, and three outbuildings I assumed must be barns. The county had assessed the value at $11,050,000. Holy shit. Campbell wasn't just rich. He was filthy rich.

Angry tapping on my driver's side window made me jump and drop my phone between the seats. Campbell stood there, wearing torn jeans and a faded sweatshirt, with a deeply forbidding expression on his face. In the rear view, I saw his truck, now parked behind mine in the small gravel space.

Oh, shit.

I opened the door and got out, thinking fast.

"What in God's name are you doing here, Natalie?"

"Oh. I, um, had another question to ask you."

"You had another question?" he demanded, eyes wide with disbelief. I inched back to the relative safety of my open car door. He was controlling his shock with difficulty.

"Um. Yes. Where do you work?"

He laughed. "You followed me—to work—to ask me where I work?"

I went with honesty. "Yes?"

"Here. I work here. I'd imagine you've figured that out by now."

"Whose house is this?"

"What, you don't think it's mine?"

"Is it? Because you just said you work…"

"Natalie, you're going to kill me. I can't keep up with the speed of your brain. Or your… your, I don't know, nerve. What the hell? You followed me!"

"I was curious. I told you I ask questions."

"You did tell me that. Fine. You want to know? I work for the Connaughtons. Here, four afternoons a week. This is their horse farm. You want to see? You want to know everything? Come on. You're making me late. Hop in," he said, gesturing at his truck. "Be careful what you wish for."

I slammed my door and jumped into his passenger seat. The cab was old but super neat. An empty Dr. Pepper bottle in the cupholder was the only sign of life. He peeled out and made a second irresponsible left turn into the long driveway. "What do you mean, be careful what you wish for?"

"You'll see. Or smell, I should say."

The driveway, at least a quarter of a mile long, wound around ancient oak trees and past a grove of smaller trees, maybe dogwoods that would flower in the spring, and came to a fork. The right fork led to the house, a huge white clapboard mansion masquerading as a farmhouse. The left fork, which Campbell took, led to a barn, painted red and white in an intentionally picturesque style complete with brass rooster weathervane on top. The barn was bigger than my elementary school.

"Come on," Campbell said, turning off the engine and stomping on the parking brake. I got out, admiring the amazing view of the Blue Ridge Mountains these people had, even from their barn.

I followed Campbell inside. Fifteen or twenty empty horse stalls spread out from a center aisle. "This is the nicest barn I've ever seen. So clean," I said.

"And bingo."

"Bingo?"

"Bingo as in you've figured out my job," Campbell said, grimly pulling off his sweatshirt to reveal a grungy T-shirt underneath and tossing it onto a hook already holding some kind of harness-looking thing. "That is my job. To keep this pristine barn pristine. The horses are in the field during the day. I don't mess with them. There's a trainer guy who brings them in after I'm done. The Connaughtons pay me, pretty good money, actually, to clean up. You know how much manure seventeen horses generate overnight?"

"A shitload?" I said, aware I shouldn't make light of it but also that it was absolutely the right thing to do.

His anger deflated and he let out an unwilling bark of laughter as he got together a shovel and a wheelbarrow. A distinct smell emanated from these. "That is indeed the exact measurement."

"So," I said, looking around, delighted. "You're a stable boy." A farm boy. Like in *The Princess Bride*. When I was younger, I used to watch that movie over and over again. Actually, at this moment, he resembled the one in the movie. Same long-in-front hairstyle. Darker hair. Greener eyes. I had the long blonde hair but was hardly a princess. I squeezed my fists in my coat pockets. Focus, Natalie.

"I get it. You don't want to go to rehearsal straight from here. That's why you're late."

"Yes. Not real excited at the idea of going anywhere near Noah smelling like this barn. That guy is… not someone I can picture here."

"Noah is a character. He's not usually too bad, but then I've never seen him when he had to do without something he wanted before."

"Huh. I'll have to take your word for it."

I sat on a neat pile of bagged feed and watched him work. With efficient movements, he shoveled heavy loads from the stalls into the wheelbarrow. I didn't fail to notice the play of muscles across his back and arms through the thin T-shirt. Even the sweat circles were hot. One formed at the front of his chest, flattening the T-shirt into the divide between his pectorals. Good God. I forced myself to focus on something else. Anything else.

"Listen. Campbell. I'm sorry. I think you could probably charge me with stalking for following you out here. I was curious, but this is way over the line. I'm sorry. Again."

"It was… I…" He gawked at me as if I were speaking Russian.

"Weird? Odd? Frightening?" I volunteered, his hesitant smile giving me courage. "I can keep going. I know a lot of adjectives. I've already written all my college application essays. I used a lot of adjectives to describe myself."

He laughed as he shoveled. "Those adjectives? I don't remember Mrs. Stevenson-Cash telling us to dare colleges to accept us."

"No. Not those. In the applications I went for the full scream-my-awesomeness-from-the-rooftops bragging."

"Where did you apply?"

"UVA, Michigan, Northwestern, and Berkeley. A few smaller schools, too, but I really want to go to Berkeley."

"Why Berkeley? It's so far away."

"I know. That's why. I want to leave here, see the world. My dad is a professor at UVA. It's his school, not mine. Here I'd always be Professor Tremayne's daughter. All the schools have good swim programs, and I'm hoping for a scholarship. At least a partial scholarship, but I'm late to that party. We'll see soon, I guess."

"Good schools. You must have good grades to get in, too."

"Pretty good. You? Where do you want to go?"

"I'm not going."

Not going? Why? I mean, I was aware that a lot of people didn't go to college, college isn't for everyone, blah, blah, but Campbell and I went to a high school that sent more than 80% of its students to four-year universities. He'd wanted to be an engineer. He took AP classes. I'd seen the contents of his backpack. He'd never have been assigned to those classes if he didn't have the grades in the lower level ones.

Even though I realized there must be some very sensitive reason for a student like Campbell not to go to college, and that the reason was almost certainly none of my damn business, it didn't stop me from asking. "Why not? Are you going in the military?"

"No. No military." He leaned on his shovel, taking a break.

"Then why not?" I stood and moved closer, into his space, until I could smell him: a combination of laundry detergent and hard work. He sucked in a breath and his gaze dropped to my lips. Everything went loose inside me. This was it. He would lower his head, and I'd...

"Hello, Campbell." A fifty-ish woman with auburn upswept hair stepped gingerly into the barn in knee-high leather boots. I jumped back. She wore a pale pink cashmere sweater with pearls and tightly fitted pants the same color as the boots and took a long look at Campbell, standing still, not shoveling. "Oh, hello! You've brought a friend today." She did not sound like friends were in any way welcome.

"Yes, ma'am. This is Natalie Tremayne. Natalie, this is Mrs. Connaughton." Campbell got back to work.

"Lovely to meet you, dear. Campbell, I came out here to ask if you'd be willing to move the feed bags over to the western door. They're in the way there and the horses kick at them as they enter the barn. They might nick one and make a mess."

He nodded.

"Thank you. And if you don't mind, let me know when you next bring a friend. I could have invited her to join me for some sweet tea up at the house, so she doesn't distract you from your work." Her brittle smile reminded me of winter ice and warmed her face not at all. I'd gotten him into trouble.

"Oh, I won't be staying, Mrs. Connaughton. Campbell forgot a homework assignment and I brought it to him. That's all. I was just leaving."

"Fine. Don't forget to pick up your check when you're finished, Campbell." She disappeared from the barn as fast as she'd appeared.

"I'm sorry, for the millionth time. I'm going to go now. I don't want to get you in trouble at work."

He paused, shovel in hand. Sweat glistened on his neck. "Okay. I was going to say before: it was kind of flattering, that you came. In a deeply weird way. But it was nice. To have someone to talk to, here."

"I'll see you, later, I guess?"

"Yeah. Please don't mention the stable boy thing to anyone at school, if you don't mind. Everyone thinks I'm weird enough. I don't need to be associated with horse manure on top of that."

"They don't think you're weird. They think you're quiet. You don't talk to anyone."

"It's probably best that way."

"Why? You don't want any friends? I could name at least fifteen girls off the top of my head who'd love for you to pay them some attention."

"Fifteen?" he asked, a teasing grin starting.

"Well, now that we know you're not gay."

He chuckled. "And how do you know that?"

"Come on. You can't tell Noah Jones you play for the other team and then expect it to remain a secret."

The shift in his posture revealed his embarrassment. It also seemed to remind Campbell that he wore clothes covered in horse crap. He moved the shovel between us.

"Listen. I've got to go. And you need to get back to work."

"I might be late to rehearsal. Cover for me with Mrs. M, if you don't mind."

That chest in the sweaty T-shirt. I couldn't take my eyes off it. "I will if you come with me and Marisa and a few others to the movies on Friday night."

He crossed his arms over his chest, smiling broadly, which in turn gave me a primitive urge to lick the sweat off his neck. "That's a pretty bold negotiation when I'm still thinking about charging you with stalking."

I shrugged with a total lack of shame. Damn. This whole new go-to-hell persona rocked. Why hadn't I been like this all four years of high school? There was nothing now I wouldn't say.

"Okay, you're going to play it that way," he said, nodding with admiration. "I can't, anyway."

"Why?"

"I'm busy on Friday nights. I mean this Friday."

"Working here?"

"I only work after school."

I didn't miss the correction. Every Friday night was booked. And not with a job. He'd laid a new mystery in front of me. No more stalking, though. I'd have to find out the old-fashioned way, by hardcore interrogation. All in good time—I'd freaked him out enough for today. "Oh. Another time."

"But, hey. Thanks for asking." He reached out as if to touch my arm but must have thought better of it. Dirt, and worse, streaked his wide hands. We grinned at each other wordlessly. He wiped his hand on his filthy pants and began shoveling out the next stall.

I took a good long look from the barn doorway and decided his rear view was almost as good as the front.

# Seven

When the bell rang Friday afternoon, I went home. We had no rehearsals on Fridays, and I had a few hours to kill before Marisa and a few others and I had plans. Movie first, then late night food, then maybe driving around to see what was going on. Nothing amazing, but you never knew.

After school, I always dumped my backpack, tossed aside my shoes in the mudroom, and checked out what was in the fridge. I'd about decided between a yogurt and some leftover cookie dough when Mom snuck on her tiny feet into the kitchen and pushed the refrigerator door closed, making me jump. She worked odd hours as a real estate agent, and I never knew when she'd be home. Dammit. The familiar stew of anger and shame rose up my neck, making me squeeze my fists.

"Honey, let's go for a walk instead. We'll be having dinner in a couple of hours."

"I don't want to go for a walk. It's freezing and I did an hour's workout already this morning."

"Fine." She didn't move, her skinny arm holding the fridge door. Seriously? She planned to hold it closed?

My brother Ethan came into the kitchen, carrying a half-eaten bag of Goldfish crackers and an empty Coke can.

"Didn't spoil your supper, did you, E?" I asked, turning my best stink eye on my mom. She had the grace to blush a little.

"Nope. Still hungry." Ethan sidestepped her, reached into the fridge for some string cheese, and went back into the family room where the TV blared. She let him.

I gave her the classic outrage face. Though the blast should have blown her hair back, she returned my stare, some guilt there now.

"Are you kidding me? I'm not allowed to eat, but Ethan is?"

"Honey. I just want to help you control your weight. Those last pants we bought you were a size…"

This reminder that I wasn't little and skinny and cute like her, like Amelia, like Marisa, like every girl my age in every TV show and movie, stirred the stew in the pot. "I know what size they were. I'm much taller than you are. It wouldn't take much to be bigger than you."

"That's not the point I was trying to make."

"Then what is the point you were trying to make?"

"It's my job to make sure you're healthy. And you're carrying a tiny bit too much weight. I worry."

Maybe this was why Campbell had plans every Friday night. And would probably have plans every night, if I asked him again to do anything. My weight. "The doctor said my BMI was fine."

"I looked it up on the internet. It's not fine. It's in the overweight range."

"I am athletic, Mom. I work out every day. It's muscle tone."

"Oh, honey…"

Fear twisted my insides. Most of the time I could blow her off when she started this stuff. Most of the time I felt good enough about myself not to care. But I'd spent the day wondering whether Campbell really had plans or had just made it up because he didn't want to be with me, and that meant I had no governor on my ability to deal with Mom's criticism right now. I squared my feet and stood my ground.

"Stop, Mom. Stop right there. I'm sick of this crap. I get it. You wanted a cute little blonde cheerleader daughter you could share clothes with and get manicures and all that, and you got me instead. If I lost thirty pounds, I'd still be ridiculously tall. I'd still scrape off all my nail polish when my hand touches the pool wall in the backstroke. I'll never be cute and little. I'm not the head cheerleader. Our head cheerleader spends every weekend drunk, and all week busy copying other people's homework. Is that what you want? Is it?"

"Natalie, that's enough. You're being ridiculous and you know it."

Now that I'd gotten rolling, it felt so good I couldn't stop, even though the sick feeling in my stomach swelled to nausea. Her face grew whiter and whiter as the words spewed forth. "No. In a few months, I'll be out of here. I won't be around to embarrass you with all my rolls of fat." I didn't have rolls. I squeezed the extra skin at my waist to make my point. "I can go anywhere if I get a swimming scholarship. Anywhere. I've got all the choices still to make. I won't be stuck here, like you."

"Natalie Catherine. You will not talk to me like that. You will—"

"I'll see you later." I spun around, picked up my backpack, and went straight out to the car. Behind me, she called my name, but I ignored her. I pulled the back door shut harder than necessary to make it bang.

Once in my car, I blew out a shaky breath. I hated fighting with my mom. It was like being hypnotized; I didn't want to do it, but I kept starting and finishing the job anyway. Where was the control? Why did I let her push my buttons like that? As I backed out of the driveway, the nausea eased a bit. I almost wanted to go in and apologize, to take away the strain and the distance, but I couldn't.

I had no idea where else to go. On Fridays at 4:00, nothing happened at school. I texted Marisa but got no response. On a whim, I turned my car toward the university, thinking maybe I could catch my father at his office hours. He'd told me once he held office hours on Friday afternoons because that would keep away the students who only wanted to suck up and leave time for the ones who really needed to see him.

The classic Palladian architecture of the University of Virginia glowed in the fading daylight, spectacular even in winter. The state's flagship school benefitted from lots of prominent alumni who gave lots of money for fancy buildings and year-round landscaping. If I didn't live right in its backyard and hadn't spent all my childhood being dragged to this faculty function and that basketball game, I might have had it at the top of my list. It was a good school, with an excellent swim team and biology department, but I'd never feel like I'd left home if I went here. I desperately wanted to leave home and not be Professor Tremayne's daughter all my life.

Right now, I was totally okay being Professor Tremayne's daughter. I parked in the permit-only lot and went straight to his office.

Not surprisingly, he sat at his desk facing the window, alone. I always enjoyed the fact that Dad bucked all the stereotypes of a college professor. He didn't wear tweed. He had perfect vision and no need for glasses. He was tall and broad-shouldered, like me. He kept his office neat and all his books carefully stowed in a bookcase.

He turned, took in the expression on my face in a glance, and stood. "What's wrong?"

"Mom."

"Oh." He gestured at the empty chair opposite him where students cried about their exams.

One more time I gave thanks for my father, who understood me so easily. When I was really small, he had little or nothing to do with me. Mom took me shopping and to swim practice and children's theater and to the doctor. She sat by my bed when I was sick. She listened to all my pre-teen problems and gave wise advice on every topic. I remembered Dad more as someone who came home at dinnertime and told me to turn off the TV.

In the last three years, all that had changed. My mom and I could barely manage a civil word, while my dad seemed to have some kind of supernatural understanding of what teenagers thought about and did. I chalked it up to the fact that he taught math to college students only a year or two older. Or maybe that his professor's brain hadn't connected until I was old enough to say something interesting.

"What's happened?" Dad busied himself by neatening his desk to end the day.

"The same old stuff," I said, picking at a cuticle. " Weight. We argued. Again. Stormed out. You know. Very dramatic. I already feel stupid and sorry, so you don't need to lecture."

"Have you ever considered trying to break that pattern?"

"Yes. No. I don't know how. I fall for it every time. She starts off and then bang—down go all the dominoes. All I ever can manage is not to scream back. Sometimes."

"It will pass." He clicked on an e-mail, sending it to the trash.

"When? Even I'm tired of it." I missed my mom. The mom I didn't fight with.

"That might be a sign you're getting ready to end it."

"Maybe it'll be easier when I'm gone from here."

"I still wish you'd at least consider this school. It's a good one, you know." He looked around, as if trying to find something persuasive in his office.

"I know, but if I go here, I'm not really leaving for college. I want to see if I can handle it on my own." The view out his small window was the same tree and brick wall it had been since I was little.

"You could live in the dorms."

"Yeah, but you'd be right up the road. I could eat dinner at home every night. You know the food here is terrible."

"I doubt you'd want to do that. I expect you'd have better things to do. You can go to school in the same town and still leave home, you know." He shut down his laptop and closed it.

Part of me, the part I liked to pretend didn't exist, did want that. Even now, having run from my mother, I recognized that I'd been blessed with a good family. The mother who'd stayed up all night cleaning up my vomit and telling off the mothers of my bullies was still under there somewhere, and even when we fought, the memories of those moments and the hope that we'd get them back someday weren't buried too deep. In a way, the degree to which I loved my family made it even more necessary to push so hard to get away. It would be easy to be sucked into staying and never finding my own way.

I played with the zipper of my coat instead of answering him, slouching in my seat.

"What else is going on?" he asked, waiting me out. He'd always been patient like that. Comfortable with silence. "We haven't talked in a while. How's the play?"

"It's fine. I've learned all my lines, and the song."

"Who else is in it? Amelia? Noah?"

"Yeah. Noah didn't get the lead this time."

"See, you're not as far away from your mum as you think. I expect she knew that. Who did get the lead?"

"This boy named Campbell Adams." Even as I said his name, and, oh, I wanted to say his name, I felt the flush creep up my neck.

He stared at me, a knowing smile starting. "Ah."

"What?" He said nothing, just smiled in that maddening way. "What, Dad?"

"You like that boy."

"I do not."

"All right. You don't." He turned his back deliberately to dump his saucer full of discarded tea bags into the trash.

"Okay. A little bit." Saying it out loud gave me a floaty feeling, like a helium balloon. I stood and went to the window. Two students walked by, holding hands.

"It's my duty here to say, 'Be careful.'"

"I don't think you need to worry. I asked him to come to the movies with all of us tonight and he said no. Apparently he has plans every Friday night."

Dad made a sound that I could have interpreted as an insult to Campbell's judgment, or that could just have been a dry spot in his throat. "Adams, you say? Who are his parents?"

"I don't know. He changed schools between sophomore and junior year. He used to go to St. Anselms. Scholarship, I think. He has a job after school, and I think he really needs it. It's kind of a crappy one," I said, chuckling at my own pun.

"Hmm. I don't think I know anyone who has kids at St. Anselms. Good school, though. I've had a lot of their graduates as students. I have a few in my first-year class now. I could check him out for you. He's a senior, I assume? They'd just be a year older."

"Dad, no. God. I'd die. Don't. It's nothing, anyway."

He laughed. "Fine. Are you coming home with me for dinner?"

"I guess."

"I think you probably owe your mum an apology."

"Probably." She'd apologize to me too, but the damage was done. God. I'd like to think in that distant time when I'd be the mother of a teenager, we'd be best friends and we'd hang out and we'd never argue.

He stood, gathering his neat pile of papers. He refused to use a briefcase on the grounds it was too professorial, so instead he carried the pile around. He dropped things everywhere and lost keys and sunglasses nearly every month, but wouldn't bend. "Come on. I'm hungry."

LATER THAT NIGHT, after I'd mumbled the required apology to my mom and returned to something resembling good terms, I picked up Marisa. We were to meet the rest of the swim team friend group at the movie theater for the 7:30 showing, but it was a ritual for us to stop by the Walgreens near the theater first for illicit snacks and gum, even when it was pouring rain.

On the way, she grilled me. I knew it was coming and I wanted to tell her.

"So, what's going on with Campbell?"

"Would you believe it if I told you we had knee sex?"

In the passenger seat, she twisted around fully to give me the full effect of her withering scorn. "Knee sex?"

Mercifully, I had an excuse to look away: the road. "Yeah. One day at rehearsal, I warned him Noah wants his part, and we sat out in the lobby of the auditorium and touched knees. On purpose."

"I bet Noah wants his part." She made a face so over the top-suggestive it made me laugh. Oh, crap. His "part." How many people had I said that to without getting the joke?

She waited, focused on the original story. The windshield wipers made four trips before she spoke again. "You touched knees? That's it?"

"We touched thighs, too. And after I found out he wasn't gay."

"Um, Nat, let me explain how sex works. See, he puts his…"

"Thanks, I'm good," I said, rolling my eyes.

"I'm not sure knee sex, while, um, super hot, is a whole lot to go on."

"You're totally right. I think I'll have to live off the memory anyway, because I asked him to come with us tonight and he made up some excuse about having plans. Every Friday night."

"Ooh. Sorry."

She took it to mean exactly what I had: an excuse. Not until now did I realize I'd hoped she'd come up with a reason he'd say that while still being obsessed with me like I was with him.

"Yep. I think the knee sex might be the pinnacle of our relationship."

"Oh. When did you ask him to come with us? You didn't tell me that."

Something stopped me from telling Marisa what I'd discovered about Campbell's job. He'd asked me not to tell anyone, and normally I would have taken that to mean everyone but Marisa. I didn't want to crack the wall around that secret, though, even for Marisa. "The other day at rehearsal."

"So, friends? Are y'all friends?"

"I guess so."

We pulled up in front of Walgreens and I parked. The rain roared on the roof and obliterated the view out the windshield. "Friends with someone that amazing-looking is better than nothing. Or maybe worse. I can't decide," Marisa said, then hopped out and slammed the door, racing without an umbrella to the entrance.

Inside the store, we dripped water and browsed the candy aisle, trying to find the movie-theater sized boxes. With time to kill, we spent a long time considering the options.

"Who buys Raisinets? Tell me the truth. They're like disgusting little chocolate-covered bugs." I chose my Junior Mints, like always, shaking the box from end to end to see if it sounded full.

"My little sister loves them. My mom buys chocolate-covered raisins for her every time she goes to Trader Joe's."

"Ugh. Well, that kid is odd." Marisa's little sister was in seventh grade, the same as Ethan. "Which reminds me. Did I tell you what my mom let Ethan—"

"Hey, look who just came in."

I glanced up from the candy display toward the automatic doors near the cash register. Campbell, wearing a hoodie with stains on the front, ducked in, shaking rain off his caramel-colored hair. He gave an impersonal wave at the cashier, who sagged on her feet while she flipped through a magazine, and then headed for the refrigerated section lining the back walls of the store.

Marisa glanced at me. He hadn't seen us. I shook my head, trying to stop her. She made a silent tsk tsk movement with her head. Oh, God. Here we go.

"Campbell!" Marisa called. Confusion passed over his face until he located the source of the sound. Faint embarrassment replaced it as he registered us.

"Hey, Natalie. Marisa."

Marisa's face had the devilish look it got when she was up to something. "And what are you up to on this beautiful rainy night? The condom section is over there, I believe."

At that, he flushed a deep shade of red. One of his fists closed reflexively. Oh, damn. What if he really had come to buy condoms? We didn't know anything about him. He could have a harem he visited every Friday night for all I knew.

"Oh, shut up, Marisa," I said, giving her a friendly elbow in the side. "What would your mother think if she knew you were so familiar with the condom section?"

Gratitude flashed across his face, and he shoved his hands into the front pocket of his hoodie. What was that orange gunk spilled all down his front?

"Milk. I have to get some milk."

"Milk?" asked Marisa.

"Yeah. I need… I mean, my mom asked me to buy milk." He fidgeted, standing there, but at the same time seemed unwilling to move. "Y'all are going to the movies tonight, right?"

"Yeah." I said, admitting to myself that he emitted some kind of electric signal that made me keep moving closer and closer. I wanted to be close enough to see the golden ring in his eyes.

"I wish I could come. Really," he said, staring back, making my pulse increase.

"You still can. We're buying snacks now. What is your opinion on Raisinets?" asked Marisa, doing the saucy flirting-on-my-behalf thing she did. I glanced at her. She'd seen his effect on me. She had her hands on her hips and watched with open enjoyment. Oh, God, I was probably panting.

Campbell dragged his attention off me with difficulty to answer her question. "I don't care for Raisinets. I prefer Junior Mints." He made sure that registered as I dropped the hand holding the box to my side self-consciously. "Thanks for the invite, but I have to get back. With the milk."

"Right. Well, maybe another time." I did a little wave thing with the Junior Mints box and stepped past him toward the register. Maybe I'd read it wrong, but he didn't seem like he was lying to blow me off. Wouldn't it have been easier to say that Junior Mints tasted like toothpaste?

"Uh. Hey. Do y'all eat breakfast after swim practice?"

Marisa stared at him in amazement, but she wasn't dumb. Or unkind. "Um. I always eat beforehand, but Nat usually brings something to eat afterwards."

"Skip it Monday. I'll bring something." He cleared his throat. "For you, too, Marisa, if you want."

"No, thanks," Marisa said. She intentionally dropped her package of Twizzlers and poked me hard in the back of the calf with it as she picked it up.

"Sure, Campbell. That would be great," I said, trying to envision eating breakfast with Campbell Adams and failing miserably. Would I have to pretend to eat like a bird, after swim practice, when I was so hungry I could eat a raw lion, mane and all? Did girls do that in this day and time? Surely not. This girl wouldn't. I might not have the best body in the world, but he saw me in a swimsuit every weekday at the crack of evil dawn, and he'd still asked me to eat breakfast.

"Good. See you then," Campbell said. "Uh, I'd better get that milk. I need… to bring it back. Soon." He did a little wave and disappeared in the direction of the milk refrigerators at the back wall.

"Oooh. Someone has a date!" whispered Marisa, her face shining in glee.

"Not a date. Couldn't possibly be. In the school? A date in a school is illegal in twenty-two states, I think."

"Date," Marisa said, using her Twizzlers like a magic wand. She waved the package with a flourish and touched me on the nose. "I have made it so."

# Eight

Campbell didn't say a word to me during swim practice Monday morning—just emerged from the locker room, dove in, and kept his face in the water for the whole workout. I spent all my minutes underwater wondering why he'd bothered to ask me to eat breakfast when he'd lied about having plans Friday. He obviously hadn't been doing anything. He'd been wearing a gross sweatshirt and had been in a drugstore buying milk for his mother. Yet he'd looked at me with… interest. I couldn't think of the right word. Like I was a *girl*.

He'd complimented my Junior Mints.

I swam six lengths of butterfly as warmup, unusual for me, so I could put my face in the water and hide my smile.

And he'd also asked me to eat breakfast. Maybe. I paused at the end of the lane, pretending to catch my breath. In the boys' lane, Campbell swam like an automaton, taking no notice of me or any of his other teammates. He'd definitely mastered the invisibility thing. Marisa pulled up in the next lane to ask me a silent question, which I couldn't answer. When the whistle blew,

Campbell jumped out of the water and headed straight to the locker room.

After practice, I took the time to put on eyeliner and lip gloss just in case. If this was a date, even a twenty-minutes-before-first-period date, I'd give it everything I had. It probably wouldn't hurt me to put on some makeup every now and then even if Campbell had totally forgotten about what he'd said.

He hadn't. Outside the locker room, Campbell waited with donuts in a greasy bag.

"Did you still want to…?" He gestured at the bag.

"Sure. Are those donuts from that place at the shopping center?"

"Where else?"

"Where do you want to eat?"

"Follow me."

We went to the cafeteria. A big open affair, the cafeteria still had a few tables tucked into corners created by the huge pillars that held up the ceiling. Because they were out of sight of anyone at the doorway, these were the ones where the Amelias and the Joes sat at lunchtime. At this hour, before the first bus arrived, the room stretched empty before us, except for the cafeteria workers in the kitchen.

As always, I was starving after practice. I ate a whole donut before I even bothered with conversation. Ugh. I glanced at Campbell. He'd eaten two. He grinned at me as he licked a crumb off his perfect lower lip. Oh my God. I forced my gaze away from that spot before I made a fool of myself.

"Thanks for bringing them."

"I wanted to apologize," he said, turning more serious.

"For what?"

"I think I gave you the impression I didn't want to hang out with you on Friday."

My stomach paused from its digestive work long enough to lurch a little at the look in his eyes.

"I did want to. Hang out with you on Friday, that is."

On the table, his hand touched mine, so lightly it might have been accidental. I glanced down, surprised, but he didn't move his away. Maybe he hadn't noticed. Some kind of longing, a need to do something, anything, filled me, but I couldn't move.

"Natalie, I like you. I really like you." His hand inched closer until our little fingers were pressed tightly against each other. No accident now. The contact made me light-headed.

"But?"

His head whipped up.

"I know there's a 'but' coming, Campbell. It's okay. Go ahead."

He took my breath away by gripping my hand. Our fingers laced together. "It's not a good idea for you to be with me."

"Why? Are you dangerous?"

"What do you mean?"

I looked him in the eyes. "There's a rumor. That you and some girl at your old school got into a fight and…"

"And?" He'd turned white. Tension tightened the muscles in the hand I held. Why?

"And that you hit her. According to the rumor, her parents charged you with assault."

His hand relaxed. "Do you believe that?"

"No, but I've got to be honest, Campbell, you're sitting here right now telling me I should run for my own good. I'm asking if it's true."

"No."

"No?"

"No. It's not true. I've never hit a girl. Except for my own sister, when she was a teenager and still lived at home. I would have been about ten. Maybe eleven. And that was in self-defense."

"Did they charge you with something you didn't do?"

"No. If people are saying any of that, it's not true. I've never been charged with any criminal offense, and I don't think I've ever committed a crime. That I know of."

"So, I shouldn't be with you because…"

"You just shouldn't be with me. I'm not the right guy for you. You can do better. So much better."

It never occurred to me to think any guy would think I was too good for him. I'd spent the whole weekend wondering when Campbell would figure out he could do better than me. Still, he didn't get to make all the decisions here. "Why are you allowed to judge that for me?"

Taken aback, he dropped my hand and put his under the table. "B-because I…" Pain crossed his features. "Can't we be friends? You said before that I should have friends."

I knew the right thing to say. I'd heard this before. Guys usually wanted to be my friends. They felt some obligation to sell their friendship to me, to persuade me with a wink that it was better than boyfriend-hood. At this point in the conversation, I was supposed to smile gamely and say, "Sure, friends."

That was before my go-to-hell attitude. I was done doing what I was supposed to do.

"It's too late for friends, Campbell. Friends don't hold hands across cafeteria tables."

Shock rippled across his face. I put my hand on the table again, palm up, open for taking. For a minute, he didn't move. He fought some kind of battle with himself—I watched the emotions cross his face. For someone who'd been such a mystery until a few weeks ago, they were easy to read: confusion, fear, decisiveness, longing, and then surrender. Every change of expression registered inside me, producing an uncomfortable echo effect that made my sweater feel too warm.

Oh my God. What if he didn't take my hand?

If he didn't, I'd get up and walk away without another word, like some trench-coat-wearing Frenchwoman of mystery. I even uncrossed my legs in preparation for standing, when he pulled out his hand from under the table and took mine. I could have done without the whole agonized-desperation thing he had going on, though.

"Dammit, Natalie. This is a bad idea. Very bad. You're going to regret this."

"As long as you're not into hurting women, I think I can handle it."

He brought his other hand up to the table and gripped my hand with both of his. "You have no idea how much the emotional stuff can hurt."

"Let me handle my own emotional smackdown, thanks. I'm pretty tough. It's time for class. I've got to go. Señora hates it when I'm late." I let go of his hand and stood, yanking my bag onto one shoulder.

He stood too, reaching out to stop me. "Wait a minute."

"What?"

He took my hand again and pulled me into a tiny little alcove behind a pillar. "If you're going to screw up your life, there are things I need to tell you, but we don't have time now."

"Why? What do—?"

"No more questions right now." He leaned in, close enough his breath stirred the hair at my temples.

"Why not? I—"

"Because." He slid his hands over my cheeks and put them in my still-damp hair, tipped my head up to meet blazing aqua eyes, and kissed me as I drew in a shocked breath.

I'd been kissed before. The usual stuff: spin the bottle in middle school, a couple of bold moves after a beer or two, the preliminaries before Gabe and I got down to the business of unwrapping our first condom. Once, even on stage as part of a one-act play.

Not like this.

His height and size, so close, made me feel almost petite. His lips were soft at first, then crushed against mine, creating a burning feeling where they touched that licked like fire through every part of me. I let the backpack slip off my arm and crash to the floor. His body pressed mine full length and anchored me against the pillar. His hands traced my spine, and I didn't know how to handle the response that had my mouth seeking frantically and my hands pulling and grabbing. Our tongues met as the kiss deepened. From the back of his throat he groaned, only barely audible. One hand made its way to twist in my hair as mine rode out the width of the muscles of his shoulders.

I'd always secretly thought kissing was unsanitary, pointless, and kind of gross.

I'd been wrong.

I was lost in a blindside of sensation.

"Get to class, ladies and gentlemen," one of the cafeteria ladies from across the room said, clearing her throat in warning.

Campbell broke away, breathing hard, freeing me from my happy little cocoon between him and the pillar. He squeezed his eyes shut, but there was no embarrassment there.

"I'm sorry," he said, pushing back a lock of hair that had come loose from my messy bun. "I shouldn't have done that."

"Did you see me complaining?" Would my pulse go back to normal? Or was this the way I was now? Forever?

He laughed, a sad little laugh that worried me more than his apology.

"After the swim meet on Saturday, would you go out to dinner with me? There's some stuff I want to talk to you about, and somewhere I want to take you."

"Can't you tell me now?"

"I can't now, because we have about thirty seconds to make it to class. I want to do it right. You have the right to decide if you want to do this. I owe you that."

"Go on, now, kids. Get," shouted the cafeteria lady.

I glanced at her and lowered my voice, not moving. "I do want to. I thought I'd made that clear."

"You can't make a decision without all the information. And you don't have it."

"I don't handle being denied information well."

"So I've heard." He chuckled. "I'm not denying it. I'm delaying it."

"Fine," I said, grumpily. "I'll wait. And yes, I'll go Saturday. But don't assume I'll leave you alone until then."

The bell rang.

"I'd be disappointed if you did."

I SAT THROUGH MY CLASSES in a haze of excitement, sparing about ten seconds to consider the idea that at a minimum, Campbell might put a real dent in my GPA. Even so, I'd heard that colleges had to think you were close to the line to bother checking the grades you submitted after Christmas of senior year. I'd worked damn hard to make sure I wasn't close to any lines.

He'd asked me on a date. A real date. I'd never been on a date before, not the stereotypical boy-picks-up-girl-and-pays-for-her-milkshake kind. Groups, yes. Parties, absolutely. The existence of a Date with a capital D a mere five days in my future, I realized, meant I'd have to tell Marisa. I'd need her help with all the etiquette. What to wear. How to act. I had no idea.

After I'd taken my turn working a problem in AP Calc, I sat back down to ponder The Kiss. In the movie version of *Beauty and the Beast*, when the Beast transforms into the prince at the end, he's lifted up and undergoes a force so powerful it shoots light from his fingers. The Kiss felt like that.

My life was filled with capital letters. It made a nice change. I wrote the word "Kiss" on my notebook. Rolling my eyes at my own idiocy, I scratched it out and then went over it until I'd obliterated it in a solid black box.

Campbell had regretted doing it. Why? It wasn't me. He was attracted to me. I knew that somehow, without a word from him. Whatever it was he had to tell me was monumental—something he thought would drive me off.

He didn't know me well yet. I was stubborn. Like a bull, or a terrier, or the Great Wall of China. It was both my best quality and my worst fault. I was the kid who'd insisted on playing Monopoly until the end. The one who learned to hold my breath the longest. The one who saved up my money for an American Girl doll my mom said I didn't need, even though it took so long I no longer wanted it by the time I had enough. I bought it anyway. It sat on a dusty shelf in my room, proof of both my persistence and pigheadedness. I'd never once even changed its clothes.

I never gave up. Even when I should have.

At the end of the day, I dashed to grab my things from my own locker so I could catch Campbell at his before he left. I should have been nervous about it, staking out where we were: had we gotten to a point where we met at lockers, did we want other people to know, blah, blah, blah. I didn't care. We'd figure it out as we went. I just wanted to see him.

And there he stood—waiting at my locker, a hesitant, possibly nervous, smile on his face. He was so beautiful. I spared a quick half second to wonder if anyone that beautiful would ever kiss me again.

"Hey," I said, stopping short, nerves walloping me out of nowhere.

"Hey," he said, clutching the straps of his backpack and making no move to touch me. All right. We hadn't reached the PDA in the hallways part yet. Elly Townsend, who had the locker on my left, raised a surprised eyebrow at me before she slammed her locker closed and walked away.

"That was definitely weird, this morning."

"Weird?" he asked, pretending to be offended, while leaning against Elly's locker.

"In all the best ways."

"It would be better if you could forget it. I won't, but you should."

"Nope. I have a memory like a steel trap."

Both of us did, judging by the dull flush on his face and the heat in mine.

He cleared his throat. "Anyway, I'll see you at rehearsal. I've got to go to work."

"Can I come with you?" I wanted to touch him so badly. His T-shirt clung in all the right places. And it was still clean. Hallways were hallways, however. One touch here and everyone would know by sundown. I pushed the flat of my hands against the cool metal of the locker bank to keep them away.

"Nope. Mrs. Connaughton made that crystal clear after you left the other day. If she saw you, she'd suspect I wouldn't be concentrating on the manure in a professional manner, and she'd be right. I need to keep the job."

"Okay." The compliment buried in there calmed me down some. I could be patient. Sometimes.

"And, Natalie," he said, after he'd stepped away. "No more like this morning until after we talk."

I let out a long groan but smiled at him as he waved.

TUESDAY MORNING IN THE POOL locker room, Marisa pounced the minute I walked yawning through the door.

"Where the hell have you been?

"In all the normal places. Where were you? You didn't answer my text," I said, dumping out my bag.

"I went home sick yesterday afternoon. My mom thought I wasn't really sick and took away my phone."

"Were you actually sick?"

"Of course not. I just didn't want to take the French test yet," she said, throwing her stuff into the back of the locker.

"Oh."

"Bruh. How could you go this long without telling me about breakfast? Come on. I can't wait another second. Spill. Was it a date? Was it date-ish?"

"Yes." I grinned at her, lots of teeth, desperate-red-carpet style.

"What?" she screeched. "'Yes?' What the hell is that? Talk. Now."

"Okay. He met me in the hall outside. He had donuts. We went to the cafeteria, he told me I shouldn't want to be with him, he asked if we could be friends, I said no, and then he kissed me."

She sat on the bench, her suit forgotten in her hands. "Whaaat?"

"He met me in the hall outside…" I started again, to tease her.

"Oh my God. Campbell Adams kissed you. How was it? Oooohhhh."

"Bruh," I said, intentionally mocking her greeting of me, "you have a boyfriend."

"I know. And I love him. But Campbell Adams. He is sculpted from gold."

"Gold? Wow," I said, laughing. "It was good. The Kiss. Very good."

Very good, ha! The English language had some major limitations. I could tell her clinical details, but there weren't any words I could use to make her understand, to feel, the way he'd looked at me, how his breath sped up and made mine do the same, how he smelled, the feel of his breathing near my ear, the strength in every line of his body.

She sighed in raptures. It was all very gratifying even without the words. I loved Marisa. She never disappointed.

"And? What's next?"

"We're going out on Saturday. He says he has stuff to tell me and wants to show me something or take me somewhere."

"Huh. That's odd. Any idea where?"

"No, and he's all angsty about it, like it's this big secret or something. Something I need to know, because he's totally convinced I'll run away screaming when I find out."

"Weird. What do you think it is?"

"You don't think he's a vampire, do you?" I asked, only 98% joking. Hot mysterious guy everyone left alone, freakishly normal girl. All that was missing was an extreme case of clumsiness.

"Yeah," Marisa said, sarcasm dripping off her heavily enough to drench the tile floor, "that's absolutely it, Bella."

"I do have a real theory." I'd only spent every one of the last twenty-four hours trying to come up with one.

"What is it?"

"I think he's poor. Like, really, really poor."

"Do you think?"

"Yeah. It fits. He has an after school job he works every day."

"What does he do?"

"Um, I'm not sure," I lied. "I'm guessing he had to leave St. Anselms because of something to do with his scholarship. He said he didn't move."

"His clothes don't look cheap. Didn't he have on a Vineyard Vines shirt before?" Marisa would notice this. She spent way more time on fashion than I did.

"They could come from Goodwill. Lots of the rich people donate their clothes to Goodwill."

"That's true. Annika got a Nicole Miller dress from Goodwill once."

"Anyway, I think he's going to take me to his house, which I'm guessing is tiny or run-down or something."

"You'd never care if he was poor, would you?"

"Of course not. But he might not know that. He doesn't know me that well."

"You're probably right. I'm sure that's it."

"It won't stop me from teasing him about this big secret. I might even check, you know, in direct sunlight. For sparkles."

Marisa used her swimsuit as a sling shot and scored a direct hit, right in the face.

THE WEEK DRAGGED ON. We had fifteen minutes in the morning after swim practice, an occasional wave in the hallways during the day, a locker visit in the afternoons, and then rehearsal which lasted until ten or eleven o'clock at night. There we were surrounded by a scheming Noah, an openly flirtatious Amelia (Joe had been caught at a JV girls' basketball game hooking up with a sophomore, breaking them up again), and an increasingly surly Finney, who sat by and watched as Amelia took no notice of him whatsoever.

Campbell said we wouldn't have time for The Talk until after the swim meet, and that we had to go somewhere specific for it to take place. It didn't stop me from trying to guess during the handful of minutes we found to be alone in the cafeteria alcove in the morning.

"You're a spy, and you're going to take me to CIA headquarters."

"Nope."

"You're a thirty-year-old narc, and you're going to show me your 2012 yearbook."

"Nope. Still seventeen. Wasn't that a movie?"

"Yes."

"Any more guesses?"

"You're a vampire."

"Uh, Natalie, that was definitely a movie. Even I've seen that one."

"So that's a no to the vampire?" I asked, keeping my face businesslike and pretending to write on an invisible clipboard.

"That's a no." A smile began to chip away at his worried expression.

"I don't suppose you'd let me look at your naked chest, out in a meadow, just to be sure?"

He choked back a laugh. "Not yet."

"A werewolf?"

"No."

"A zombie?"

"No."

"The Dread Pirate Roberts?" I asked, smiling at him, delight washing through me.

He leaned in and gave me a heart-melting expression of longing, just like in the movie. Damn. Noah had his work cut out for him if he thought he could take a part away from this god of a guy in front of me.

He did the slightest of bows. "As you wish."

He could quote *The Princess Bride.*

My knees actually wobbled.

Saturday couldn't come soon enough.

## Nine

Our school had paper-thin walls. The babble of the crowd outside the locker room in the pool area rose steadily louder. I wasn't ready to go out there yet. Instead, I skirmished with myself to get to a place where I was ready for the meet. I hoped the greenish cast to my skin came from the dank lighting and not my mental state. I'd hate to have to answer my parents' questions about it afterwards.

My parents had never missed a single swim meet since I was little and swimming for our neighborhood pool team. They yelled my name so loud I heard it even underwater. They used to wear T-shirts with my name on them in Sharpie marker until I made them stop. Though I wouldn't have minded if they ignored me and wore them anyway.

The meet Saturday marked the midpoint of the swim season. Virginia swim meets, and all swim meets, I guess, had a specific order of events to allow swimmers to rest between events. Coach put my name down to swim four events: the opening medley relay, my individual medley, the backstroke, and the closing freestyle relay.

Today we'd be taking on our arch-rival school from across the county, along with two smaller schools who wouldn't be a factor. We needed every race to rack up the points to advance toward the state level. I tried not to think about my date tonight. Coach would be pissed if he knew his best swimmer was fully and completely distracted by thoughts of a boy. He never got tired of teasing, in kind of a not-very-funny, desperate sort of way, everyone on the team with a known boyfriend or girlfriend. He begged us to concentrate. He said things like, "True love you'll remember today, but the regional meet you'll remember for a lifetime!"

None of that had ever applied to me before.

I paced a course on the tiled floor of the locker room, unable despite my best attempts to get into the zone. My zone, a carefully built haven of controlled and directed aggression I harvested from every little slight I'd experienced since I swam the last race, worked for me. It tensed my muscles and made the adrenaline surge. Today, however, even my usual bass-heavy pre-race playlist and my superstitious spot in the corner where I dressed did nothing to keep the races at the forefront.

Campbell hadn't let me kiss him since Monday. That drought had to end tonight because he'd been killing me all week. We sent each other hundreds of text messages that weren't quite R-rated, but definitely weren't appropriate for general audiences. He preserved a distance in the hallways, but at rehearsals we'd hung out in the lobby, side by side on the benches, thighs touching, heat building.

On one occasion I'd replayed for Marisa about a thousand times and at night in the dark a million more, he'd walked me to my car after rehearsal, and waited, silent except for his sped-up breathing, until everyone left. In the dark, broken only by a distant streetlight, he'd pulled me closer until our feet intertwined, close enough I could feel the pull like a magnet. His breath on my face ruffled my hair, but he'd never kissed me, only stroked my back and whispered what he wanted to do in my ear. That one burned almost hotter in my memory than the actual Kiss.

The fire had raced through my veins ever since, incinerating my concentration and ability to sleep.

Now all I had to do was kill it in four swim races and all restrictions would disappear.

Or try to kill it in four swim races.

Somehow.

Marisa knew better than to talk to me before a meet. She left me alone, as usual. I left the locker room last, finally managing to corral some tiny piece of my control.

Poolside, the boys waited, stretching and jumping, swinging their arms wildly to loosen the joints. The other team did the same, adding as much bluster and threat to their performance as possible. I twisted my hair and put it under the swim cap, which I always saved for outside the locker room at meets. It would have been easier to do it in front of the mirror like the other girls, but I'd always done it this way and always would. I spotted Carrie DeMarco, who'd been competing with me in the backstroke since we were little. The mere sight of her, tall and rawboned in her suit, allowed some much-needed adrenaline to blast through my veins.

Campbell stood apart from the rest and smiled at me. I went over to him, breaking my usual routine. I didn't have to check to know Marisa had watched all of this with interest.

I stood on my tiptoes and whispered in his ear. "Good luck."

He turned and did the same to me, allowing his lips to brush my ear and sending a happy shiver down my spine. "You too. Still on for tonight?"

"Of course."

He squeezed my forearm, and I went back to the girls, passing Coach who glanced between me and Campbell, eyes narrowed. Both Campbell and I swam the 200 medley relay, which was the first event, first the boys, then the girls. Too late, I remembered my parents, who'd have had a terrific view of the whole exchange from the sidelines. If they'd noticed, it would be their first visual proof I had hormones. I waved at them, aware my face was red, and noted their intensely curious faces. Oh damn.

The announcer did the timer check and called the swimmers in the first race. In this race, each swimmer did two lengths, starting with the backstroke. Campbell swam the anchor leg—the last stroke, freestyle. He lined up behind the others.

Usually, I hated having to wait for the boys to swim this event before I could do mine, which came next. Now I appreciated the opportunity to stare without any need for an excuse at him—I mean at our four-person team. Three, after our backstroker, Adrian Barrett, dropped into the water.

How had I overlooked Campbell as long as I had? Why, come to think of it, wasn't there a herd of girls and a Hollywood casting agent following him everywhere he went? He was perfect. Even in a shorts-length Speedo and a rubber swim cap. Taller than the rest of the guys, he seemed bigger and older than they were. Older especially than Sam Young, whose name went with a baby face and a skinny body but who swam the breaststroke better than anyone else.

"Take your mark!"

The buzzer went off and Adrian splashed off backwards in a bad start. He fell behind before he'd gone a half-length. Annoyance doubled as Annika Anderson, who swam the breaststroke for the girls' medley, pulled me aside and distracted me from my view by insisting on commenting on every single thing whichever boy in the pool did. It meant I had to watch the person swimming, not the one waiting at the end of the line for his turn.

"Sam got off a good dive. I don't think it's enough to make up for that clown show Adrian just pulled off, though. Nope. He's not making up any ground at all. Dammit. But he didn't lose any either. Come on, Trace! Go! Dammit. He's gaining a little, but eff it all, he's going to have to swim the best 50 he's ever done in his life to catch up. Gah! Here goes Campbell. Go!"

At that point I abandoned any attempt either to remain calm or to keep my feelings on the down low. I got as close as I could get to the pool edge and yelled for all I was worth. "Go! Campbell! Goooooooo!"

He had an excellent start and began catching up almost immediately. Tension rose in the room, and the crowd yelled his name, if they knew it. I jumped in place, screaming. I didn't realize I'd dug my fingernails into my palms until the dull ache surprised me. Annika turned to goggle at me.

In the pool, Campbell's beautiful stroke steadily gained ground after a perfect flip turn. Unless something went wrong, he'd win. "He's winning! They're going to pull it out! Go, Campbell!"

"What's with you? What happened to the zone? You're swimming next. Like, right NOW," Annika said, grabbing my arm to remind me that I had to line up. The backstroker swam first in the next race.

Which meant I got to stand over the end of the lane when Campbell won and vaulted easily out of the water. His victory had fired him up. He and the other guys slapped hands and hit each other's shoulders. Excitement crackled in the air. Instead of beating his chest or pumping a fist, a huge smile split his face and he grabbed me in a bear hug. None of the other three girls waiting for the medley relay bothered to hide their shock. Campbell never interacted with anyone on the swim team. I didn't care. I got to hug his shirtless chest. It worked for me.

"Swimmers, you may enter the water."

Crap. Just when things were getting good. I broke away, catching one last glimpse of Campbell's face, glowing like the sun, and dropped into the water for my two lengths of backstroke. What happened to Adrian wouldn't happen to me. Hayley MacLaren, who swam the fly, was a little weak, but nothing I could do about that except give her as big a lead to erode as possible.

"Take your marks!"

I gripped the handles at the bottom of the block and set my toes. When the buzzer went off, I arced backwards and took off. Swimming is an unusual sport. If you're doing it right, your head is in the water, and you're unaware of the other swimmers for the most part. Turning your head to look can cost valuable hundredths of a second. I didn't need to. Carrie swam this leg of the event, but I'd beaten her before. I'd beat her today. I rolled to my stomach for my flip turn and timed it perfectly. When my wrist hit the starting block again, I squeezed tight against the wall so that Annika could dive over my head. I wasn't surprised to see I'd given my team a third of a length advantage.

I levered myself out of the pool, water pouring off me. Campbell waited nearby, but he knew I had a job to do, and that was to urge on Annika, Hayley, and Ainsley. We watched Annika keep my lead, Hayley chip away at it to a worrying degree, and then Ainsley touch an arm's-length ahead of the swimmer in the next lane, pulling it out.

Campbell and I congratulated them and then he pulled me aside slightly. "Without your lead, we would have lost that one."

"Thanks. Right back at you, for yours."

We stood too close. People were looking. My parents were looking.

He leaned down to whisper in my ear. I'd never get used to anyone being tall enough to lean down to whisper in my ear. "I want to kiss you."

A shiver of excitement made the fine hairs on my arm stand on end. "Fine by me," I teased, knowing he wouldn't, not here in public.

"Tonight," he promised.

"Adams," interrupted Coach Phillips. "Your mother wants to talk to you."

"Now?"

"Yeah. She's over there."

A woman stood at the rail separating the spectators from the pool deck. Beautiful for her age, she wore obviously expensive stylish clothes and a leather coat and had blonde hair groomed within an inch of its life, like Amelia's. A big diamond winked on her elegant left hand.

Campbell wasn't poor. At least his mother wasn't. They didn't sell diamonds like that at Goodwill.

He touched my arm briefly and went over, where he had a short but intense conversation over the rail.

"That's Campbell's mom?" I asked Coach, who watched this conversation with almost as much interest as I did, but for different reasons.

"Yes. She's my son's pediatrician."

Not poor.

Campbell grabbed his towel off the rail and returned. His face had gone tense and upset, and much, much older.

"I really hate this, Coach, but I have to go. Right now."

"You're joking, Adams. 50 free is up in just a minute, and then the free relay. I need you here. Can't it wait?"

"No. Family medical emergency. I have to go now." Campbell's face was creased with worry. He wasn't making it up. "Right now. I can't wait for the 50 free."

Coach saw it and recognized defeat. "Dammit. Fine."

I touched his arm. He avoided my eyes. "Who is it? Your dad?"

"It's complicated. I'll tell you later. I'll text you."

"But Campbell…"

He didn't hear me. He'd already raced off to the locker room.

Coach paced next to me, flapping his clipboard agitatedly, in the first stage of grief. "We're screwed now. Adrian sucks at the free. And I'm going to have to reshuffle everything." He'd forgotten I stood there and dashed off to the officials' table to begin substitutions.

"What's going on?" Marisa, who swam the butterfly, not particularly well, had a good twenty minutes before she'd need to line up.

"Campbell had to leave. Something bad. His mom came to get him."

"He didn't say what?"

"No. Only that it was a family emergency. They're not poor."

"Yeah. Not by the look of his mom. You can't get that handbag at Belk," Marisa said, a trace of envy flitting across her face.

"I noticed."

"What do you think he's going to tell you then? If he's not poor?"

"I have no idea. Nothing tonight, I'd guess. He said he'd text me. Date is off, I assume." A leaden lifelessness swamped me.

From across the pool, Coach Phillips, now truly frazzled, bellowed my name. "Where is your head, Tremayne? Why is your butt not in line? 200 IM is up. Get going."

I SWAM IT, and the other two races, well enough to win them all, but not with my usual times. No PR today. The boys' team as a whole, however, lost the meet by only a few points, which made the veins in Coach's temples vibrate and swell to a truly alarming degree. Had Campbell swum the 50 Free, or the 100 Free, which were his best events, and won them, it would have made the difference. Adrian was a poor substitute.

During the after-meet meeting poolside, we all sat quietly, unhappily kicking the poles that supported the benches, the weight of the loss on our shoulders. Coach opened his mouth a few times, unable to speak. My shoulders should have felt pretty light, given that I'd won all four of my races, but for some reason I felt all the guilt for Campbell. I swear I caught Coach glaring at me once he finally found his tongue and got his rant rolling. Poor Adrian got assigned extra practice, which might even have been a relief after the tongue-lashing he took.

In the locker room, everyone dressed and showered in silence, trickling out with little to say. I checked my phone obsessively after every article of clothing I put on, but no message from Campbell came in. It had been nearly three hours. Marisa waited for me.

"What's really going on? What do you know about his family? Who could have had an emergency?"

"He lives with his mom and dad. There's an adult sister and brother-in-law in North Carolina. I guess there could have been a car accident or something. I think his mom was here watching the meet, so she must have gotten a text or a call. That's all I know about. He doesn't talk much about his family."

"Huh."

"Coach said his mom is a doctor. A pediatrician. I didn't even know that much." At that moment, my phone dinged in my hand. "Here it is."

"What does it say?"

I didn't want her to see it before I read it and realized how odd that was at the same time I thought it. I'd never hidden anything from Marisa before. I shielded the phone slightly as I read.

*Campbell: I'm so sorry.*
*Campbell: I have to cancel for tonight.*
*Campbell: I promise I'll tell you what's going on, but don't worry. Nothing life-threatening.*
*Campbell: I still want to take you to dinner. And the other stuff.*

"What does it say? You're not going to let me read it?" Marisa stared at me, incredulous.

"It says nothing life-threatening but he has to cancel for tonight." Relief flooded me that nobody was dead or dismembered, but God. Cryptic much? I wanted to punch something. He knew I wanted to know everything yesterday, or better yet six months ago Friday.

I sucked at waiting.

Now I'd have to wait not just for the knowledge I craved, but also for the things he'd promised in my ear that night at my car. An uncomfortable spurt of... of longing, or something, robbed me of breath.

"Are you going to text him back?" asked Marisa, completely unaware of my Trip Through All the Emotions At Once. "Are you going to ask him what the hell is going on?"

"What? Like demand to know who it is and what specifically happened? He knows I want to know. We've even discussed that I'm not the world's most patient person. He didn't want to tell me. I'll look needy and unhinged if I go off on him."

"So?"

"So, I'm not needy and unhinged. I've gone this long without a guy. I'm good if he walks away right now."

Marisa snorted. "You're such a liar."

I sagged. She was right. I was lying. To myself as well as to her. I already cared more about Campbell than was comfortable. It gave him power over me. I hated anyone having power over me.

"I could walk away," I said, assuring myself as much as Marisa.

"You could not."

"I might have to, so let's quit with the 'you can't' stuff, okay? This isn't *Romeo and Juliet*, you know. Nobody dies if it doesn't work out. This is real life. And let's be honest, Marisa. We're seventeen. We're kids. My parents got married at like twenty-five. That's really young, and it's still eight years away. We're not going to marry Campbell and Ron. No way."

Marisa opened her mouth, to object probably, but my mom opened the door to the hallway and peeked her head in. "Honey?

Everyone is gone. Are you almost done? Are you interested in dinner?"

I glanced at Marisa, pleading for escape. She shook her head.

"Sorry. Ron and I are going to some family thing of his. You're on your own."

"Crap," I said, in a low voice. "Yeah, Mom. I'm coming. Dinner sounds fine."

AT THE BRICK OVEN PIZZA PLACE Ethan asked for, we crowded around a four-person table.

"You swam well today, honey," Mom said.

"Thanks."

"The boy who left in the middle—did that mess things up? The woman in front of me got a call and stood up in a big flurry."

Dad gave me a measuring glance. "Campbell Adams, right? Wasn't he the same one who won the relay in the last leg at the beginning?"

"Yes. And yes, Mom, his leaving made a difference. He's our best freestyler."

Ethan, who'd been building who knew what out of pixels in Minecraft on his iPod, looked up. "Is that your boyfriend? He hugged you. The really tall one, right?"

"He's not my boyfriend. We're friends."

"He's certainly good-looking," Mom said, trying to kindle a little girl-camaraderie spark. For a minute I wanted to let her.

"Kind of seemed like more than friends from where we were sitting," Dad said, watching me closely. I focused on keeping my body language indifferent.

"Well. Right now, we're friends."

"Do you know his parents, Tracy?" Dad asked Mom.

"No. The woman in front of me was alone. I didn't recognize her. I'd say she lives a little fancier life than we do."

"She's a pediatrician," I said. I didn't volunteer that I'd learned this from Coach and not from Campbell.

"Oh. She must not be in the practice we go to. I've never seen her. And with Ethan's asthma, we've seen all the doctors in ours."

"I don't have asthma anymore," Ethan said, scowling but not lifting his eyes from his screen. He hated to be reminded of his diagnosis and had stopped speaking to Mom for a week after she ran across the soccer field during a corner kick to give him a puff on his inhaler. "And how come you're here, anyway? You said you were going out tonight."

Dammit. I'd needed to tell someone I had a date, even if I couldn't bring myself to say "date" or "boy" or "Campbell." Choosing Ethan was a bad idea. I forgot he wasn't a normal human. He saved up everything I said for future ammunition.

"Did you have a date tonight, Natalie?" asked Mom, joy transforming her features. I hated that expression. The expectations and hope ratcheted up the Perfect Daughter pressure to a deeply uncomfortable degree. "With Campbell?"

So much for *we're just friends*. "Um. Yeah. We did, anyway. He had the family emergency and obviously it's off now. Calm down. This was literally going to be the first date. No need for the meet-the-parents deal. It could crash and burn out of the gate."

"I'm sure it will be fine, honey," Mom said, restraining her fist pump with difficulty.

Dad looked a little less thrilled.

"Make sure you use a condom," Ethan said, making the game beep.

I threw a sugar packet and hit him in the nose. "God! Ethan! Make him stop, Mom."

"Good advice, honey. Do use a condom, Natalie."

My dad remained silent but burned a couple of holes through Mom's forehead with his death-ray glare.

"Oh my God. Please stop," I said, looking around at the other tables for anyone I knew.

"Yes. Please stop," Dad said to the ceiling.

I let out a long sigh. "Third degree over. We've established: I know Campbell. I might date Campbell. It is super early. And condoms are good. Can we eat now?"

# Ten

Things didn't get better from there. On Sunday morning, during church, I got a text from Campbell. I'd forgotten to turn off the sound, and it dinged in my pocket right in the middle of the prayer. My mother turned bright red and elbowed me. I read the text before I put it away, aware of my mother's rage. She hated any kind of bad behavior in church. Ethan had learned to sleep with his eyes open.

The text read:


***Campbell: Dealing with a lot of stuff. Probably going to be out of school a couple days.***
***Campbell: We'll talk soon.***


No apologies. No more information.

And he knew it was killing me.

I rode home determined to find out something. Anything. Anything short of demanding answers from Campbell. I didn't want him to know it mattered so much to me. In the backseat, as my parents discussed the sermon and whether it had a point and a narrative arc, I texted him back. It took a lot of deleting and rewriting, but in the end, I was satisfied.

**Me: So sorry you're having a crap weekend. I hope whoever it is gets better soon. See you when you get back. :-)**

I couldn't think of any subtle way to ask what was going on. If he wanted to tell me, he would.

At home, I skipped the chili in the crockpot and took a peanut-butter sandwich up to my room.

On my laptop, I checked the local news. No mention of any car accidents or anything else that would have taken Campbell away from a meet before it was over. I couldn't remember the name of the town in North Carolina where his sister lived or her first name, let alone her married name. I'd never asked, and he certainly hadn't volunteered. I pushed away from my desk in disgust. So much for being nosy—Campbell had distracted me so much I'd forgotten to ask him anything important. All the power of the internet under my fingers and I didn't know even enough information to get more.

I'd have to manage patience.

CAMPBELL MISSED SCHOOL MONDAY and Tuesday, as well as the rehearsals on both of those evenings. Mrs. M chewed her lip. Noah played Campbell's role, pretty well for the most part, but I had to turn away to hide my giggles when he did his constipated Beast-Is-Tortured expression.

My part was coming along well. I knew my lines, which is more than I could say for Amelia, and brought the house down the first time I sang the title song with piano and correct blocking. I'd even managed to conjure up a decent Cockney accent for the spoken parts, after watching scenes from *Oliver!* on Prime a dozen times or more.

During practice Tuesday for a scene between the Beast and Belle, I sat in the auditorium studying for my AP Gov test the next day. Finney came and sat down in the row in front of me.

This couldn't be good.

"What've you done with Adams, Tree Trunks?" He leaned in, his face close enough to spot a zit on the side of his nose. Onions. He ate something with onions for dinner. Yuck.

"Your mouth is moving, Finney. You might want to shut it."

"It seems impossible to believe, but I heard a rumor that you and Captain America have something going on. What's the deal? Is he blind?"

I didn't look up from my book and leaned back to evade the onion stench. "I'm sorry. Did you say something?"

"You heard me. What's up? Is he slipping you the hot beef injection?"

"Aw. You watched *The Breakfast Club*. One step closer to culture. Congrats."

"Fine. Be like that. As a matter of fact, I'm all for it, Trunks. You lock up Thor, and I get Amelia."

It was like speaking to a member of a lower species. I didn't bother to hide my smile. "Yes, I'm sure Amelia has *you* penciled in directly below Joe and Campbell."

"Whatever. He's clearly nuts, but I couldn't be happier for you. You have my blessing over your union."

"It's like someone is talking, but I can't hear anything." I held my hand up to my ear like my grandma.

"Later. I've got to get something out of my car."

"Good to know." No doubt he had a joint out there. He usually did.

He stood, waiting for me to say something else. I stared at him, expressionless. He got the message and went away.

A rumor? Of me and Campbell? How would he have heard it? I rolled my eyes at myself. He could have heard it a million different ways.

I stretched, pleased. Even if I didn't technically have a boyfriend yet, people thought I did. It made it seem real.

It was a good shot in the arm at a time when I needed one. Campbell hadn't been in any contact since Sunday.

ON WEDNESDAY MORNING, Campbell returned to swim practice. Coach Phillips, who had an unfortunate grudge-holding problem, refused to speak to him. The mood at practice was tense and silent, all of us swimming our distance with ruthless efficiency to get it over with.

I swam with nausea rising in my throat. Campbell wouldn't look at me or speak to me. He didn't seem angry. Anger I could confront and deal with; he acted like I didn't exist. We'd returned to where we'd been before I'd seen that cast list. The Kiss, and all the movement since, disappeared in a puff of smoke.

I couldn't let it go that easy.

After practice, I changed faster than I'd ever managed before and caught Campbell in the still-empty hallway outside the boys' locker room.

He gave me one anguished look and tried to keep walking. The hurt banged around in my rib cage and made me reckless.

Apparently, I could say anything. I had nothing to lose if I'd already lost it. I deserved to know why.

"No way." *What happened to 'I still want to take you out'?* I grabbed his arm. He blinked, and then pulled wordlessly away to start down the hall again.

"Nope. Not that easy, Adams. You're going to talk. What is going on?" Even with my long legs, I had to jog to keep up with him. If he didn't stop, we'd be out the door and halfway to the middle school.

"I can't do this. It's not a good idea. I shouldn't have—"

"You did, though. And now I want you to tell me what you were going to tell me on Saturday."

"No, Natalie. There's no point. Go back to your regularly scheduled life. It'll be easier."

The hopeless expression on his face stopped me in my tracks and let all the air out of my self-pity. Something big was bothering him. It scared me. For him.

"Okay. It's not about me. I get it. We're still friends, right? Tell me. It looks like it's killing you not to tell someone."

He stopped walking a few yards ahead and turned back toward me. "I can't." A lie. He wanted to tell me. The want screamed from every line of his body.

"You can. I won't even expect dinner after." I approached him slowly, as if he might bolt.

He gained control again, smoothed out the mask of his face. "Just stop. Stop… needing to know everything all the time. Please."

"Campbell, I can't just let you walk away, looking like that, without—" I'd grabbed his arm again, desperate to keep him there.

He shook it off, gently. "You absolutely can. See you." He stalked away, in the direction of the school library.

I went to my locker and sat down on the cold linoleum in front of it.

A weary, sick feeling flooded me like when I had a fever and had swum too hard trying to ignore it. I recognized it as loss and misery. Campbell was done with me. We hadn't even gotten off the starting block and it was over. An unfamiliar pricking at the corners of my eyes let me know I'd fallen harder for him than I'd thought. I didn't cry. I never cried.

To distract myself, I went over the clues to the Mystery of Campbell once more.

Okay. Campbell had a doctor for a mother. He wasn't poor. I snorted at myself for even considering any supernatural option. Whatever he hid was torturing him. And it was bad. For a moment I reconsidered the story Kameron had told me. But he wasn't violent. He couldn't be. Under stress, right now, he'd gently removed my hand from his arm. Was someone else violent with him? I'd never seen his father. His sister had moved far away. Maybe Campbell lived in an abusive home.

That couldn't be it. He'd been planning to tell me whatever it was, and something had happened to stop him. Announcements related to child abuse didn't usually precede a dinner date.

I did a lot of sniffling before Spanish and almost convinced myself I had a cold coming on.

THAT AFTERNOON, I came home before rehearsal and slung my backpack beside the door. I headed straight for the refrigerator like usual, only to be met by both my parents sitting at the kitchen table, side by side, heads bowed with stress. Dad never came home at this hour. My throat tightened and dried. Had somebody died?

"What?" Last I heard, my grandma was finishing up a singles cruise in the Bahamas. She wasn't even seventy yet. She couldn't have died.

"Sit down, honey. We need to talk to you about something." My mom bit her lip. Okay.

I sat.

My dad cleared his throat. "It's about Campbell Adams."

A buzzing noise filled my head. With difficulty, I said, "What about Campbell?"

He didn't meet my eyes. "You mentioned his name before, and I told you I had some students who'd gone to St. Anselms." He paused a moment, then went on, embarrassment and Englishness making him over-enunciate everything. "When I—I mean we—saw at the meet that you had developed, ah, feelings of some kind for the boy, I thought I might ask round and see if anyone knew him. One young woman, a freshman, did and spilled out quite a story."

"Oh, God, Dad. You didn't."

"I'm afraid I did."

"And? What did she say?"

"My student, Morgan, said that she'd been close friends—soccer teammates, I believe—with Campbell's ex-girlfriend, Isabelle."

"Is this that old story about him hitting her? Because I asked him about it, and he—"

"Hitting her?" My mom exchanged worried glances with my father. "You didn't tell me that part! Oh, heavens. This gets worse and worse."

"It's not true, Mom. I asked him."

"Let's return to the point, shall we?" asked Dad. "Morgan said nothing about violence. She did, however, say something about pregnancy."

Pregnancy.

Pregnancy.

Pregnancy. The word echoed in my head until it lost its meaning and sounded like gibberish. I couldn't make it function, couldn't make it convey its meaning to me.

A silence descended. The wind blew a branch against the window over the sink. I needed to cut my pinkie fingernail. My head buzzed. I couldn't say anything. Words wouldn't form. A girl, and Campbell, and Pregnancy. With a capital letter P. I shoved down a wild desire to laugh at that. A life full of capital letters, that's what I had.

Dad went on, taking my silence as permission to tell the story. I didn't have the power of speech to stop him even if I'd wanted to.

"Morgan said that when she came back to school for her senior year, Isabelle's junior year, Isabelle was gone. Her parents had pulled her for homeschooling, the story went. Everyone believed it because her family is very religious. But Morgan and Isabelle were close, and Morgan went to Isabelle's house to see her. Isabelle said she was three months along, and her parents didn't want anyone to know. She wouldn't be returning to school, and by soccer season in the spring she'd be a mother."

I opened my mouth, only to have one of those arid desert spots attack my throat and make the words dry up again. A baby. The family emergency. And he bought milk. At Walgreens. Babies drink milk. His sweatshirt had been stained with… Oh God.

"Morgan said Isabelle told her Campbell was the father. Everyone at St. Anselms knew, she said, that Campbell and Isabelle had been serious. They stood out because they were so young, only sophomores. Campbell was removed from St. Anselms as well. He, of course, transferred here."

"He's got a baby?" My voice sounded like somebody else's.

"A son, apparently. A year old now."

For some reason, I concentrated on how often I blinked. It seemed like a lot. I could see my own eyelashes when I concentrated. The refrigerator hummed. I traced the wood grain of the table with a chipped fingernail.

A baby.

"Honey, we just wanted to make sure you knew what—"

"Don't worry about it, Mom." My voice sounded dead, even to me.

"I hate to mention it, Natalie, but given the school board, and my opponent's position…" Dad reached across the table for my hand. I pulled mine off the table, weirdly unable now to feel the surface of the wood under my skin.

"I said, don't worry about it. There is *nothing* to worry about." The words fell out like I'd spilled them. I couldn't get back any power over them. *Nothing* was right. Well, a baby was definitely *something*, just nothing to do with me.

A baby.

Their sighs of relief echoed in the silent kitchen. Idly, crazily, I wondered what they'd done to Ethan to get him out of the way for the exorcism.

"I know it hurts. When I was—"

"I don't want to hear it, Mom." I looked at my dad, who'd had the nerve to bring up his damn school board seat, like it mattered, like it meant something, at a time when… and I got back emotions. In a flood, they returned and roared out of my mouth like flame from a flamethrower. His fault. His fault for being nosy and finding this out. "And, Dad, next time, keep your nose out of my business. I don't need you to babysit me or do background checks on everyone I know. I don't want to talk to you, and I don't want to look at you." I stood up, shoving back the chair, reaching blindly for the doorway.

Anywhere but here.

"That's enough, Natalie," my dad said, his tone as harsh and as unfamiliar as mine. "You should be glad I did. You obviously didn't know about the baby. And I doubt he was planning to tell you."

He was. But not anymore. He walked away from me. Because he knew what a big deal this would be. Because he didn't want his problem to become my problem, even a little...

On the third stair from the top, the first tear dripped off my chin.

# Eleven

Upstairs in my room, once my hand stopped shaking, I texted Noah and told him I had a migraine and wouldn't be able to be at rehearsal. I'd never missed a rehearsal. Ever. At least no one was angling for my part. That I knew of. Who'd want it? Giant costume, old lady. It had my name written all over it.

I didn't usually wallow, but I figured this once it ought to be allowed. I got under all the blankets on my bed and wondered idly if it was possible to die of mortification. Out there somewhere a religious ex-soccer player pushed a stroller with a baby in it, drooling or something, and Campbell had provided half the DNA.

I'd kissed somebody's father. At seventeen.

A father. A dad. A child called him Daddy. Dads were old guys, with baggy jeans, Old Spice scents, and belly overhangs. They tried and failed to use cool slang and told boring stories about how, back in the eighties, they'd had heavy metal hair and played a mean electric guitar. Their knees cracked when they crouched, and parts of their scalps shone under fluorescent lights.

Campbell was a dad.

If only he'd been a vampire.

With a wild laugh into my pillow, I realized I had the answer to the question of whether Campbell had lost his virginity. Um. Yeah. In a pretty big fucking way. One question answered.

He'd be at swim practice tomorrow. I had until then to get it together and decide what to do about this horrific knowledge that… coated me like sludge. The most attractive option, the wisest one maybe, was to ignore it, hope no one else found out about it until after graduation, and escape from here off to college without anyone knowing I'd kissed somebody's dad before my eighteenth birthday. Attractive or not, I hated that option. I hated not dealing with things. Embarrassment was not my natural state.

The only other option was to confront Campbell about it and demand to hear the truth from him. Maybe my dad had it wrong. Please let him have it wrong.

I rolled over onto my stomach, putting my head in my hands. Did the fact that he had a baby, if (could I still hang onto the "if"?) he really had a baby, make Campbell a different person than he'd been yesterday? Maybe the baby made Campbell the person he was. The one I'd gotten obsessed with.

Oh my God, a baby. If Campbell had a baby, his life was so different from mine that we might as well live on different planets. All the stuff I'd thought we had in common: swimming, the play, our classes—those things meant everything to me and probably nothing to him. They had no importance compared to the responsibility of being a parent. He was on another level.

I flopped onto my back and reached for my stuffed dog. Amy stayed on my bed, as "decoration," I claimed, but she came in handy at times like this. And besides, I couldn't possibly be expected to be a mature adult at this moment.

Why hadn't he told me? Why had he changed his mind? He'd been planning to tell me. I'd bet my life on it. And then he walked away. It had killed him to do it. Didn't I owe it to him to listen? Oh, God, something this specific couldn't possibly be false, which meant Campbell had been keeping this secret for almost two years. Didn't he need someone to talk to about it? Even if just as friends?

I let out a groan. Why did it have to be me?

Four months. Four months and I'd walk away from here. After graduation I'd get some stupid stress-free summer job, and see people from school like once a week, maybe at a picnic where we'd say how much we'd miss each other while lying through our teeth. I'd text my future college roommate, finding out if we liked the same music, and we'd buy matching bedding and decide if we wanted beanbag chairs and fairy lights or not. Marisa and I would say we'd stay in touch, and we'd mean it. I'd report early to campus for swimming, and orientation, and consider whether to rush a sorority. I'd decide against it in the end, because whatever, sorority girls are shallow, but I'd have a good time coming to that conclusion. I'd go to some parties and drink some beer. I might hook up randomly. I might find one of my classes fascinating and change my major.

It had all been planned out, for years. I'd been on this same path, no variation, since sixth or seventh grade. I'd never considered any other scenarios.

It all depended on there being nothing to keep me here.

Campbell had plenty to keep him here. No wonder the college conversation went nowhere.

If I asked Campbell about it, if I heard the story, I'd be involved. I might already be involved. Dammit. If I had any brains at all, if I had any sense of self-preservation, I'd show up for swimming tomorrow morning and ignore the very existence of Campbell. He'd given me permission. He'd said we were done. I should take him at his word and be done.

Doing anything else would be idiotic.

The screech of the wheels coming off the rails echoed in my head.

POOLSIDE, THE NEXT MORNING, I stalked right up to Campbell, who stood alone and a little forlorn.

"Meet me after practice. In the hall. And we're going to talk."

"I can't today." He turned away, as if one of the championship banners on the tile wall had become fascinating.

I leaned in close, on tiptoes to make sure he heard me. "Yes, you can, *Dad.* After practice." I didn't leave room for any argument. He'd come.

He turned around fast enough he didn't have time to wipe all the shock off his face. It didn't take long. His face went impenetrable. "There's nothing to say."

"Yes. There is. But not now. I need to concentrate during practice. You, too, probably. You can shave at least five tenths off that 50 free." That was rude, but I didn't know what to do with the anger. It made me gnash my teeth and say awful things to people I cared about.

"Fine," he ground out.

We pivoted in opposite directions. If I'd had this much emotion during the meet, I'd have had four PRs. When Coach blew the whistle, I dove in and swam as if my life depended on it. When the hour was over, my muscles were weak and exhausted, but none of the anger disappeared. My temper burned slow. I'd never had a flash fuse. I had a hard time getting rid of it once it started.

This time I had no idea who I was angriest at: Campbell, for lying; my parents, for telling me; or myself, for letting him in.

Except Campbell hadn't lied. And my parents had to tell me once they knew. The only asshole in this scenario was me.

Marisa asked me what was wrong fifteen different ways in the locker room. I told her whatever I could think of to distract her. I'd never done that before, but I couldn't tell Marisa something like this before I got the truth from Campbell. Having to put off my best friend made my fists clench. If I didn't get things under control, I'd knock his head off.

Why hadn't he told me? I'd practically begged him.

"Want to go get a soda?" asked Marisa, once our wet hair was twisted back up.

"No. I need to talk to Campbell."

"Okay." She let me pass, aware on some level that something was up.

Outside, Campbell leaned stiff as a poker against the wall, resentment written all over him.

I walked up to him and intentionally into his personal space. "So, I'm guessing I know what you had to tell me?"

He stayed silent, watching my face. It didn't take long for me to regret the personal space decision, because the space between us crackled and buzzed. Damned if I'd back off now, though.

"I assume from your silence that you are, in fact, the father of a child?"

His lips worked for a second or two. "Come with me." He took my elbow and towed me down the hall. We found a spot at the landing of a staircase and sat, a good four feet apart. "Yes. I have a son. Is that what you wanted to hear?"

"Well, to be quite honest, no, it isn't. I really, really, really wish you'd said, 'No, Natalie, I have no idea what you're talking about. I did not father a child at sixteen. The stress must be getting to you.'"

"Sorry. I did father a child at sixteen. I'm terribly sorry if that ruins *your* day," he said, his lips twisting into a grimace of bitterness.

The pain on his face deflated all my ridiculous self-righteousness just like that. God. He'd kept that secret all this time. With no one to talk to.

"Campbell, I'm an asshole."

He glanced up, surprised.

I took a deep, cleansing breath. "How old is he?"

He twisted the hem of his T-shirt.

"He had his first birthday a few weeks ago."

"Dammit, Campbell," I said, all the sustaining anger draining away. "Didn't you think this was the kind of thing you ought to have mentioned?"

"I told you not to get involved with me. That I wasn't the right guy for you."

"You're not still with… his mother, are you?"

"No. Of course not. What do you take me for?"

Though the anger had gone, my sarcasm never quite deserted me. "I have no idea what to take you for. I assumed you were a normal high school student. Now I find out—from my dad, by the way, that the things I didn't know about you outnumber the things I did by like five thousand to one."

He said nothing for a few more seconds, twisting that shirt until I wanted to yank it out of his hands. I wished I had even a tenth of that ability to tolerate quiet. Impatience: yet another flaw.

Finally, he looked up at me, those remarkable eyes full of honesty. "She broke up with me that summer, when she found out she was pregnant. When her parents found out, they freaked out. Her parents are major Southern Baptists. He's a deacon and she runs the vacation Bible school. Pro-life everything. They told my parents. I'd like to block out forever how bad that meeting was. Her parents decided their lives would be over if anyone knew, and mine agreed to keep it quiet, so we got jerked out of school. I'm under strict instructions not to tell anyone. Ever. It's easier if I just don't talk about… anything." He blew out his cheeks, his body rigid with frustration.

"What's his name?"

Campbell took a second to register the question, and pulled his knees up to his chest, like a little kid. Protecting himself. "Oliver. His name is Oliver. But not Adams. Isabelle's parents didn't want her to give him my name. To keep it nice and quiet. His last name is hers, Barringer. It's like he's not allowed to have any part of me. She didn't argue. She doesn't, usually, not with her parents. She was sixteen. We were sixteen, I should say. And what could we do?"

"Do you still see her?"

"Yeah. I have visitation with him every Friday night. And Sunday afternoon."

Friday nights. "So that's why we saw you…"

"In the store? Yeah. When babies turn a year old, they can drink regular milk instead of…" He trailed off, embarrassed, as my stomach recoiled at the thought of the word he was about to say. Oh my God. If I'd ever thought about it, which I definitely hadn't, I'd have hoped not to have to be involved in any conversation in which the words "breast milk" would be used for at least ten more years. "We were out and I needed some."

"So, you've been taking care of him? Every weekend? For a whole year?"

He sighed, heavily. "For a lifetime, Nat. He's my child. It's diapers and bottles now, but soon it'll be walking and toys and preschool and kindergarten and on and on. It isn't a game. Isabelle is homeschooled. Studying for her GED. She takes care of him the rest of the time. I'm lucky. At least I get to go to school, feel 50% normal. That's all over for Izzy."

I'd never felt younger in my whole life, but I plowed on anyway. "And college?"

"There's no going away to college. I have a 4.2 GPA and it doesn't matter. I have to pay child support. My parents can afford college. They have plenty of money. They're both doctors. They could afford to pay the child support, too, if they wanted. But they don't. It's my mess, they said. Mine to take care of. And they're right. It is mine. My fault. My child." He came to a halt, guilt across his features. "And he's great," he added in a whisper. "My son."

"How…" I started, through dry lips, "how did it…"

"Happen?" He barked out a short laugh. "I expect you can guess. We were stupid. We'd been dating a while. I was horny. She was curious. I thought I loved her. We used a condom, but condoms aren't 100% perfect. Izzy never got on the pill. She thought it would make her seem… I don't know. Like a girl who was looking for sex. And if her parents found out they would have gone ballistic. It's exactly what usually happens to people who are stupid like that."

A memory flashed of Gabe, wrestling awkwardly with the condom. I'd giggled. He'd turned red. Even at the time, I knew that if I'd said the word, he would have tossed it aside. He'd asked if I took the pill first and been obviously dismayed when I said I didn't. Marisa told me once that Ron hated to wear a condom and that on occasion she forgot to take the pill. A sudden urge to warn her rose in me. I pushed it down. For now.

"It's not that stupid. It's common. You were young." I pulled my knees up to my chest, too, though I had no idea what I was protecting.

"God, Nat. I'm young now. There's no planet on which seventeen is old enough to be a father. I love that kid, but I'm automatically the world's shittiest father because I don't know anything about being a father. I wasn't prepared. I'm still not prepared."

I pondered that for a while. I couldn't imagine myself as a mother at all, now or in the future, shitty or otherwise. I was closer to Oliver's age than my mom's. And so was Campbell. "So, you … change diapers and everything?"

"Of course I do. When he's with me, I do all the stuff. My mom watches him if I have to run out for milk or whatever, but otherwise, she makes me do everything. My responsibility. Didn't you ever babysit or anything?"

"My brother is almost six years younger. I changed his diaper once. And yes, I babysat, a little, but never any kids young enough to be in diapers. I know nothing about babies."

"You learn quick. I'd never seen a baby up close before that day in the hospital."

I didn't want to learn. There were so many things I needed to learn before babies should cross my mind. I wanted to ward off that kind of responsibility with Jedi mind tricks. Every part of me screamed to run. He read it in my face and smiled sadly.

"Now you know why I told you to go. To get away from me. This isn't for you. Not in a million years. You'd never be so stupid to get yourself into a situation like this. You're the smartest girl I've ever known. Don't get me wrong. I love Oliver. Sometimes it hurts how much I love him. But I'd tell everyone the same, if I were allowed to talk about it at all. Wait. Wait 'til you're ready. Walk away."

"What was the emergency?"

"Emergency?" Something wistful softened his face.

"Yeah. At the swim meet."

"Oh. Oliver was with Isabelle. He woke up sick on Saturday morning, and within a couple hours, his fever had spiked to 104. At the hospital, they said he had pneumonia. He scared us: he kind of flopped, sort of. No energy and such a high fever. Izzy freaked out and wanted him to stay with me because my mom's a pediatrician. He's okay now, getting better."

"Oh." I thought about all the times I'd told the nurse at school I was sick, and my mom or my dad had dropped everything to come and pick me up. It never occurred to me before they might have been doing something important.

"It's not a shocker or even all that unusual for a parent, but it is for a high school student. My life is not like yours. Swim team, the play, all that has to take a backseat to Oliver's stuff. Those things are just for fun. They're not real life. I only get to do them because Izzy has primary custody."

"God, that sucks. I can't even imagine."

"I don't want you to imagine. You shouldn't imagine. You need to get out of here for college."

I wanted that, too. Even more desperately now that I'd seen this alternate universe. "Am I the first person you've told about this?"

"Obviously our parents know, and some of the relatives, and my sister and her husband, and Izzy's best friend. And probably a few others who've heard from one of them. But you're the first person at this school I've told."

"Oh." For a second I tried to imagine it: no one to talk to, alone in a school of 1500 students.

"I had a lot of friends, you know, back at St. Anselms. I let them all go. A couple of them tried to keep in touch, but my parents made me get a new cell number. Stay off social media. Better for nobody to know. Or very few."

He squinted at me thoughtfully. "I guess a few more people know than I'd thought. Your dad, for one. How did he find out?"

"He's a professor at UVA. One of Isabelle's friends is in his class." I felt the red creep up my chest as I anticipated his next question.

"Just curious. How, exactly, did that come up?"

"Umm." Heat rushed into my cheeks. I held my knees closer. "My dad saw us at the swim meet and asked me for your name. He had a St. Anselms kid in his class. I guess he did some checking."

Campbell colored to match me. "And he thought…?"

"Yeah. He thought."

He considered that for a while, then relaxed his leg, letting his foot stretch out toward me. He kept it away, though. "Listen. It's not fair of me to expect you to keep this secret. You can tell everyone, and I can't stop you. I don't even have the right to ask."

"I'd like to talk about it with Marisa, if that's okay. But that's all."

"Definitely. Tell her if you want."

"Okay. Nobody else. I promise. So, we're friends?"

"If you're willing to be. But nothing more, Nat."

Now that he'd mentioned "more," all I could think about was his lips. I tried not to stare at them: relaxed now, no longer anguished. An echo of the Kiss sent a tiny thrill through me, but I couldn't summon up the all-consuming passion I'd had before.

Now the idea had baggage and weight. It was less attractive. At least for now.

"Yes," I said. "We can be friends. You probably could use one."

"I'm sorry. For getting you involved. For everything."

"Apology accepted. And I'm not involved. I'm here to listen if you need an ear. And that's all."

Even as I said it, I knew I was lying. Keeping myself aloof wasn't in my DNA. I always had to know everything. To master every situation. To be involved in everything up to my eyebrows. I'd appoint myself Official Confidant and get all offended if he didn't tell me everything. God, I wished I'd never heard any of this.

So much for a quicksand-free march to graduation.

# Twelve

*I* sleepwalked through my classes the rest of the day. Once, I passed Campbell in the hall, both of us carrying piles of books. He waved, and that one wave was so sad and lost that my heart squeezed.

After school, I found Marisa.

"Bruh." She grabbed my arm. "Are you going to tell me what the hell is going on now?"

"Yes. But not here. Let's go get donuts."

I left my car in the parking lot while Marisa drove us to the donut shop, where they sold the same cake donut to everyone, but would dress it up with frosting or coconut or even bacon bits if you wanted them. I ordered one with white frosting and coconut and one with cinnamon sugar. Marisa got three plain cake.

"Okay. We have food. We're away from school. What. The. Hell. Is. Going. On?" she asked.

"It's about Campbell. Before I tell you, I need to swear you to secrecy. Promise that you and I will be the only people to talk about this?" I stared at her. Her nose wrinkled. "Promise."

"Okay. Anything. Talk!"

"My parents sat me down yesterday after school. They want me to stay away from Campbell."

"Why? Your mom's always after you about getting a boy-friend."

"I'm getting to that. You remember I said Kameron told me he went to St. Anselms before here? A girl who knew him there is in my dad's first-year calculus class. My dad saw me and Campbell at the swim meet, and he—"

"Bruh." Marisa slapped her hands onto the table, making my donut bounce. "Wait. I didn't see anything at the swim meet. Was there something good to see?"

My eyebrows drew together in frustration. She always wanted all the details of everything, while I had a tendency to want to spill details as fast as I could make my mouth move. If I didn't spit out this information in the next ten seconds, it would choke me. Didn't she see that? "Um. No. Not really. He hugged me. And we, like, whispered in each other's ears. But apparently it was enough to set off the parent alarms."

Marisa made short work of her second donut and spoke with her mouth full. "So, anyway, Dad wanted to check on you."

"Right. And—oh God." She'd derailed me, and now I lost the ability to speak calm English. I blurted it out. "Campbell has a baby!"

"A what?" She froze, like an animal about to be shot.

"A baby! He got his ex-girlfriend from St. Anselms preg-nant, and she had the kid, and now he's the father of a one-year-old baby."

If I hadn't been so upset myself, it would have been funny to watch Marisa deflate in shock. She dropped her third donut half eaten onto the wax paper and kind of melted into her seat, making her look small and defenseless.

Her throat worked. "Oh my God. Oh my God. Oh, Nat. Does he have anything to do with it?"

"The baby? Yes, he has custody part of every weekend, and he works so he can pay child support." I toyed with the edge of my wax paper, rolling it into a tiny cylinder. "He says he can't go to college. He's not supposed to talk to anyone about it, so that's why nobody…" *Knows him. Sees him.* "It's got to be terrible."

Marisa's face blanched. "I don't even know what I'd do, if Ron and I…"

"You better damn well be careful. That's all."

"Yeah." She swallowed hard. "More careful than I've been. Holy shit."

"Right." Irrational urges to buy out Walgreens' whole shelf of condoms and fling them like confetti through the hallways zipped through my head.

"Bruh. What are you going to do?"

"Me? It's not my problem. I don't have a baby." Thank God in the Highest Heaven Above.

"About Campbell, dumbass. You totally knew that's what I was asking."

I focused on the frosting donut, still untouched in front of me. "I don't know."

"Okay, well, I'll come right out and ask. Have you done it?"

"Sex, you mean? With Campbell? No!" I'd said that too loudly. I looked around, but everyone was engrossed in their designer donuts.

She laughed. "Okay, born-again Victorian maiden. Dial down the drama. You've done it before. He's done it before, obviously. You have a pretty major thing for him. You definitely were headed that way before. Before all this."

"I told you about the Kiss. That's about all. Almost right after that, he started with the whole noble 'you shouldn't be with me' thing, and damn, Marisa, he's right! Being with him would totally derail my life."

"It doesn't have to." Marisa reached over and calmly broke off part of my donut, popping it into her mouth and then scrunching up her face at the taste of the sugary-sweet frosting.

"What do you mean?"

"Let's get to that later. What would you feel for him if none of this had happened?"

"But it did." My sweating hands had made wet spots on my pant legs. I moved them.

"Pretend it didn't."

"That's a hell of thing to pretend doesn't exist. Okay, fine. Since it's all hypothetical, then, I liked him. A lot. We were getting close. He… mattered to me." I bit my lip when I saw the surprised interest in hers, beyond embarrassed that I'd actually said that. "Is that enough? Yes, dammit. I wanted him. For a boyfriend, and all the rest, too. What would it have hurt? I would have had a fun end of senior year, and then we would have gone our separate ways, and then…"

"Why can't you still have that?"

I closed my mouth. "Because… because…"

"Because nothing. If you like him, be with him. He's been trying to push you away, even though obviously he doesn't want to. Looks like you matter to him, too. He'll be okay with an end date. There was always going to be an end date, right?" She ate the rest of my donut.

"Right." Even as I thought about it, an end date seemed cold and heartless.

"Then enjoy it. He's stuck here anyway, so why wouldn't he be willing to take what he can get? Go play with the baby.

Babies are cute. Hang with Campbell. Hug his spectacular half-naked swimming body. Do more with it than that, if you want. Then go to college, like you planned."

"You think?"

"It's up to you, but I can't see what it could hurt."

CAMPBELL MISSED THE FIRST TWENTY MINUTES of rehearsal. When he got there, I was on stage with Amelia and Tyler, the seventh grader who played my teacup son. Tyler was a sweet kid, tiny for his age. He and my brother Ethan both played soccer. My mom said that Tyler's mother had gone to Juilliard and hadn't given up trying to force her kids to be stars.

I lost my Cockney accent without warning at the sight of Campbell, showered and in a long-sleeved T-shirt and jeans. My subconscious had been up to some naughty stuff, because as soon as I saw him, the word "sex" settled in my mind. Then I forgot all my lines, too.

No. NoNoNoNo. This had to stop. Campbell had messed up more days of school for me than I wanted to count. He'd been distracting me in class. I'd had to stay up late studying to catch up about half the time, and that made me sleepy, which made me crabby and hungry, and that made me disoriented. I would not let him mess up this play too.

I took a deep breath and pulled the lines out of thin air somehow, getting through the scene on force of will, though the Cockney accent went way too Dick Van Dyke. Mrs. M stared at me, brows drawn together.

"I need to go to the bathroom. Sorry. Too much Diet Coke."

"All right, dear. We'll move on to the opening song. Take your time."

I wasn't in that one. I'd have at least thirty minutes. Campbell wasn't in it either. I'd be interested to see what he'd do with that break.

"Campbell, I thought we agreed you'd be on time from now on. I really need you to be here precisely at six." Mrs. M frowned at him. As I passed him on the way to the lobby and the bathroom, he bit the inside of his cheek.

"It's no problem, Campbell," sang out Noah, lounging on the stage edge as if he owned the auditorium. "I'll be happy to handle your part if you're not here."

Amelia looked up. "Mrs. M. It was fine. We didn't do any of the Beast scenes yet. We were doing the Mrs. Potts one. Campbell didn't…"

I banged out the door, unwilling to listen to what now sounded stupid. I couldn't believe I'd ever been at a place where my biggest worry was that Noah might get Campbell kicked out of the play. Campbell wouldn't even care. Not that much, anyway.

By the time I came back from the bathroom, Campbell sat in our now-accustomed place on the bench outside the auditorium with his books. He gave me a half smile of greeting.

I sat down next to him.

He glanced up from his work, setting it aside. "Hey."

"Hey."

"So, friends, right?"

My conversation with Marisa replayed through my head. I hadn't decided yet. I could keep my options open. "Friends."

"I forgot to write down the module we were supposed to read in Physics. Did you get it?"

"Yeah." I rummaged in my backpack for my planner to let him copy it down. While his head was bent over his own planner, I stared at his thick, blond-streaked hair. "You have chlorine hair."

He glanced up, amusement on his face. "You do, too."

"How long have you been swimming?"

"Since I was a kid. My parents signed me up for lessons when I was five, after I fell off the end of a dock on the Eastern Shore that summer. I used to be kind of silly, or at least that's what my mom says. I was clowning around, pretending a shark was waiting to eat me. I don't remember it, but my sister jumped in and saved me. I spent the next two weeks at the Y, taking lessons."

"I don't remember learning to swim. I feel like I've always known." I laughed at how stupid that sounded. "I took lessons when I was maybe three."

"You're really good on stage, too. How'd you get into that?" he asked, gesturing toward the auditorium door.

"Thanks. I used to put on little plays in my garage for my parents with my friends. Sang at church. Then I did middle school chorus and children's theater. I used to dream of being on the Disney Channel."

"You're talented. Is there anything you're bad at?"

Flustered, I didn't know how to answer that. Inspiration struck. "I'm good at most of the things that can be worked at. I'm bad at most of the things that are supposed to come naturally."

"That's an interesting answer."

"I do my best. So tell me. How on earth did you come to audition for this play?"

He laughed, pushing back his hair self-consciously and looking down at his planner. "I like to act. I was in plays at St.

Anselms. I checked before auditions when the rehearsals were, and they're not on Fridays, or Sundays, or right after school, so I figured why not."

"You didn't do it last year."

"No, last year the baby was due. I didn't know how it would all shake out. There was court, and…"

"Court?"

"Yeah. Once the baby was born, the Barringers made Izzy file for child support in court. In the end, we worked it out. Or, I should say, my parents and hers worked it out. I think I'm paying more than what I would owe, given that I'm a minor and didn't have a full- time job at the time it was calculated."

"Oh. Can't you do something about that?"

"I guess I could. I could re-file in court and let the judge decide, but hell. Why shouldn't I have to pay? Babies are expensive. There's diapers and clothes and bottles and all kinds of stuff. The worst part of court was…" He broke off, unwilling to go any further.

"The worst part was what?"

"My parents insisted on a DNA test. Izzy's parents went nuts over that—turned it all on her like she was some kind of slut who'd been with a dozen guys. I tried to tell Izzy I knew she hadn't slept with anyone else, she was sixteen, it was stupid, but we did the test anyway. God, it was horrible, sitting there in the hallway at the courthouse while a stranger swabbed my cheek, and Oliver's, and Izzy's. Like we were criminals. And Izzy refused to speak to me for a long time. She thought I'd told my parents it wasn't mine."

"Were you absolutely sure? Really?"

"Yeah," he said, shortly. "I was sure. The only doubt I had was when she told me."

"Doubt?"

"It felt unreal. Like a dream. I didn't really think she'd lie to me about being pregnant, but I kept thinking unbelievable denial-type stuff, like it wasn't possible. Stuff like 'but I still have braces.'" He rubbed his nose. "Like braces are some kind of protection against pregnancy."

"Yeah." I almost understood what he was saying. I had a zit starting on my forehead. It would be an easy jump to think it might serve as some kind of amulet against adulthood. "You don't have braces now. They must have done the job. Of straightening your teeth, if not stopping your sperm."

I sucked in my breath with a sharp hiss. Oh my God. What a thing to say.

Visions of my state-sanctioned but still controversial Family Life class from middle school raced through my head. Diagrams of the fallopian tubes and a bunch of body parts which all started with the letter V. An egg, waiting for puncture. Sperm, dancing eagerly on the microscope slide from the video they'd shown us. So much sperm. The vision finished up with the sticky condom Gabe had unrolled after that bizarre and bloodless occasion.

I wanted to cut my tongue out. I'd said "sperm" to Campbell Adams. Maybe I'd die, mercifully, right now. Dying would be less gross than cutting out my tongue. Gah.

Heat hummed in the air from our blushing.

After the two most mortifying seconds of my life, he cleared his throat. "Um. Yeah. I got the braces off in the summer after tenth grade. Right after I found out about Izzy."

"You have good teeth."

"Good sperm, apparently, too."

We stared at each other for one horrifying beat, then burst into laughter so loud it bounced off the empty lobby walls in an echo. I laughed until my stomach muscles ached and my cheeks felt tight. Campbell Adams had a wicked sense of humor. He rolled back and forth on the bench, gasping. I stood up and bent over, trying to catch my breath. I sat back down and hit his shoulder by accident. We bounced apart as if burned.

I dared a look into his face. The laughter melted off, leaving something tentative and hesitant behind. A thrill, uneasy and forbidden, rolled through my midsection. My hands, holding my knees, squeezed as I tried to keep them from touching him. Oh God. I'd have to decide quick if we were going to last as friends for more than about ten more seconds.

More time. I needed more time. I jumped to my feet.

Campbell stood, too.

"Hey," I started. My voice wouldn't come out breezy and confident, like I wanted it to. It was low and nervous. "I... Campbell. I want to..."

"I want to..." His voice had dropped an octave, too.

Hands at our sides, the eye contact flared and burned. His dark pupils expanded, pushing aside the yellow ring of his iris and leaving all sea blue. If I just...

No.

I stepped backwards. He blinked, shaking his head slightly.

"I think we need time to process. To see what we're doing here. To make sure..."

"That we want to be friends?" he asked, still low.

"That we don't want to be more," I managed, before turning to the doors of the auditorium. To run.

I CLOSED THE KITCHEN DOOR with a silent click that night past ten thirty. As we got closer to the opening of the play in

April, Mrs. M stretched the rehearsals as long as she could. Most of the time my parents had already gone to bed.

This time, my mom sat at the kitchen table, on her laptop. Facebook, maybe, or Instagram. It embarrassed me that she was so active on social media, even though when I was in a rational mood, I knew she had every right to post about the time Ethan and I ate the cake she'd made for her coworker's birthday, or the TMI details of her chigger bites.

She closed the laptop as I hung up my coat. Briefly, I wondered if my mom ever did anything on her computer she wanted to hide from people. Maybe she was flirting with some high school boyfriend or something. Not likely. Probably scrolling Zillow.

"How was rehearsal?" Whatever she'd been doing, it had given her some kind of fortifying glow. She seemed calmer, less tightly wound somehow.

"Good."

"Is the play coming along?"

"Yes. Slowly. Noah's being a dick to Campbell." I stood next to the table, awkwardly wondering whether I should sit. I sat.

"You know I don't like that word."

"I know. Sorry."

"Honey, you're... okay about Campbell, aren't you?"

"I'm fine. We're actually..." In my pocket, my phone dinged. I pulled it out to read the text, even though I knew how much my mom hated it when I read my phone when she was talking to me.

The text came from Campbell. "Come over Friday. Meet Oliver. Just friends. Nothing weird. My mom will be here."

"I'm actually..." My brain whirled. Meet the baby? "I'm actually..."

"Is that text from Campbell?" she asked, reading it on my face. At times like that, I still responded to the tug of the connection between us.

"Um. Yeah."

"I thought you said you and Campbell were finished?"

"We're just friends." We weren't. We hung, suspended in a no-man's-land of confusion. She'd see that.

"Natalie." She cocked her head to the side, waiting for the truth.

"What?" I sucked at lying to my mom. I wanted to be great at it; my life would be so much easier if I were great at it, but nope. She saw through me every time.

"Something is still going on, isn't it?"

I sat down at the table. "If I say yes, will you talk about it like a normal person? Not lecturing and telling me what to do?"

That stung. I watched the dart hit its target. She'd been nice and non-judgmental and so happy I'd joined her at the table to talk. It generated a bigger twinge of guilt than usual. I blinked. Why did I say things that hurt her?

She absorbed the blow. "I can try."

"Okay. We're friends. He's got a baby. Yes, I checked; everything that girl told Dad is true. He has custody on the weekends. But, I…" *I want him. He wants me. We have no idea what to do about it. Or if we should do anything about it.*

"What?"

"I still like him. And I think he likes me."

She leaned forward, resting her chin on her hands, relaxed in a way I hadn't seen for way too long. A rush of love all tangled up in resentment and confusion shot through me. "It was bound to happen, sooner or later. With somebody. It would be so convenient if you could pick some perfect catalog model with no past and nothing but promise in his future, but it doesn't work that way, does it?"

"No."

"I remember."

"Will it really mess up Dad's school board deal if I'm friends—maybe more than friends—with Campbell? Do you really think that guy, the guy who's running against Dad, would care?"

"Let's take it one step at a time. I don't see any reason you and Campbell shouldn't be friends—you're already in the play together, and on the swim team. I'll talk to your dad." She opened her laptop enough to peek at the screen to see if it was still on. "But Natalie. Be very careful. You've worked so hard for everything you have. I've been so proud of you. Make sure you don't throw that away."

"I won't." Without realizing I was doing it, I glanced at my phone. Campbell's text needed answering. What he'd suggested was a pretty big deal.

"Go, honey. Go answer him. I trust you to know what you're doing."

I stared at her in shock, wanting to say something else, but the call of the phone was too strong. She smiled and opened her laptop, and I took the phone and left.

In my room, I dawdled by checking Facebook and Instagram. I read Campbell's invitation six times. I typed several responses before I settled on one. I hesitated before I hit send.

If I went over there and saw the baby, then walked away from Campbell without a backward glance, I'd hurt him. Badly. He told me he'd gone two years almost without telling even his former best friends. Now he'd invited me to meet his son. In his house. With his mother. This wasn't just a pretty big deal; it was a ginormous, galaxy-sized deal.

If I went over there, I'd be involved. Way past my eyebrows.

If I went over there, Campbell wasn't the only one who could get hurt.

I read the text one more time and added a silly emoji to lighten the mood. It wouldn't fool him in the slightest.

I hit send.

# Thirteen

*I* followed Campbell's car through the cold rain to his house on Friday afternoon. Somehow, despite our warm and fuzzy chat, I hadn't mentioned my plans to my mom. I told her I'd gone to Marisa's, without knowing why I'd lied.

Nerves roiled my stomach and made me clench my steering wheel. This had to be the most bizarre first date in the history of the world. Before I could get too weirded out, we pulled into a subdivision way north of town and far from our high school. His house met all my expectations: big wide yard, nice landscaping, faux columns, and expensive brick. The house of two doctors and their teenage son. And his son.

I took two seconds as I parked on the street to fully embrace the Bizarro. Then I got out, prepared to meet a baby and the mom of a guy I spent way too much time thinking about.

Campbell waited for me on the front steps after ditching his car. He ran his fingertips down my upper arm as he let me pass to go in first.

The woman from the swim meet opened the door. She wore a Habitat for Humanity T-shirt and yoga pants, nice ones, the kind people wore who actually did yoga. "Hi, you must be Natalie. Campbell's told me a lot about you. Cam, Oliver's still down for his nap. He should be up soon."

To me, Campbell said, "Izzy brought him by earlier so he could take his nap here. Thanks, Mom, for watching him."

"He was no trouble. Been asleep all this time."

"Usually, I pick him up after school, but today, because, well… We did it this way."

Because it would have been beyond awkward for me to go with him to Isabelle's house to pick up their baby. Yeah, made sense to me, too.

"It's nice to meet you, Dr. Adams."

"Call me Beth."

Which meant I would call her nothing at all. I smiled at her as politely as I could. She was being very friendly, given what Campbell had said about how his parents didn't want anyone to know.

"You have a lovely home." I rolled my eyes at myself. *You have a lovely home?* Who the hell says that with a straight face?

"Thank you," Dr. Adams said over her shoulder as she disappeared into the back of the house.

"Yes, well," Campbell said. "Want to see the baby?"

"Sure." I followed him upstairs. "How did you get your mom to agree to let you tell me?"

He paused at the stair landing. "I told her I was tired of living in a world made up of six people. And I deserved to spend time with someone other than my parents, Izzy, and Oliver. She couldn't come up with any argument."

My mouth dropped open. "You did that for me?"

"Well, and for me. It's true. It's ridiculous how small my world had gotten. I don't want Oliver to grow up in a bubble, like he's some kind of skeleton in a closet. It's not fair to him."

We'd come to a door left ajar. "Shhh." Campbell pushed it open silently.

The room was a beautiful nursery, like something out of a Pottery Barn Kids catalog. Stars and the moon danced across the ceiling and walls, and it had the mark of a real mom—Dr. Adams, I presumed—all over it. Campbell hadn't earned the money for this stuff shoveling horse manure.

On the wall opposite the window, a white crib sat in the dim shadows created by the pulled shades. A baby, much larger than I'd been expecting, lay asleep in the center, no blankets or anything. He wore tiny blue corduroys and a gray football shirt.

Campbell went to the side of the crib and motioned for me to come closer. The baby's head was perfectly round, like a piece of fruit, and his damp hair was blond like Campbell's. He breathed silently through parted lips, his cheeks red and his chest rising and falling. His eyelashes lay on his cheeks like a doll's.

He was beautiful. More than beautiful. Like… like a perfect thing. I tried to find words for the tightness in my chest but couldn't come up with a single one.

I'd obviously seen babies before, in diaper ads on TV, crawling with forward-thinking purpose and no leaks. A lot of the time the real ones I saw in Target in strollers more elaborate than my car tended to be crying, or covered in the remnants of whatever they'd eaten, or stained in some wet stuff I didn't want to think about.

Oliver, sleeping here in the silence, the huge crib mattress surrounding him, looked simple and clean like something from one of the fairytales I'd loved when I was small. I wanted to touch him, with the same desire I had to put my fingers in the frosting of beautifully decorated wedding cakes in the bakery window.

Campbell reached out for him, and I let out an involuntary gasp of dismay, stopping his arm.

"Oh, don't. He's so peaceful."

A surprised smile, making him look younger, lit up his face. "No, it's time for him to get up. If he doesn't, he'll stay awake partying all night and everything will come crashing down. That's one of the places where Doctor Mom and Izzy agree: babies need schedules." He bent over the crib, his height making it easy to reach down to the mattress and picked up the baby under the armpits.

Oliver let out a small noise and curled himself into Campbell's chest without waking up substantially. Even I could see that Campbell had become an expert at baby-holding. He could have stepped out of one of those ads intended to emphasize masculinity by contrast—hot guy with a puppy, hot guy with a flower, hot guy with a baby.

Those ads are marketing genius. The real thing in front of me dried up my throat.

Just when I thought I'd gained control, Campbell dropped a kiss onto the top of Oliver's head.

"You..." It came out too rusty. I tried again. "You really know what you're doing."

"This? This is the easy part." Campbell shifted him slightly, jouncing him some to wake him up. "You should have seen him when he was sick and had green gunk coming out of his nose. You want to hold him?"

I did. So much that it felt like a blow to my midsection. I shrugged totally fake blasé consent and held out my arms. Oliver had begun waking now and made noises Campbell could probably interpret but wasn't awake enough to protest being handed to a stranger. He weighed more than I thought, all of it warm and cuddly like a kitten.

We stood there in the quiet for a second. Oliver figured out something was different. Smell, maybe. Who knew? He straightened, almost like a tiny adult, and looked me in the eyes, his wide and questioning. My mouth opened.

The baby's eyes were twins of Campbell's—blue with a yellow ring, long dark blond lashes ringing them. I looked up into the more adult version. "Yeah. The DNA test was really unnecessary, wasn't it?"

"You mean the eyes? Yeah. They're like mine, I guess. To be fair, they didn't look like that when he was first born. They were kind of this brownish-bluish color."

"They change? I didn't know that."

"Yeah. Stuff changes a lot. Every time I think I know what's going on, something changes."

I liked holding the baby, and he didn't seem to mind me either. I liked it so much that I handed him back to Campbell. We headed for the stairs.

"So, what do you and… Oliver do on Friday nights?"

"Um, I fix him dinner. It used to be nothing but bottles, but—"

"Ba!" Oliver said.

"—now he's technically a toddler and allowed to eat regular food. So I'm learning to cook stuff. Macaroni and cheese, baked chicken, cooked vegetables. Apparently it's all about the choking now. Tiny pieces of everything."

"Really? You cook?"

"Yeah, and feed him, and maybe play a hot game of blocks or something, read a board book, and then he goes to bed at like eight o'clock. Then I sit here and watch sports or Netflix with the baby monitor on. You have no idea how exciting it is."

"By yourself?"

"Sometimes my parents are here. Mostly not."

"Wow. Sports or movies?"

"Huh? Oh, you mean which do I prefer? Both. I watch like five movies every weekend, plus college basketball, and in the fall, college football and the Steelers, and baseball before that. It's amazing how much time TV can suck if you make a real commitment. And have nowhere else to go."

"You never take Oliver anywhere?" I watched as Oliver sat on the floor at Campbell's feet, pulling himself up on Campbell's jean-clad legs, babbling to himself in a language only he could understand.

"No. The parents didn't want…" Campbell squinted at me. "Anyway, it's a pain in the butt to take him somewhere. You have to pack a bag. Like a suitcase. It's easier when I have him stay here."

"Okay," I said, wondering if he heard himself. And what the hell their parents were thinking.

Campbell's cell, tossed onto the coffee table in front of us, flashed a text. He picked it up. "Izzy found Oliver's eczema cream in her car. She's bringing it by. I hope you don't mind."

Here? "Do you want me to go?"

"No. Of course not."

"Does she know I'm here?"

"No. I'm sure she'll be fine."

Right.

We sat for two extremely awkward minutes side by side. Campbell ruffled Oliver's hair while Oliver sucked on his first two fingers and stared at me.

At long last the doorbell rang. "Can you watch him for a second?" asked Campbell, picking up the baby and depositing him on my knees. Oliver's stare continued unbroken. I wondered when humans learned that staring was rude. Clearly no one had clued this baby in. Not that I minded. Once Campbell rounded the doorway toward the front hall, I pushed the tip of my index finger into Oliver's round cheek to see what it felt like. He giggled.

I glanced up in time to see a small skirmish break out as a tall red-haired girl slipped around Campbell to come in the room. He'd been blocking the doorway, but she ran around him toward the baby and pulled up short when she registered me.

I may not know much about guys. I'd be the first to tell you that. I do know girls, though, and had no difficulty reading every expression that crossed her face. Her first glance went to Oliver, and then to my knees where he sat. As she took the next two steps close enough to snatch him from me, terror, betrayal, possession, and then determination flashed in quick succession. By the time she had her hands under the baby's armpits, I had an enemy.

An enemy built exactly like me. I might have been a shade taller and a hair heavier, but I had no trouble seeing the formidable soccer player Isabelle Barringer once was.

"Hi, Mister Sweetie! I missed you!" She cuddled him close, giving him a big smack on the cheek I'd touched. Oliver, that little traitor, put his face in her neck and filled his hands with her hair, pulling down on it with enthusiasm. That had to hurt. If it did, she didn't give it away. She cuddled him close. "Hi."

"Hi. I'm Natalie."

"Sorry to bust in like this," she said, not sorry at all, "but Oliver has the itchies, don't you, baby? Here's the cream, Campbell." She reached into her coat pocket with her free arm and lobbed a metal prescription tube to Campbell with impressive athleticism. "You didn't mention you had a friend coming over. Make sure you don't forget to watch the baby."

"Give me a break, Iz. You were just leaving, right? Say goodbye to Mommy, Oliver."

She made a big show of kissing the baby all over his stomach and face, making him laugh, then another big show of handing him back to Campbell, not me. She stood in the doorway, pretending to zip her coat, while giving me a killer warning death-ray from frosty hazel eyes. Then she was gone, the front door slamming behind her.

Campbell put Oliver down and spread out a blanket on the floor, piling it high with amazing amounts of bright-colored toys. Oliver crawled over to it with as much purpose as those diaper-ad babies.

"Sorry. I wasn't prepared for that."

"For Isabelle hating me?"

He slumped backwards on the sofa.

"She didn't hate you."

I slumped backwards too, suddenly exhausted and wondering why I'd come. "Okay. Maybe she didn't hate me, but she did not love me being here, touching her baby, distracting you from your job as Dad. Or, let's be honest, me being here."

"I think what bothered her most was the idea that I might have been having fun. Neither of us has had much that resembled a normal life for a while. She's a good person. Her parents have kind of smothered her now that she doesn't go anywhere. I think they're happy she's home all the time. Fewer bad influences from the bad people on the outside. It must drive her nuts. She's had a lot of responsibility and not much in the way of fun."

I thought it was more than that, but I let it go. "Why aren't you together? I think she'd still like to be."

Shock rolled across his face in a wave, more of it than I would have liked to see. "No way. She broke up with me. That was a year and half ago. And since then, I don't know. It feels over. Played out. We have this huge thing that maybe we should have done together, but we were too young, and we didn't, and now it's too late."

"People get back together all the time."

"Maybe," he said, turning to me, hitching his leg up onto the sofa. "But I don't want to get back together with Isabelle. I don't feel that way about her anymore. Too much has happened."

"Where's my little Ollie?" Campbell's mom said, coming into the family room from the back of the house. She leaned over and scooped him up, tickling his stomach and making him giggle. Child and all, she managed to sit gracefully on the sectional.

"Mom, are you going to be around all evening?" asked Campbell.

"Why? Am I annoying you?"

"No, I just wondered if you'd be willing to watch Oliver if Nat and I went for a walk."

She bit her lip and squeezed Oliver. "Ah, Cam, I believe your father and I've made it clear: this is your responsibility. You get yourself into a situation like this at your age, you can't count on Mommy and Daddy bailing you out. You have Ollie tonight."

Campbell, who'd been sitting tall with hope, sat back, defeated. What kind of grandmother refused to watch her grandson for the duration of a twenty-minute walk? I watched her blowing zerberts on Oliver's stomach. She clearly loved the child. Maybe she thought Campbell and I would dive into the nearest shrubbery and have at it, producing another grandchild in nine months. Maybe she had good reason to think that.

"Natalie, tell me about yourself. I understand you're a swimmer? And going off to college in California?"

I glanced at Campbell, who stayed silent. He'd certainly talked about me. "Yes, ma'am. About the swimming. I don't know which college I'll be going to until April when the regular decisions get released."

"Sounds like you're quite a student if you're considering Berkeley. Campbell's dad and I went out there, what, two years ago? To help out with the wildfires. Beautiful area. Excellent school."

"Yes, ma'am. Did you say wildfires?"

"Right. We try to do our bit to help out when there's a natural disaster like that. We're doctors, and it's only right that we use what we're fortunate enough to have to help the less fortunate. We operated a free clinic down in New Orleans after Katrina before Campbell came along, and occasionally we go out of the country. One time to Haiti and more places than I can name off the top of my head. It's important that young people like you do the same. The world is only as good as we make it. Right, Campbell?"

"Right, Mom." Campbell's voice sounded like something was stuck in his throat. "Nat, want to help me get started on Oliver's dinner?"

"Sure."

Dr. Adams laughed and stood up. "I can take a hint." She gave Oliver a big smacking kiss and set him on the floor, taking a magazine with her on her way out.

The baby crawled over, babbling away, and pulled himself up on Campbell's calves again. Campbell scooped him up, stuck him under his arm like a football, and disappeared on the way to the kitchen.

"Are you coming?"

"Yeah. Just a second."

I needed a minute to compose myself. Watching Campbell handle Oliver was hot. Me thinking it was hot felt wrong. This attraction was dangerous, and I needed to get it under control. I'd thought coming here today would give me a dash of reality. I thought there would be vomit or snot or screaming. I thought I'd come to my senses and realize I didn't want any part of this whole steaming mess.

Instead, here I sat, running my memory over the freestyle-honed muscles of Campbell's shoulder as he slung Oliver over them, over the gentleness of his hand in the wispy blond hair. Desire sang through my veins in a way never before inspired by an actual person, and not as seen on TV. Adrenaline had actually flowed when Isabelle got territorial. I'd been prepared to fight her for him.

And where the hell would any of that get me? In disgust, I stood up, wiping my hands on my jeans. Was I planning to throw away college so I could stay here and play house with Campbell and a baby, fighting off weekly incursions by his stir-crazy ex? Did I not see how it was?

There could still be a sliver of hope. Isabelle looked pretty tough. She still might be able to take me down.

It was becoming increasingly clear that someone needed to.

# Fourteen

od, I loved to sing. I loved how right it felt to hit notes on key, to feel the power coming from my diaphragm, to modulate the volume and the vibrato at the ends of notes. The title song was fun to sing and right in my range, however it had the distinct disadvantage of being the accompaniment for the romantic waltz of Campbell and Amelia near the end of the play.

I tried not to watch as I sang, usually, but now that I'd seen Campbell hold the baby, I couldn't resist. He held Amelia like a precious glass Christmas tree ornament and danced with a grace surprising for such a big guy. Amelia was the perfect contrast: her dark hair so different from his, her tiny frame so delicate and protected in his arms. Mrs. M had been right—they did look beautiful together.

I wished it were me. I wanted to dance with Campbell. I wanted his arms around me.

The song came to an end.

"Beautiful, Natalie! Very nice," Mrs. M said from the orchestra pit. Arnold the piano player sat back. Mrs. M glanced around, furious. "I need townspeople! Where are the townspeople? Amelia, wait just a second."

Campbell and I exchanged awkward glances as the underclassmen took the stage. We descended the steps back to our backpacks in the audience. We both had to study for the calculus test scheduled for the next day.

We got in about ten minutes before Finney wandered in from the hallway. I'd never caught him studying, and he spent most of his free time at rehearsal saying insinuating things to Amelia without much progress. Amelia vacillated between Joe and a remarkably clueless pursuit of Campbell. It dawned on me that perhaps, since Joe wasn't in the play or at rehearsal, Amelia may have been pretending interest in Campbell to avoid having to deal with Finney.

The toad with that name seated himself in the seat in front of us and turned around, resting his hands on the seat back.

"Is that math?"

"Yeah," Campbell said. I'd noticed he'd been talking more to other people. "Calc."

"Ugh. I took Trig and that's it. Calc is for geeks."

"Or, more specifically, for people who want to go to college," I said, dry as a desert.

"Yeah, yeah, Tree Trunks. We all know what a genius you are."

Finney didn't register Campbell tensing in the seat beside me. I did.

"I'm going to ask you nicely, man, not to refer to Natalie that way again." His voice was calm. I heard the steel behind the calm.

Finney laughed, loud and raucous. "Oh, so it's like that, huh? You and her? I get that you're a big guy and all, but damn. You'd have to get a running start to climb on that fat ass thing."

The air crackled and popped.

Slowly, as if his joints hurt, Campbell stood up. Finney jumped up, his squat little muscles flexing as well.

"I said before you were a tool, but that doesn't come close to covering it, does it, man?" asked Campbell in a conversational tone. "You're like a piece of dog shit left out in the rain. And you're going to apologize for what you just said right now."

Finney barked out a laugh, straightening up and clenching his fists. "The hell I am."

"You're going to apologize. On your knees."

"Maybe I need to be clearer. I said fat ass. I meant giant, lardy, whale-size, morbidly obese ass. And I am not. Going. To. Apologize."

I broke in, putting a hand on Campbell's arm. "No, Campbell. Don't. He's not worth it. He's *so* not worth it."

"Anywhere, man. Any time." Finney, who was at least six inches shorter than Campbell and fifty pounds lighter, had clearly allowed the bloodlust to go to his head. He actually smacked a fist into a palm, managing to resemble an undersized gorilla even more than he usually did.

"Now?"

"Fine." Finney headed for the exit, overflowing machismo making him even more of an idiot than usual.

"Campbell." I gathered a handful of his sleeve in my fist, restraining him from banging out the door after Finney. "Campbell. Do not do this. Zero tolerance, remember? If you're caught, you'll be expelled. You won't graduate. You need this diploma, Campbell. Please."

He looked down at me, through the glaze of bloodlust that matched Finney's. I thought maybe I'd gotten through to what little bit of rational brain was left to him after the tsunami of testosterone had rolled back out to the ocean.

"He's not going to talk to you like that."

"It doesn't matter. He's been talking like that to me and to everyone since middle school. He is a cretin. I admit, it bothered me when I was twelve, but damn, Campbell. Life is full of assholes. He is not worth you messing up your chance to graduate!"

"I've already messed up all my chances. What's a little more?"

"No! Stop. Stay here. For me." I squeezed the shirt tighter and whispered. "For Oliver."

Then he shook my hand off and followed Finney out the doors toward the parking lot.

Son of a bitch. I hadn't really entertained delusions that because Campbell didn't mind cuddling a baby like a forty-year-old man, he'd been entirely stripped of all the idiocy of a seventeen-year-old guy. Had I?

Now what? I dithered in the row of seats and considered Mrs. Murchison. She'd stop the fight all right, but if they didn't make it off school grounds before exchanging their supermasculine blows, they'd both get expelled. She'd have no choice but to enforce the zero tolerance policy. It didn't even matter who started it, or if it was self-defense. Anyone caught fighting would be kicked out. No, not Mrs. M.

I scanned the rest of the cast. Noah wouldn't be remotely motivated. He had a well-developed sense of physical preservation and would be more inclined to go out and egg them on. Campbell being expelled could only benefit him, and I spared a wild thought to wondering if he'd created the entire situation. I considered Garrett Pannell, the junior who played Gaston. Nope.

Like his character, Garrett was an idiot and a brawler. He'd jump in and make it worse. The rest of the freshmen and sophomores would follow Noah's lead and form a cheerleading line.

As I was on the point of dashing after them myself to use my own not-inconsiderable strength to pull them apart, the door flew open again. An untouched Campbell stalked in, vibrating with unrelieved aggression.

"What happened?"

"I walked away. Dammit. It killed me. I told him what, precisely, he could do to himself but that I wasn't going to throw away my life on a piece of horse manure like him."

"What did he say?"

"Don't make me repeat it, okay? A lot of smack that just about made me change my mind." He ran his hands through his hair, standing it on end. Tension hummed through every line of his body.

"You don't have to defend me, you know. I've been doing a pretty decent job of it for almost eighteen years."

He glared at me, frustration and rampaging testosterone crowding out his usual calm. "Let's talk about that. In the hall."

"Where's Finney?"

"Out in his car smoking a joint, I presume."

"Okay. You go. I'll meet you by the doors."

He turned and left silently. He needed to calm down. A lot. I couldn't rule out the possibility he'd still snap and go after Finney.

"Um, Mrs. M? You need me any time soon? I dropped a folder upstairs, I think."

"No, dear. You go ahead."

Out in the deserted lobby, most of the lights were out, and daylight had long since faded, blackening the walls of glass doors and turning them into mirrors. Campbell didn't sit on the bench right outside the doors to the auditorium where we usually went to talk. I started around the curve of the carpeted area, in search of him.

At one of the alcoves between two other sets of doors to different seats in the theater, a hand shot out. I stopped.

"Okay. I have a few things to say," Campbell said. He hadn't calmed down much.

"I'm listening."

"First off, you have no idea how hard it was to let him get away with throwing shade like that." He flexed his hands, as if he hadn't quite decided to let him get away.

"I have some idea."

"Secondly, I know you can defend yourself. You're awesome at defending yourself. You are one of the toughest, most together people I've ever seen."

"Thanks." The compliment warmed me.

"How do you do that?"

"What?"

"Just… handle things. You handle everything. Finney, the swimming. Things. Me. I've thrown some unbelievable crap at you and every time you… stay there."

"I don't know. What's the alternative? Flying to pieces? What did you do when you found out about Oliver? I'll bet you didn't fly to pieces." I leaned against the wall nearer to him. Some of the tension had gone out of him, but not all. I traced the width of his shoulders with my eyes, and he caught me. He swallowed, making his Adam's apple bob.

I swallowed too.

"No, I…" He smiled. "Actually, I went out driving. It was summer. I'd just gotten my license. I stopped at Target and stood in the baby aisle and stared at everything. For an hour.

Wondering what the hell it was all for. I left when I got to a section that sold some product called Boudreaux's Butt Paste."

"I don't know what that is."

"You don't want to know."

I let that pass. Everything would be so much easier if I didn't feel the tug of want, of longing every time I came near him. I loved standing with Campbell. Just standing here. I liked breathing the same air. He met my eyes. The stew of emotions reflected back at me changed and focused.

Enough to make me draw in a breath and lean towards him. He bit the inside of his cheek but moved closer to me as well.

"Nat," he whispered. "We shouldn't… But I can't… I want to… do you…?"

He reached out a tentative hand to my shoulder, letting it slide gently down.

"I do want to." I touched his cheek, unable to put up any resistance. Such a relief to let my hands loose, to touch any part of him. My other hand went up all by itself, fingertips feathering on his collarbone.

His arms went around me, pulling the small of my back closer, just as I'd been wishing minutes before. I had half a second to throw all my agonizing, and every other thought, straight out of my brain before his lips were on mine. He let out a groan and deepened the kiss, running his hand up my back while pressing closer and closer.

The desire I'd held in check shot through me, singing with the sound of the blood racing in my veins. This was a kiss. A Kiss. We struggled, trying to find places to put hands and thighs and chests closer and closer. I felt the wall of the alcove against my back and was grateful for the support. I'd never been good at kissing; I'd always been unsure where to put my tongue or how much to open my mouth. Now there was no need to wonder. It just happened and it was right. Gasping for breath, we pulled apart for a second. I allowed my hands to trace the muscles of his upper back and neck. Heat spread where I touched, where he touched me. His eyes were wide, dilated to make the yellow ring disappear. Surprise, and something else, was written there.

I didn't have time to wonder what before he ducked his head again, to kiss my cheek beside my ear, and then work his way back toward my mouth. Oh God. We had to stop, or Finney would come stomping in from his car and find us both here naked on the carpeted floor of the school auditorium lobby. Much longer and I wouldn't even care.

"Campbell." I gasped for breath. "I can't think. You're making me stupid."

"I'd say you have a few IQ points to spare." He kissed my jawline and I had to force my hands away.

"You're making me want to do this forever. But…" I cast an anxious glance at the doors to the parking lot where Finney kept his car and his habit.

"I know. I'll try to stop," he said, grinning at me and kissing my temple. All I wanted was to stand there touching as much of his body with mine as long as possible. "I'm trying. I promise."

"I don't need any more time. I think friends might possibly not be an option anymore."

"No. Not an option. I don't want to be friends with you."

"Oh, God, Campbell. I'm going to go off to college, and swim, and it won't be here. And then what are we going to do?"

"We'll worry about that when the time comes."

"But I don't want to hurt you." *I don't want you to hurt me, either. And I'm so afraid it's too late.*

"You won't."

I had never felt like this before. I had to kiss him again. He didn't seem to mind much. This time he allowed his hands to venture beyond my back and neck. The touch of his hands on me, even through my sweater, made me gasp. I put my hand over his, to prove it was really happening.

After a remarkably long time without oxygen, we came up for air again.

"What about Isabelle?" I asked.

"What about Isabelle? I don't want Isabelle. I want you. I'd think that was obvious."

"No," I said stupidly. I had lost IQ points. More than I could spare. "About how she wants you. Won't I mess up your relationship? And don't you need to get along with her?"

He pulled back just enough that all my emotions stopped clanging around inside me like birds trapped in a building and I could think. "Yes. I need to get along with Isabelle. It's better for Oliver that way. And she's going to have to get used to it. It's been only us and our parents, taking care of a baby and doing nothing else for so long. It'll be a big change. But she can't possibly have thought I'd never date anyone, never have a relationship with anyone else."

I thought maybe she might well have thought that, but I kept silent.

"Okay. We'll figure it out," I said, as he came in for another kiss, his thumb grazing my collarbone, heading south.

"Um, guys?" came a piping prepubescent voice. We jumped guiltily apart. Tyler Donaldson, the seventh grader who played my son, stood there, managing to look guilty, grossed out, and delighted at the same time. "Mrs. Murchison says she needs you both for the next scene."

"Okay. We'll be there." Campbell let out a resigned breath and gave me a half smile. "Could have been worse, right? It wasn't Finney."

"No. Not Finney."

Campbell gave me a quick kiss on the side of my head, in my hair.

THE NEXT MORNING as we hung around our lockers before first period, I told Marisa what had happened.

"So, okay, the douchery of Finney is unacceptable. I totally agree Campbell shouldn't have beaten his ass, for Campbell's sake, but damn, I would have loved to see Finney come in here with a face like a pork tenderloin." The war-like expression on her elfin face was funny.

"Right? It almost hurt to stop him." She was right. He needed to pay. But how, without getting into trouble?

"We could TP his house. Start a rumor that he has no testicles on Snapchat. Oooh. We could slip an anonymous note to the office about the stash in his car."

"No. I don't want to sink to his level." At that moment, a horrible, wonderful idea came to me. "I've got it. Come on." I grabbed her hand and towed her in the direction of Mrs. M's classroom, down the hall.

"Mrs. M. Good morning."

She looked up from her computer screen. "Natalie. And Marisa. What's up, dear? Don't you need to be moving along to first period?"

"I wanted to share something with you." Teachers loved it when you used the word "share." It made them feel like they'd taught us something.

"Yes?"

"You know the elementary outreach? For the play?"

"Yes. That's coming up in two weeks."

"I know. I'm not going to be able to do it after all. Swimming. But I spoke with Max Finney after rehearsal, and he wants to do it. He doesn't know how to tell you. And I think he's a little nervous. You know, that people might think it's uncool."

"Well, I don't want to make him uncomfortable."

I did. Finney had made me uncomfortable in a thousand tiny ways over the years. The mental picture of him in a clock suit dancing for giggling children would go a long way toward making me much more comfortable.

"You won't. Like I said, he wants to do it, but he can't admit it. Just tell him he's going to. Point out what an honor it is. He'll do it if you make him feel like he has to. He'll be so great in his clock costume at the elementary schools. It's the best costume in the show. The kids will *love* it," I said, thinking how much more I would love it.

"Thank you, dear. I'll tell him. I hate that Max has felt that way quietly. What a shame."

"It'll be so fun to get to watch the video afterwards." The bell rang. Marisa and I waved and left.

"Bruh. That was awesome. He'll absolutely hate that, but even Finney won't be able to say no if she asks him directly. That was genius," Marisa said.

"I'm glad it wasn't Finney who caught me and Campbell, or else we'd be dealing with a lot more than getting him back for being a general dick."

"You said that kid Tyler was the one?"

"Yeah."

"Isn't he in your brother's grade? I'm pretty sure he was in my sister's class in fifth grade." Marisa gave me a meaningful glance.

"Yeah, I think so."

"Huh."

The first bell rang. She didn't elaborate. I didn't ask, because I didn't need to.

If Ethan found out and told my mom I'd been kissing Campbell, she'd back me up.

Wouldn't she?

# Fifteen

"**D**o you have a minute, Tremayne?"

Coach Phillips grabbed me in the rush of the hallway at a class change. I had lunch next, so I nodded and followed him back to the study hall which served as his classroom.

"Here's the deal. You're swimming better than you ever have. It's a banner year for prep swimming around here. Berkeley is sending a scout to the state meet Saturday."

Shock glued me to the desk chair. A scout? All the way from California? "Are you serious?"

"That's what I understand. A low-level scout, but a scout just the same. And don't think it's only because of you. There're two guys from Northern Virginia who are killing it, and a girl who swims fly from some little town I've never heard of. UVA will also have somebody there, but of course they send people to the state meet every year. Hardly a long trip."

"Oh God."

"You'll be fine. You made it on your own to states for the back and the IM, and the women's relay got there because of you. Make me look good, okay?"

"Okay." Inside, my empty stomach writhed. All of a sudden, lunch seemed out of the question.

"One more thing. I know you have your heart set on California. I want you to promise me you'll take a good look at Virginia. I know the coach. He's a good guy. You'd do well with him. I think his style would work with yours." Coach leaned back and balanced on the back two legs of his chair. I'd never seen him go over, but it made me nervous.

"Oh, Coach, I know, but my dad is a Virginia professor. I kind of wanted to get away from here."

"I think you're forgetting how large that campus is. No law says you have to take your dad's classes or live with your parents." The chair creaked as he rocked.

"How did you…?"

"What? Know that you want to get the hell out of your parents' house and see a little of the world? Because I was, believe it or not, eighteen once too. Hightailed it straight out of Tallahassee as fast as I could. Shook the dust of that major city off and all that nonsense. Once I got to Georgia, I realized my parents weren't quite as bad as I thought. You'd be amazed how much of the money I earned in the dorm cafeteria went toward bus fare and catching rides with other students home again."

Ugh. I hated it when adults gave me the "I was your age once" speech. Coach had gray tufts of hair above his ears and a definite paunch, which put him way closer to forty than eighteen. It had been so long since he'd been eighteen, he couldn't possibly remember the first thing about it.

"Um. Okay. I'll think about Virginia." Virginia meant Campbell, but I didn't want to let go of my Berkeley dream. For the first time, however, the thought of staying here didn't sting, and that brought chagrin. I'd mocked girls who made college choices because of boys. Now here I was.

"More than think about it. I want you to talk to the people on Saturday. Go kiss Berkeley's ring if you want, but then come on back and talk to them." The front chair legs hit the ground with emphasis.

"Okay. I gotta go, Coach, or I'll miss lunch."

He saluted me away, and I went to the cafeteria to find Campbell. He'd finished his lunch, the paper bag crumpled at his elbow.

I pulled up a chair across from him. "Coach says there will be scouts at the meet."

"I figured. Not that it does me much good. I can't go away to college. I can't leave here. I might do some community college, though. Good for you."

"Why can't you go away? You could take Oliver with you if you lived in an apartment."

He gave me a sad smile that made me feel too young to understand again. "I can't take Oliver away from Isabelle. I'm literally not allowed to move away from this county without a court saying it's okay, not if I want to take Oliver. And I can't go without him. It's in the best interest of the child to see both parents regularly, and I wouldn't want to leave him. I'm stuck here forever unless Isabelle and I randomly want to move to the same place."

The implications of that sunk in. Even apart, parents had to stay near each other for the benefit of the child. Forever. At seventeen, Campbell already knew he could never leave the town where he'd grown up until Oliver reached adulthood, not if he wanted to see that happen. I stood up to go to the counter. Campbell followed, tossing his trash.

"I hope this isn't prying too much, but is there a reason you can't go to UVA? One of their scouts is supposed to be coming. Here in town?" I didn't glance at him as I paid for an energy bar I could carry with me.

"I can't afford it. I can't even begin to afford it. And I'm not good enough for a scholarship."

Um. How to say this delicately? Never mind. Delicate was not my middle name. "Your parents can afford it. They're doctors. Even if…" I surveyed the emptying room, lowered my voice. "If there were no, um, Oliver, wouldn't they have sent you to college?"

He stuffed his hands into his pockets and gestured at a seat with a pointed elbow. We sat again.

"Yes. If everything had been different, normal, I'd have graduated from St. Anselms, had access to their spectacular college counseling services, been accepted at Duke or Brown, where my parents went, and had my tuition paid for. Like all the other rich kids at St. Anselms."

"So then, I get that you need to stay here, but we have a great university in this town. Why won't they do what they would have done before?"

He sighed. "Because. You don't know my parents yet."

My heart picked up on the "yet," but I remained silent.

He went on. "They grew up wealthy, both of them. Privileged. They've always felt kind of guilty about it. They met at a Habitat for Humanity build during medical school. They're both big champions of the underprivileged. You heard my mom talk about Katrina and the wildfires. They use their vacation time to go to natural disasters and third world countries and provide medical care. It's a thing in our family. My sister is in medical school down at UNC, preparing to do the same thing. She met her husband in Teach for America. My parents don't have a lot of sympathy for the problems of rich kids, even their own rich kid, who went out and knocked up his girlfriend like a damn idiot. Especially after they'd given me a blistering lecture on birth control and a fistful of condoms two weeks after I started to date Izzy."

"Oh."

"When I told them, they went into, like, a white-hot rage at me. Stupid, they said. They didn't cut me any breaks for being sixteen. They never have cut me many breaks. What's that line? 'To whom much is given, much is expected.' Something like that. Anyway, during the rage-filled part of the proceedings, my dad said if I wanted to go out and make a grown man's mistakes, I could damn well live a grown man's life and pay for it. College was out unless I paid for it myself." He focused on the table, where he traced some ancient graffiti with his thumb.

"But they let you stay in the house, didn't they?" I kept talking, though the picture he'd painted depressed me.

"Yeah. My mom talked Dad down from that ledge. He was ready to kick me out. She's a little less militant and begged him to let me stay in the house until I graduated from high school. He finally agreed, but he didn't back down from the college thing. I'm on my own for that."

I kept my opinions on Campbell's dad to myself. It was obvious Campbell loved him and even admired him for the hard line he'd taken. It would have been easy, however, for the Adamses to make Campbell's hard life a whole lot easier. I didn't understand people who would do that to their own son for a principle. It occurred to me to wonder what my own parents would have done.

"But what about loans?"

"I'm afraid of loans. Afraid that I'd go to school, then not be able to find a decent job because I can't move anywhere, and then what? Shovel horse crap to pay both child support as well as college loans?" He stood up. I followed suit.

"You're so smart, Campbell. You can't let that go to waste."

"I'm trying to figure a way out, but I haven't found one yet." He smiled at me bleakly. "But I'm open to suggestions." He let me lead the way out of the cafeteria.

I STOOD, staring into the refrigerator, hoping something appetizing for dinner would materialize before my eyes. It didn't. I pulled out a carton of yogurt and some lunchmeat, and as I whirled around for the bread, Ethan walked in to pour himself juice to go with the almost-empty package of donut holes he held.

"I was going to eat some of those," I said, reaching for them.

He held them behind his back. "Nope. I'm a growing boy."

"Whatever. By the way, I found my Patagonia jacket scrunched up under that pit of a bed of yours. You keep yeeting my stuff, and I'll need to inform the parents." He kept taking my jacket. It was a mens, because I liked the color of it.

"Go ahead," he said, eating a donut hole with great showmanship. "I have some info they might find interesting too."

My stomach clenched. He knew. "What are you talking about?"

"Wouldn't you like to know?"

I stepped closer. Ethan would likely be tall, like me and Dad, but he hadn't gotten there yet. I topped him by at least seven inches and a dismaying number of pounds. I grabbed the front of his hoodie in some ridiculous urge to force his silence. "Yes. And you're going to tell me, right now."

"You got caught making out at school."

Son of a bitch. That didn't take long.

"Let me guess. Tyler Donaldson?"

"Yeah. He's in my math class. Says you were two seconds away from having sex."

That little turd. To think of the sweet way he played the little teacup. All the while, unsuspected evil coursed through his veins. Maybe his stage mother was onto something. He was a theatrical genius.

"I was not. You think I'd be that stupid at school?"

"I don't know how stupid you'd be somewhere other than here. How much do you want me to keep it secret? Enough to give me the Patagonia jacket?" He grinned at me in a way that made me want to slap him.

"I'm not giving you my Patagonia jacket."

"You will if you don't want Mom to know."

"Don't want Mom to know what?" asked my dad, ambling in through the side door.

"Natalie?" asked Ethan, making clear I'd need to decide, now. I shook my head. Even if I didn't like the jacket, I'd never let that little dirtbag have it. Not after this. He gave me a smarmy little smile while my dad went through the mail on the table, and then adopted his best helpful choirboy expression.

"Natalie doesn't want Mom to know she got caught making out at school. In front of an impressionable twelve-year-old."

"Oh, please. You're twelve. There's nothing impressionable about you!"

"Doesn't sound like that's the most relevant part of this conversation." Dad put down the mail and gave us his full attention. "Uh, 'making out'? Is this true?"

"Ugh. Dad. Really? You want to hear this?"

He shuddered. "No. I definitely don't want to hear this. I would prefer to drink Drano in a cocktail glass. But I feel that I must. Explain."

His job done, Ethan picked up his glass of juice and headed back for the TV. Dad grabbed his shoulder before he made it out of the kitchen. "You'll want to mind that tattling, Ethan. Twelve is a little old for that, don't you think?" Dad cuffed him on the head and pushed him out of the room. I wanted to give him a hard boot to the backside. My thoughts of violence meant I wasted time I'd have better used to think about how to spin this. Absolutely nothing presented itself.

"Dad, it's not a big deal. Campbell and I were talking, and—"

"Campbell? Tell me it was someone else. I'll just pat your hand, clear my throat a lot, remind you to be careful generally and appropriate at school, and we'll go on our merry ways."

"It's Campbell."

His shoulders dropped. He pulled out a chair at the table and sat, every movement deliberate and weary. Motioning at the chair opposite, he said, "I thought we talked about this."

"We talked about Campbell having a son. You didn't forbid me to talk to him."

"I highly doubt this would have come to my attention if what you were doing was talking. And besides, you told me you weren't… talking."

"Um. We started talking again."

He stared at me like he did when he worked on a particularly difficult calculation for his job, rubbing the bridge of his nose. "But… Campbell has a child."

"I know, Dad. I've met him. He's adorable."

"What! When did you meet him?"

"I went over one afternoon after school when Campbell had him. Don't worry. His mom was there."

"Okay. Let's unpack this. Campbell might be your age—he is your age, isn't he?"

"Yes. He's five weeks older."

"But he's living the life of a much older person. And that will always be true. He has serious responsibilities to a child. You're at different phases of your lives. It would be so much easier if you break it off now."

"I'm aware of all that, Dad. We're not getting married. I'm not throwing away college."

His face-rubbing moved to his temples, letting me know he was moving beyond concerned into worried. "It's not only that. Bryant—my opponent, you know—has started posting things on the blog on his campaign website. Anecdotal stories about teen sex. Horror stories. Right now, he's getting them all from generic websites, but they all have one thing in common. The condom broke and they ended up pregnant. They went for an abortion at age sixteen and nearly died of infection. The pill didn't work and then the two promising athletes were forced to raise a special needs baby they weren't ready for. All kinds of stuff like that. Deadbeat dads. STDs. All designed to show that abstinence education, and then total abstinence observed, is the only way to preserve any kind of normal future for teenagers."

"Dad, you know that's all ridiculous. It all shows he doesn't have any other ideas for what he would do on the school board."

"Be that as it may, I'm having to deal with where he's taken the discourse. Bryant's supporters are beginning to make noise at the meetings. Campbell's situation is not exactly the world's best-kept secret, is it? And what do you suppose Bryant will do with the information that *my* daughter is dating somebody's teenage baby daddy? You're exactly the kind of promising scholar-athlete whose future is derailed by sex. You'll be the star of his blog in a matter of minutes."

"Relax. Nobody at school knows about it." My stomach gave an uneasy clench. Except for me. And Marisa. And probably Ron, now. Marisa told him everything. And no doubt Kameron, whose curiosity fuse I'd probably lit. And whoever Ron told. Oh God.

"Let's keep it that way. No more discussion. And whatever you do, don't tell Marisa. Her mother is one of Bryant's congregation." He gave his temples one last massage, then met my eyes.

Oh no. Too late.

"And Natalie? No more Campbell. I don't give a lot of orders, but I'm giving one now. Not because of my school board position, but because my daughter is dating a boy who I know is sexually active and irresponsible about it. Don't argue," he said, holding up a hand as I started to sputter. "We have incontrovertible proof of that, don't we? He's about a year old."

"Are you kidding? You're saying that I can't be responsible! You're insulting my intelligence!"

"I'm not. I'm saying Campbell is irresponsible. I'm saying find another guy."

"Dad, you can't stop me. This is ridiculous. Mom said…"

"I don't care what your mother said." By the expression on his face, he did care and would be interrogating her later. I felt bad for throwing her under the bus. "And I can stop you. You are still seventeen. Until May 21. Still a minor. You live in my house and you will live by my rules. And those rules include no dating anyone who has gotten anyone pregnant out of wedlock."

I'd never heard anything so grossly unfair. It couldn't be possible to be any more responsible than Campbell: I'd seen it. He was raising that child. Maybe not full-time, but he changed diapers and cooked soft vegetables and shoveled poo to pay for his food. There wasn't a boy in my entire high school who had a better idea of responsibility than Campbell.

I respected authority, but not this kind. Not the kind based on fear and shame and… general wrongheadedness. Nor did I have the guts to tell him off, which left me with no other option than to stalk off to my room, no dinner in hand.

Me: *What are you up to?*
Campbell: *Nothing. Sitting here with O. Watching TV. Just a regular Friday.*
Me: *Marisa ditched me for Ron tonight.*
Campbell: *Oh. Sorry.*
Campbell: *You're welcome to come over and hang out with us.*
Me: *Oh. Isabelle isn't there, is she?*
Campbell: *Of course not. But my parents aren't here either.*
Me: *Give me fifteen minutes.*

*I* tossed aside the phone onto my duvet cover. Oh my God. I thought when Marisa ditched me that I'd be hanging out here, in my room, watching my Insta feed scroll by, punctuated only by an occasional TikTok video. Ethan had gone to somebody's house overnight. No way would I go downstairs and hang out with my parents. They fought over having told me different things about Campbell, but Dad had prevailed. Mom chose her battles, but not this one: no more contact with Campbell.

The fact that this came from Dad, had originated with him, burned. I was used to fighting with Mom. We sparred so frequently that we danced around like familiar boxers, each knowing the other's best moves. There was something almost reassuring about it, automatic, like knowing how to do the proof for a geometry problem.

Dad, on the other hand, hadn't issued any dadly dictates since middle school. We'd been almost buddies in the last few years. He listened to me complain about my mom. He acted like he thought my ideas were worth hearing. He respected my independence. I thought he had my back. It hurt, knowing I'd been wrong.

I'd never imagined he had some weird Victorian thing about his daughter dating, but that's all I could come up with to explain it. Until now, I'd never put him to the test. He didn't know about Gabe. I'd never gone on a date. Maybe he thought he'd reached the last mile of the parenting marathon and was ready to send me off to college, to do who knew what with who knew who, as long as he didn't have to know what or who.

Now the question remained. What, exactly, did I plan to do with Campbell at his house tonight? I'd made all the moves up until now, or almost all, and I suspected I'd be making whatever moves would be made tonight. Without making a decision, I stripped off my nondescript shirt in search of a better-looking, lower-cut one. While it was off, I considered my bra, trying to imagine what a guy might think of it. If a guy were, by some chance, to see it. Blue. Underwire not protruding anywhere. Good enough. I raised my arms. Yep. Everything shaved.

Just in case.

I headed to the bathroom to brush my teeth and think of a lie to tell my parents about where I was going.

CAMPBELL MET ME AT THE DOOR. The muted sound of the TV, playing some basketball game or another, came from the family room.

"Hi."

"Hi."

We stared at each other, uncomfortable. The weight of the lie I'd told my parents sat heavy on me.

"Where are your parents?" Even with the TV audible, the house felt empty. Houses without parents always had an odd desolate vibe.

"Out of town. They went to help with the flooding in the Midwest."

"Do you ever go with them for that kind of stuff?"

"I used to. Sometimes. I've built a lot of Habitat houses and written down names at health clinics. Now there's school, and Oliver, and I don't have time."

"Does Isabelle have Oliver tomorrow? You are going to be at the meet, right?"

"Yeah. I have Friday nights and Sunday afternoons."

"I guess your parents aren't coming to see you?"

"Nope." Campbell tried to sound like he didn't care. He did, though.

"They'll miss the state meet?"

"Yep. Remember? I'm a grown man." Now the bitterness rolled out into the open.

"Yeah, but to leave you home by yourself? My parents would never do that."

He laughed, a dark expression on his face. "Uh, yeah, a party is unlikely with Oliver here. A party is nothing compared to a teenage pregnancy, anyway. The worst has already kind of happened. They're banking on the hope that I won't be stupid enough to produce a second child out of wedlock."

I was the only person here who could help him with that. I made my face carefully blank and suppressed a wild desire to laugh. The hysterical shriek died in my throat as I looked up into Campbell's eyes. The yellow ring had disappeared. They'd gone dark in a way that sent a shiver echoing in my ribcage. He stood close, his nearness making my pulse pound. I needed time. "Where's Oliver?"

"In bed. Seems to be asleep."

"Can I see him? Just peek?"

"Seriously?" he asked, surprised. "Okay. Come on."

We climbed the stairs. I made my footfalls silent. Not waking up Oliver seemed like the most important thing in the world.

The door to his room was again ajar, and Campbell pushed it open. I leaned around the doorframe, nudging his shoulder with mine. An owl-shaped nightlight cast dim light into the room, enough that I could see Oliver's outline in the crib. His chest rose and fell steadily. A noise machine made a waves-on-the-beach sound. The sense of peace I'd felt when I'd been here before stole over me again. I watched for longer than I'd expected to want to.

Then I turned, to find Campbell looking down into my face, very close to me. For a second, it felt real, like we were parents and this was our child. Too real. I backed away, out into the hallway.

"Campbell, I…"

He blinked and stepped back. "Come on. Let's get some ice cream. We can watch the game."

I swallowed. "Sure."

The silence stretched long and awkward as we went back downstairs. Something hummed between us, but what? How did I address it? Somehow, I couldn't picture gossiping about the junior who'd been caught selling trigonometry tests or mentioning that it might reach seventy degrees tomorrow.

I chose silence.

In the kitchen he scooped chocolate ice cream into bowls. I watched his forearm flex as he wielded the scoop and took my time taking in the muscles of his shoulders and back as he concentrated.

"Do you want sprinkles?"

"What?" Relief flooded me that he'd spoken, and I laughed. "You have sprinkles? Yes, please!" I hadn't had sprinkles for years, but I'd loved them way past the time most kids stopped getting them. The prospect of sprinkles lightened my mood to a surprising degree.

"I have a kid who discovered ice cream last month, Nat. It's a whole new world. Of course I have sprinkles." He added some to the top of my bowl. I dug in. We ate, standing up, leaning against the side of the pristine white marble kitchen island. Campbell was a hell of a housekeeper.

I watched him eat. His lips were perfect. So perfect. Oh God. I wanted to run my fingers over his lips, feel the cold from the ice cream. Hell. I wanted to run my hands all over him everywhere. My eyes widened when he saw me staring and parted those lips, spoon in midair. He leaned in, making me catch my breath and put down my bowl. Keeping my hands to myself was becoming more unnatural by the minute.

"You have some ice cream on your chin." Campbell pointed with his spoon, mischief sparking in his eyes.

"Where?" I asked. I could feel the spot of cold stickiness just below and to the left of my mouth.

"Right there," he said, moving even closer to touch it with his finger.

I gave him a dare in an expression. "Where, exactly?" I lifted my face. Come on, Campbell. Where are those famous seventeen-year-old hormones?

He got it. Understanding flashed in his eyes. "Right there." He put his fingers under my chin and moved closer. His breath whispered against my lips. I held his gaze, drowning in the blue as he licked off the ice cream, then kissed the spot where it had been. Then I closed my eyes and lost myself in his kiss.

His hands traveled slowly down my back, reaching the hem of my shirt. They stayed respectfully outside it. I reached down, grabbed one of his hands, and placed it under the shirt, against the bare skin of my stomach. His breath rushed inward with a sharp hiss.

"Nat..."

"Campbell. Remember when I asked you if I could check out your chest in a meadow?"

"Yes?" His lips were warm against mine.

"Meadows are kind of uncomfortable. Sunburns and bug bites. Here might be better."

"Hmm." He put one hand in my hair to keep my lips closer, the other hand now exploring my ribcage freely under my shirt. His hand made swooping motions, getting ever closer to my bra with each one. "You think so?"

"I know so. Come on. I've seen you in a Speedo before. This is nothing." I shuddered deliciously at the memory. Touching was way better than looking. "You're sure your parents aren't going to come back early, right?" My hands had sneaked under his shirt as well, roving over the muscles of his lower back, tempted, so tempted, to let them descend into the loose waistband of his jeans.

"They won't."

"Then off with that shirt." I felt him hesitate against me. "Come on. You've showed the whole swim team." I stepped back to watch. He reached for the back of its neck and pulled. Ohhhh. My God. He was so beautiful. Perfectly carved, like a marble statue. Of their own volition, my hands went forward to touch. Mine. For right now, at least, all this was mine. I squelched Isabelle, who chose that moment to make an appearance in my thoughts. For all I knew, he'd slept with fifteen girls, but I doubted it.

He pulled me close and kissed down the side of my neck. I dodged him, took his hand and pulled him into the family room, then down onto the wide sectional sofa. He braced above me, eyes wide and blue. There was fear there. "Nat. What are we doing? This isn't…"

I sat up, enough to make him rear back to avoid a collision of foreheads and ran my hands over his shoulders. Keeping eye contact, I twisted my shirt off over my head. His eyes went dark, and I watched the pulse beat in his neck as his Adam's apple bobbed.

"Oh God. You…"

Joy bubbled up inside me as I watched his face. No horror or disgust. He thought…

"You're so beautiful. Your skin is so… so smooth. Perfect." He reached out and then curled his hand into a fist, stopping short. I took control, grasping his hand and placing it on my breast. I wanted this. I deserved to enjoy this.

For the first time.

Had Gabe bothered to pretend he thought I was attractive? I couldn't remember now. It didn't matter anyway, as I got lost in the sensation, long forgotten and never this good, of having someone touch me with wonder. With… I struggled for the SAT word, just out of reach. Veneration. I lay back down, pulling him with me, one hand in his hair. His kiss grew deeper, more desperate.

"I haven't… not since Isabelle broke up with me. It's been… so long," Campbell said, breathing hard and fighting for control. "Have you…?"

"Once. A long time ago. Nobody important." We couldn't keep our mouths apart long enough to utter complete sentences. I wanted him touching every part of me, my whole body, so badly. I'd never felt it so strong before.

"We should stop," Campbell said, breaking off a kiss and sucking in gasps of air. "This isn't…. But I don't think I can. Ahhh!" He gasped, lost, as my hands reached a previously unexplored wonder.

"We should." Oh God. I hadn't planned to let it get this far. To get so out of control. "But I don't want to, either." We'd stop later, somehow. For now, I reveled in discovering the *why* of sex, when I'd only learned the *how* before.

Conversation, even attempts at conversation, stopped along with all but the most instinctual functioning of my brain. Zippers unzipped. Buttons popped. It became hard to breathe. And then…

The low static-y buzz of the baby monitor turned into something more. Crying. Full-throated wailing.

There is no sexual buzzkill like a crying baby. A bucket of ice water over the head wouldn't have had half the effectiveness.

Campbell rolled off me. We focused on fixing clothes and replacing what had been tossed aside as if the other one weren't in the room. He was faster and disappeared in the direction of the stairway, still yanking his shirt into place.

I sat there, alone on the sofa, alternating between wanting to grab my bag and go, and reprimanding myself for that cowardly thought, until Campbell padded barefoot down the stairs. He sat silently, feet from me down the length of the sectional. Despair had written itself across his features.

"Is he okay?"

"Yeah. Bad dream or something."

"Good."

"You know what we were doing?" he asked, with so much bleakness in his voice it was a blast of cold air. "It leads to that," he said, pointing to the ceiling in the general direction of Oliver's room. "That's where it goes. Is that what you want? You want to be stuck here, like me?"

"Campbell. It doesn't. Not even most of the time."

"Are you an expert? In my experience, it's led to that a pretty high percentage of the time." He clasped his hands between his knees, but not before I caught them shaking.

"Hardly. It's called birth control. I'll get some," I said. Why was he making this such a big deal? Didn't he know how amazing he'd made me feel?

"You didn't have a condom, did you? I didn't."

I didn't either. The implications of that hit me. Baby or no baby, we would have had to stop, and we'd rapidly been approaching a point of no return. Oliver had saved us from ourselves.

He bit the inside of his cheek, his expression unreadable, then sat with his head in his hands. I sat quietly, waiting for him to speak. After long seconds, he raised his head. "God, I wish things were different. Five minutes ago, I couldn't think about anything but you, naked. Sex. I haven't seen a naked girl since I was a sophomore. It kills me at swimming, seeing you with your legs bare, in that suit, cut down to…"

"Down to where, exactly?" I asked, moving closer to him on the sofa. I was still surfing the high of being wanted, of being attractive, of electrified nerve endings I hadn't known I had. All I wanted in the world right now was a tiny taste of that feeling again.

Campbell blushed, actually blushed. It was adorable, but he made no move to touch me.

"Come on, Campbell. So, Oliver woke up. He's asleep again, isn't he?"

"Yes, but…"

I moved even closer, and picked up one of his hands, clenching his kneecap over and over. "Show me where the suit is cut to." Please.

He moved our hands back to his knee, where he held mine still.

"Campbell. Sex is… it's not wrong. It's not… not a…" What was the word? Sin? Shame? "It's not weak."

"It was for me, Nat. And for Isabelle. It was a mistake. I lost…" He rubbed his nose, looking away from me. "I lost a lot because of it."

"You gained a lot, too. You have Oliver who'll love you forever. You learned responsibility because of it. I trust you."

"I never wanted the responsibility of a person who will love me forever. Not yet."

"You might not have wanted it, but you've got the responsibility now. And aren't most of us going to have it one day? You just got there first."

"The truth is, I don't trust me. Not anymore." Anguish bleached his eyes, making them look like the winter ocean. He raised his hand toward me, and I pulled his head to mine. We kissed, deep and sweet, but it lacked the hunger and the urgency from before. He'd locked the doors.

"I'm sorry," he said. "I think we'd better call it a night. Before you do something you'll regret seriously. The state meet is tomorrow. You need sleep. I need sleep. And besides, I'm sure your parents will expect you back soon anyway."

I checked my phone. "It's only nine thirty. They think I'm out with Marisa. They told me I wasn't allowed to have anything to do with you."

His eyes went wide and his mouth went slack. "They did? When did that happen?"

Oh crap.

"Um. The other day. Tyler spilled the beans about the auditorium lobby. To my brother. Who tried to blackmail me."

"Didn't they already know about Oliver? I thought your parents were the ones who told you." Campbell stood up and began pacing from one end of the room to another.

"Yes. But my dad didn't know about us. Or that we…"

"That we…?"

"That we were still talking until Ethan…" I winced as I said it.

"So, because of Oliver, you're not allowed to have anything to do with me, is that it?"

"Pretty much."

"Let me guess. I deflower and impregnate maidens, and he worries that I'll do the same to you?" He stopped, running his hands through his hair.

"Um. Kind of."

"Then why are you here?"

"Are you kidding?" I asked, amazed. "Do you think I'm going to respect some kind of … like, Puritan pronouncement like that?"

"He's absolutely right. I guess your mom agrees with him?"

"Yeah, though she was okay with us until he went ballistic. And he's not right—it's insulting to you and me both, really. He's making too much out of a mistake you made as a sophomore, and he's assuming I'm too stupid to do everything to prevent it from happening to me!"

Campbell raised a warning eyebrow. I should have noticed the banked tension in his body language before, but I'd been too busy defending myself. "Too stupid, huh? Nice. I guess that makes you *so* much smarter than me."

"Well, I'd like to think it wouldn't happen to me. I do know about multiple forms of birth control, you know."

"Oh, and I didn't?" he said, eyes blazing.

"Did you?"

"Yes!"

"Every single time?"

Campbell's lips pressed together, muscles tense.

Then I knew. "The condom didn't break, did it? You did it without one, didn't you?"

His posture sagged in defeat. "Once. Only once. But that's all it took. We ended up alone at her house and hadn't expected to be. Exactly like tonight. I didn't have anything. Neither did she. Like now. We..." He stood up straighter. "We did exactly what you and I just did, what you wanted to start up again, and we didn't stop when we should have. We thought one time wouldn't hurt. All those people who are infertile. Izzy's cousin had just adopted a baby because she couldn't have one."

"Well, then."

"Well, then, what? I'm stupid, I guess. Yep. Here's a news flash, Nat." He stepped closer, anger, or more, tensing his body again. His nearness affected me again and made me want to plaster myself to him. "When you're into it, I mean really into it, and you pass a certain… point, it's hard to stop that train, condom or no condom. Before, we didn't get close to far enough. Sex makes people stupid. Possibly even you. Of course, maybe you weren't into it."

Not into it? The idea was ludicrous. Even now, having him lecture me on the birds and the bees, I wanted nothing more than to strip off all his clothes and mine and sink back down onto this sectional sofa. He was right, though. If Oliver hadn't cried, Campbell's overachieving sperm might even now be boring a hole in any egg I had loitering around. I didn't think I'd had it in me to prevent it.

I would not have stopped him.

I'd suspected it before, but his words confirmed that Gabe had done nothing for me. There'd been no moment during that entire encounter when I couldn't have happily stood up and walked away. I'd never felt like I was on an unstoppable physical train, and now I wanted that experience as much as I wanted to win tomorrow or get into Berkeley.

"I was into it." It was the truth. I knew it was true, because I understood now how sex without condoms happened to smart people. Without Oliver, I would have agreed.

"Then you're even less experienced than you claim."

"Fine. So I'm inexperienced. I told you I was inexperienced."

"You did. But I didn't realize you were essentially a virgin."

"A what?" I'd had sex with Gabe so that I could get rid of my virginity. I'd hated not knowing what everyone else seemed to.

"Listen. All this just goes to show your parents are right. I'm a bad influence. Look what we're talking about the minute we're alone. I've got a kid. I have stupid sex. You can do so much better. Go on, Nat. It's time to go home." He stood up and walked me to the front door.

I grabbed my bag, holding it like a shield. "You don't get to decide that for me. I think we discussed it before. I'm part of that decision."

"I'm not trying to make your decisions for you. I'm trying to help you see why you should make a better one."

"Look. I came over. We made out. We had to stop. It happens. It happens to lots of people without a baby upstairs, for a million stupid reasons. Like not having a condom. It doesn't mean we're done. Sex doesn't have to be stupid. You think that one stupid mistake means that all sex is stupid. Only sex without protection, without a plan, is stupid." I stared at him. He bit his lip but said nothing.

"Okay. You win, for tonight," I said. "We have the meet tomorrow, and I will see you there." I refused to give up. I stepped close and kissed him. He responded, but with a lot less passion than there'd been before the baby monitor. "You're making too big a deal out of it."

He opened the door and pressed a kiss onto my forehead. "Unfortunately, Nat, there's very little about my life now that isn't a big deal."

# Seventeen

"**I**s the scout here?" I paced back and forth in the locker room, sick with fear. Marisa peeked out into the pool area. I'd been too afraid to open the door.

"I can't tell who are parents and who are scouts. Wait. Coach is talking to some guy wearing UVA stuff, but then again, everybody wears UVA stuff. No idea," she said.

"Oh God. I'm going to throw up."

"You're not."

"You're right. I'm not. But I'd feel better if I did."

"Probably. What's going on with you and Campbell?"

Excellent question. I left last night under deeply confusing circumstances. I didn't know if we were on or off, ramping up or ramping down. And I had no time to deal with it now.

"Nothing, officially. I'm under orders not to speak to him. But of course, I am. We argued a little last night, but it's fine, I think."

I hope.

"Ooh! What did you argue about? Ron and I go on and on about horror movies. He loves them. I can't stand them."

The idea of describing what we argued about filled me with horror. Another little secret pushed itself into the gap between Marisa and me where there used to be none. "Nothing major."

"How's the… the…?" Marisa lowered her voice, scanning the empty locker room.

"The baby is fine," I said, giving her a side-eye. "I assume, anyway. He was asleep last night."

"Oh."

"Okay. I'm ready."

"You're going to be awesome."

I took a deep breath and opened the door into the pool area. The crowd was loud and much bigger than usual. No way would anyone be able to tell which of all these adults were scouts. That anonymity reassured me. I'd never be able to resist trying to watch their facial expressions for clues if I knew who they were. Marisa and I threaded our way through all the coaches and parents and stroke judges and timers to the staging area in the gym. Because this was the state meet and so many schools sent teams, it would last all day, two or three heats in every event. We'd hang out in our roped off area, waiting for the call for our events and heats. The parents and volunteers who ran these things could easily compete with the people who put on the Macy's Thanksgiving Day Parade.

Coach Phillips caught my arm. "Tremayne. Your best chance to show off is right out of the gate in the 200 medley because you're the first swimmer in the first girls' race. Thanks to you, we're in the top heat. We have an excellent seed time. If you can best your personal record, I think these scouts will take notice."

"They're here, then?"

"They are. Do me proud."

I nodded, too nervous to say anything more. Ignoring everyone else, I went straight into the corner of the gym with my headphones in, trying to find some aggression to distill into victory.

I couldn't find any. Only smoky, vision-darkening confusion lurked in the corners of my brain. I tried focusing on the cement walls of the room. Nothing. Behind me, swimmers yelled taunts to each other and gossiped about the best-looking people on the other teams. I couldn't shut out the bits of conversation like usual. One girl described the muscles of a guy's legs to her friend, in over-excited detail.

Which, of course, took my brain directly to the guy whose muscles had been under my hands fewer than twenty-four hours ago.

Okay. Sexual frustration. Wasn't that a thing athletes used? I'd heard stories of baseball players denying themselves sex to funnel the tension into their game. I could do that. I might be able to harness last night into something useful.

The loudspeaker went off. "Event 1, all heats, men's 200 medley relay. Please line up."

Our team cheered for Adrian, Sam, and Trace, as well as Campbell, as they stood, adjusting swim caps over their hair and pulling goggle straps tight. Even in the fluorescent lights of the gym and with a winter-pale skin tone, Campbell was so beautiful. Muscles, indeed. He raised his hand to me in a subtle salute as he passed me on the way to the on-deck area.

"Good luck."

"Good luck to you too." Nothing there to give me a clue as to where we were. Watching him go, I had no trouble summoning enough sexual frustration to light up the city's power grid.

Big meets were always an exercise in long stretches of boredom punctuated by short bursts of terror. The pool areas are universally too small for all the teams to watch the races, so we had to stay where we couldn't watch until called. Most people had brought headphones, or books, or even homework.

Because of the relative weakness of Adrian Barrett, our men's 200 relay was in one of the slower heats, which were all arranged based on the times done during the regular season. They'd only just called for the women's teams to line up when the four of them returned, jubilant and slapping Campbell's back.

"Dude! That was awesome! I saw a couple of people in the audience writing on some little clipboard! You smoked them!" Adrian, while not a terrific swimmer, could always be counted on for support.

"What happened?" Annika and I stopped on our way to the line.

"We won the heat! Best time yet this season, and Campbell smoked the last leg. PR, right?"

"I think so." Campbell was trying for humble, but the thrill of achievement lit up his face.

I had an excuse to touch him. I clasped his upper arm. "You did? That's awesome! Congratulations."

"We won't win the event." He gave me a smile, boosting the longing I'd been channeling, as well as the confusion. This smile was about athletic triumph. It wasn't directed at me.

"Who cares? You got a PR!"

The loudspeaker blared again. "Women's 200 relay. Last call."

"Come on," Annika said, pulling my wrist. I hung back. The other guys went on, to find the rest of our team.

I stepped close to Campbell.

"Good luck," he said, close to my ear. "You can do it." He didn't touch me, though. Then he was gone.

The wait was interminable for the last, and fastest, heat. When our turn finally came, I dropped into the water and popped up again, adjusting my goggles. Now was the time to focus my energy on winning. Think about Campbell, and that body in the swimsuit. The way he'd swum in his race, the whisper in my ear. Adrenaline began to flow. I concentrated on pumping it through my veins, visualized it lighting up my muscles as it went. All I had to do was think about how much I wanted what I hadn't been able to have last night.

I'd wanted it, but had he? Could he have sent me off like that if he wanted what I wanted? Maybe he didn't. He was a nice guy. The kind who'd break up so sweetly the pain was delayed. Had I been an idiot? Had I been dumped and I didn't even know it?

Oh my God.

"Take your mark."

I pulled my hands up onto the block bars and braced my feet, desperately struggling to find the surge of energy. I almost had it, and then…

Somewhere in the crowd, a baby made a fussy noise. Without warning, my thoughts veered into what happened after we stopped, and how we'd argued. He'd dumped me. I was sure of it.

The buzzer went off, and I missed it. I missed it! I'd thought about something besides the buzzer. I missed it by far less than a second, but it was enough to kill my leg of the race, and probably that of my entire team. Dammit. I splashed backwards, already two or three feet behind the other swimmers.

Some days, this wouldn't have been much of a problem, but this was the state meet, and the fastest heat of the state meet, and these other girls in the pool with me now were the best five backstrokers in the state, at least for high schools this size. I couldn't count on catching them.

At least now I had my usual rage to fuel me. Rage all directed at myself. My arms windmilled furiously, while anger at how much I'd allowed Campbell to unravel my life buzzed through me. I was lying to my parents. Fighting with my dad. Unable to concentrate in class. And now losing a race that should have been mine.

Too busy marveling at the horror of the loss of everything I'd worked for, I timed the flip turn slightly wrong and lost another fraction of a second. My shoulders burned and my breath came short as I fought my way back to the block. As I approached, I watched the other teams' breaststrokers dive around me like shadowy water-stained pterodactyls, and touched in third-to-last place. A desperate Annika dove over me, and I climbed out to greet the anguished faces of the frantically cheering last two swimmers on my team.

I glanced at the crowd. Wherever the scouts were, they wouldn't be interested in me. When the race ended, I stalked off, straight past my team's surprised faces, and Campbell. I held up my hands to keep them all away, hoping to make it to a deserted stretch of hallway before someone spoke to me and I bit off a head.

Campbell didn't take a hint. He followed me.

"Nat. Wait."

I walked faster.

He caught up with me near the water fountain. "Campbell. I'm not in a good place right now. I lost. The team lost. It was my fault. Because I was distracted. My fault."

"Everybody gets distracted now and then. Nobody is perfect. You're too hard on yourself."

"You weren't distracted," I said, remembering his glee at his personal best. The thought made my blood pressure rise even higher.

"What was bothering you?" he asked, touching my shoulder. I shook off his hand. He pulled it back as if he'd been burned.

"If you really want to know, *you* were bothering me. I realized right before the race that you dumped me. You were so smooth about it that I didn't even realize it. I'm obviously not too bright. Took me a whole day for it to penetrate my brain."

"What? I didn't say anything that—"

"That's not even it anyway. I heard a baby cry. It distracted me. I wondered if it was Oliver, or I was thinking about Oliver, or whatever. It messed up my start. I never got it back."

He said nothing; he just stood there, watching. A miserable montage assembled itself in my mind. Campbell, winning his race. Me, letting him into my life to tangle up, at the last possible minute, all the neat little threads I'd spent years pulling straight. Parental ultimatums, blown swim starts in front of the very scout I'd been praying for years would watch me, babies, a college dorm room in the same town where I'd lived all my life.

I looked at Campbell and his intense eyes and his perfect lips and his ridiculously wide shoulders and I blamed him. If I'd never met him, everything would have been fine. Everything would have gone according to plan. I'd be doing the same thing I'd done all the years I'd been in high school: hanging out with Marisa, building a killer college resume, and planning my escape.

Even as the unjustified anger at Campbell almost choked me, I knew the rage was really at myself. For being weak. For being affected by him this way. For letting anything derail me from my goals.

In the end, I couldn't scream it out at him when I knew it was my own fault. Our gaze held for a second, maybe three, and then I ducked my head and escaped into the girls' bathroom, leaving him standing empty-handed in the hall.

MONDAY AFTERNOON, I left the locker room after turning in my locker key. Swim season was over. I'd been right. We'd lost that race, and although I'd done well in the other races I swam, the echo of that loss took the edge off. No personal records. Second place in the backstroke was the best I got.

Coach didn't bother to introduce me to the UVA scout.

Campbell didn't call or text all the rest of Saturday or Sunday.

We still had rehearsal at six on Monday, but I planned to drive around aimlessly until then. I didn't want to go home where my parents would likely continue their weekend-long Pep Up Natalie efforts.

Outside in the school parking lot, I dug for my keys in the bottom of my overstuffed backpack. It took me a minute to see her, in too-tight jeans and a sloppy hoodie, leaning against my car.

"Hi," Isabelle said.

What the ever-living hell was she doing here? At my car? Great. That's all I needed. To have Isabelle get territorial, when I wasn't sure where I was with the guy in question. I needed Isabelle today like I needed a lobotomy. On second thought, the lobotomy might be a blessed relief if it would help me stop thinking for two seconds.

"Hi," I said, looking around. "Where's Oliver? And how did you know which car was mine?"

"I saw it in Campbell's driveway that day. It's pretty unusual to see a car other than his or his parents' there. And Oliver is home, with my mother."

"Okay. Listen, Isabelle, you'd better tell me whatever it is you want to tell me. I've had kind of a bad day and I'd like to get out of here."

She took in the brick of the school and the tennis courts nearby, clearly in no hurry. "That's funny. I'd give almost anything to get to come here every day, and you're on fire to leave."

"Really?" I tried to see it as she did, instead of as the boring scenery of my life. "You'd get sick of it in no time, I'm sure."

"No. I loved St. Anselms. I was somebody there. I played soccer, outside. With friends. I was president of my sophomore class. Did you know that? Now I'm just the person who takes care of Oliver and helps my mother with the housework. My whole life is about doing things for other people. I don't even know how to talk to people anymore. I'm going to miss everything. Prom, graduation, class ring, everything. I passed my GED last week. Not that I have anyone to tell about that."

"I'm sorry." I thought about telling her she wasn't missing much, but no point. "Congrats on the GED. And Oliver is adorable."

"Of course he is. I don't mean to complain. I wanted to ask you what's going on between you and Campbell."

I did tell her to get to the point. "Why don't you ask him?" *Yes, ask him. Then tell me.*

"I did. He said it's none of my business."

Nobody could say she was shy. "Well, I hate to be rude, but is it any of your business?"

She picked a fingernail, choosing her words. "Normally, it wouldn't be. But with Oliver, Campbell and I are stuck together for the rest of our lives. It absolutely is my business who is around my son. You were holding him that night, so…"

The horror of that struck me with a wave of nausea. One day, Oliver would have parent-teacher conferences and little concerts they'd both attend, then there'd be sports, and graduation, and a wedding, and grandchildren. Isabelle and Campbell were yoked to each other forever: it seemed impossible to believe. And she was right. She did need to be concerned about who'd be spending time with her child. Oh God.

"Let's see. I'm pretty tame. I swim, and I'm in the play, and I go to class. I have an irritating brother and two meddling parents."

"You didn't answer my question about Campbell."

Yeah, intentionally. She was direct, that was for sure.

"Campbell and I are… figuring things out. I promise, though, I'd never hurt Oliver."

"Okay."

We kind of grinned at each other, feeling our way around this. I felt a bout of massive nosiness coming on. Isabelle wasn't the only one who could be direct. "Why did you and Campbell break up?"

Her eyes turned wistful and she fiddled with the side mirror on my car. "God, I loved Campbell when we were together. He's so noble and… I don't know. Grown-up, maybe? He seemed like so much more than the boys in our grade. He had plans, and like, goals. Sleeping with him seemed obvious, somehow. Like that's what you did with a man, and Campbell was easily the closest thing to a man that the tenth grade at St. Anselms had to offer. Most of the guys there are rich, of course. I was a scholarship student. Campbell is rich too, but he never seemed entitled or full of himself like those other boys. He never acted like he thought I owed him sex."

"No." Ugh. Just when I'd worked myself up to walking away, she'd gone and reminded me of all the things that had attracted me too. Trying not to make a thing of it, I pushed the mirror back to where it had been.

"Now I know it's because his parents are all do-goody and bend over backwards to make sure Campbell never is one of those rich kids who has everything. Hell, I know people in trailers whose parents give them more than the Adamses give Campbell."

"Yeah. I kind of got that," I said, thinking they might try to find unfortunates they could help a little closer to home.

"Anyway, I broke up with him because I was pregnant, and sixteen, and scared of Hell. I never thought it would happen. And then I freaked out about having the baby and even thought about getting an abortion. But my parents are Baptists. I knew in my heart they'd never allow it, and I wasn't old enough to do it without their permission. I didn't have the guts to go before a judge all by myself."

"Wouldn't Campbell have supported you?"

"Yeah, he would, and he did, but it wasn't long before we were arguing over every little thing. Stupid things. What brand of diapers to buy. What names to give the baby. And everything else too. What movie to see. He was always talking about some book he'd read, and he'd want me to read it too, and I didn't really want to read it, and we'd argue about that. We used to argue about politics. About my parents. Just dumb stuff. It was obvious we'd never make it. He's a brain. I'm not. We did fine when everything was easy. We fell apart after. I let him go."

"And now? No offense, Isabelle, but I'm going to come right out and ask you. Are you really done with Campbell?"

For a long moment, I thought she was going to mark her territory. Say something threatening to get me to back off. She did, after all, have an ace in the hole. Part of me even hoped she might.

"Yes. I'm done with Campbell. When I'm with him I think about being scared and unhappy and guilty and stupid. I want to start over." She smiled, lightening her serious face so that she looked like a completely different person. "I met somebody, too. Campbell doesn't know, but he'll find out soon. Tell him if you want."

"Is he a nice guy? Good to Oliver?"

"Yeah. He's older. He knows about kids. And goodness knows, I need a reason to get out of the house."

"Sounds intriguing. I won't tell Campbell, though. That's for you to do."

She laughed, not much humor in her tone. "Oh, I'm not telling my parents about it, but I don't care if Campbell knows. Listen. Thanks, Natalie. I'm sorry I was such a bitch to you the time we met before. It was before I met Tommy, and I was having a moment where I thought Campbell might be better than being lonely. But now it's all good."

"Um. Right."

"And I'm glad…" she started, shyly, "that Campbell isn't quite so lonely anymore, either."

I gave her a watered-down smile, which, in light of how crappy I now felt about what I'd said to Campbell at the swim meet, took a lot more effort than you might expect.

Isabelle waved and walked away across the parking lot.

I got in my car and drove, thinking about her. Stuck at home with the baby the bulk of the time, home-schooled and kept away from other kids. Campbell was lucky by comparison.

I liked her but didn't trust her entirely. Something hungry and desperate lay in wait behind her eyes, like a prisoner homing in on a weakness in the fence. She said she didn't want Campbell now that she'd met this Tommy, whoever he was, but she'd admitted to wanting him as recently as a couple of weeks ago. She wanted to keep him in her back pocket, a reserve boyfriend. She could afford to be generous, for now, but she'd be watching.

But she'd been right about Campbell. And I'd been an idiot.

# Eighteen

The weirdness started at lunchtime the next day, like the dream where you walk the school halls with no pants on. I ran into the cafeteria late and went through the checkout line with my sandwich and bag of chips and noticed the turned heads. Kameron Moody, sitting with her circle of gossip-collectors, chattered away behind her hands, her eyes bright and fevered. Charlie and Marquez, from my seventh period AP Lit, goggled openly at me, not even trying to hide their avid expressions. Everywhere, people pointed and whispered. I didn't have time to sit, and my usual table was empty by now anyway.

I went back to my locker and checked my phone. Marisa had texted me, but it didn't help at all: "OMG SO SHOOK!!" Whatever it was, she knew about it, but she'd be on the other side of the building on her way to French. I hadn't seen Campbell since this morning.

Damned if I'd ask a random person. I could find out what the hell was going on, and if not, I'd find Marisa before seventh period. I collected my books and went to class. My AP Gov teacher, Mrs. Samuels, talked loud and long, so desperate for our attention every day that she dialed her animation up to an eleven, managing to look like a marionette in the hands of a two-year-old. Even with that distraction, the room felt full of whispers and glances, pinging off the walls in every direction. Every time I turned my head to catch one, all I saw were students wearing the attentive mask, gazing at Mrs. Samuels.

The rest of the afternoon went on that way. Campbell had disappeared from the hallways. He didn't pass me as he usually did between Gov and Physics. I raced for the sanctuary of Marisa's locker, located near my seventh period, like one of those cartoon characters crawling toward water in the desert. Her eyes were wide, and she had the appearance of a survivor from some dystopian novel.

"Oh, my God, Nat. No one will shut up about it. You must be dying!"

"Please, if you care about me at all, clue me in. People have been pointing and staring all day and I don't know why. Am I naked all over Instagram or something?"

"You don't know? Oh, shit. Oh. It's Campbell. Everybody knows about the baby."

Ah. My stomach clenched and sweat beads rose under my nose, even while my rational mind knew, had always known, that discovery of Oliver by first the school, then the world, was only a matter of time.

In a lot of places it might not be particularly exciting news that someone got pregnant or became a parent as a teenager. According to TV, in some places it was so common that it was boring.

Not at our school.

For the most part, we'd avoided whatever teen pregnancy epidemic justified reality TV shows and *US* magazine covers.

Here, going to college was paramount. Our parents were motivated to remove every possible obstacle between their kids and higher education and the kids were brainwashed into adoration of UVA or another school from the cradle. We got our sex ed talks around fourth grade, and most parents preached birth control from early on. If anyone did get pregnant, whispers occasionally reached us of a trip to Planned Parenthood. Only one girl in my grade had gone ahead and had the baby, and we never saw her again afterwards. We never knew who the father was. There was talk she didn't, either.

Her departure made Campbell the only parent in the building under the age of eighteen.

If everyone knew Campbell had a child, they also all knew…

"Also, that you and he are a couple. No one can believe it," continued Marisa, hesitantly.

"What exactly?"

"That you'd… you'd… Um. You're so, like… level-headed, and…"

Anger boiled under my skin, raising the hairs on my arms. "You mean they think I didn't know. That I found out today. That I'd never have been with him if I did."

"Um. Something like that."

"Where is Campbell? I haven't seen him all day."

"I heard he went home after first period."

Oh God.

"Do we know how the news broke?" I asked.

"No. I heard it from Kameron way before lunch."

"Well. At least I know why everyone is staring now." The bell rang. Marisa gave me a quick pat on the arm, and we scuttled off in different directions for class.

That night before rehearsal, I waited in the lobby of the auditorium to talk to Campbell. I'd sent him six texts but got no reply to any of them. By the time I'd thought of going to the Connaughtons to catch him at work, it was too late to be at rehearsal on time.

One minute after Mrs. Murchison had told me to get on stage for the third time, Campbell came in, his face wiped clean of any emotion. He didn't acknowledge me as he passed. Finney's grin split his face as he nudged Amelia, whose distress made her clench her fists. Campbell's careful blank expression sent ice water running through my veins. It had to be tough to have succeeded so long in remaining invisible, only to have it be ruined so close to the end. With a pang, I realized it was my fault. If he'd never met me and told me the secret, he probably would have been able to stay under the radar the whole school year.

I'd never know how the school found out, but all roads most likely led back to me.

And now that they had, Campbell and his family could shout it loud and proud. No more secrets.

"Campbell, thank you for being close to on time," Mrs. M said. "If you'd told me early on what you have going on at home, I'd have been more understanding. And I'd like for you to stay after rehearsal a few minutes so we can discuss the impact the news might have on the play."

Campbell's face turned an ugly burgundy, and he nodded and ducked his head, leaving no doubt he'd like the floor to open and swallow him whole. Snickers erupted in the ranks of the underclassmen. Noah sat, poised to pounce, his expression making clear he thought Christmas had come early.

"Fine. Everyone in the last number on stage."

That was me, and Campbell, and Noah and Finney as well as Amelia.

"What is she talking about?" asked Tyler Donaldson, possibly the only person in the building who hadn't heard the story by now.

Noah stage-whispered to him. "Campbell is the daddy of a baby. I think he must have missed that part of Family Life class. Make sure you pay attention, Tyler, hear?"

"Shut up, Noah. Don't be a dick," I said.

"Darling, I am far too tickled to be able to zip it at this point. It's absolutely beyond me. Ask me next week."

Campbell still wouldn't look at me. The rehearsal proceeded like that—me anguished, Noah adding 37% more gesture to each gesture, Campbell wooden and silent as the grave. Tyler stayed wide-eyed, Finney malevolent, and Amelia mortified. Her dance with Campbell at the end of the show was almost laughable—like watching a kid in a restaurant with slow service try to animate her silverware. Mrs. M bit her lip and ran her hands distractedly through her hair, knocking her glasses off her head twice. She called a halt an hour early, aware everything was off kilter.

I took my time packing my backpack, hoping to catch Campbell before his little chat with Mrs. M. Everyone else left, in high spirits, laughing and punching each other. There's no better misery than somebody else's misery.

"Campbell. I need to talk to you." Desperate for him to hear me, I grabbed his elbow.

"I can't right now." He bent over to tuck a stray notebook into his backpack, not meeting my eyes. "Mrs. Murchison wants to see me."

I stood in the row, blocking his way, on purpose. He'd have to climb over the seat to get around me. "You know this doesn't change anything. And now, since everybody knows, you can…"

"There's nothing to change. I think we've gone as far as we can go. Oliver killed the mood the other night. You were pissed about something at the swim meet. Isabelle told me she talked to you, and that you didn't exactly seem thrilled about me. 'Figuring things out'?"

"What?" That bitch. "I didn't really feel comfortable going on and on about the wonderfulness of you to your ex-girlfriend."

"Whatever," he said, as if he were a thousand years old. "Everyone knows now. They all think you must be stupid to be with me, with the baggage I've got. And they're right. You made it perfectly clear at the swim meet that thought's occurred to you, too, more than once probably. And let's be honest. Not like you're actually with me. We've never gone on a date. Never… well, you know."

That stung. "Wow."

"I told you at the beginning. You can do so much better than me. I really don't know why you've wasted your time. I assume you think I'm some kind of do-gooder project. Something you can add to your sparkling high school resume."

I didn't miss his assessment of the height of the seats in the row in front of us. He wanted to get away. His attitude shot sparks of rage through the black when I closed my eyes for calm. He hadn't let me tell him what I'd realized about Oliver. He'd hear it anyway.

"Fine, Campbell. You're like this sad cloud of Eeyore self-pity, nobly keeping everyone away so they don't get tainted with your shame and embarrassment. Did you ever think that your shame and embarrassment has a name, and it's Oliver? When are you going to stop thinking of him as a mistake, as something to be hidden away? When are you going to decide that you shouldn't have to, like, flagellate yourself forevermore? So you have a kid. Are you under some clueless impression that you're the only person at this school to have sex without a condom? The only difference is that you have proof. You have a kid. A great kid. He deserves parents—and grandparents, for that matter—who are proud of him. Who want to show him off. Parents who take him to the park and the mall and the grocery store and everywhere else. If you can't stop the pity parade, then you don't deserve him. None of you."

"Are you done?" he asked, scaring me with the dead sound in his voice.

"Almost. Everyone knows now. You need to tell everyone in your life to go to hell by screaming out how proud you are of Oliver."

"I'm only going to say this once, Natalie," he said, leaning in, his voice losing the dead tone and going harsh and raw. "You have no idea what you're talking about. You don't have a clue what my life is like. You don't have a child. You still get to *be* a child. You've got everything handed to you for the asking. We're not the same, you and me. You're not capable of understanding me, or my parents, or Oliver."

"Are you done?" I demanded.

"Yes. I'm done. And so are we." His face had gone blank and he refused to make eye contact.

"Good." Lie! Such a lie! Not good; terrible. A shaft of guilt ripped through my insides, sudden and burning strong as lightning. I'd wanted him to start over with me, with Oliver, but instead of saying it to him in a persuasive, rational way, I'd thrown it at him like I wasn't the pot calling the kettle black. Oh God. I'd hardly behaved well myself, ignoring him at the swim meet, blaming him for my lack of focus, judging him.

I'd judged him without the first tiny piece of a clue. I was drowning in shame. He was right. I was a child compared to him. A stupid, clueless, spoiled child.

The fact that he was absolutely right made it impossible for me to say anything at all.

I moved, letting him get past me, out of the row.

Out of the room.

Out.

EVEN FROM THE DRIVEWAY, I knew something was wrong at home—even more wrong than the apocalypse I'd already weathered at school. We'd gotten out of rehearsal early, but it was still late enough to be odd that every light was on.

My parents sat at the kitchen table, eyes trained on the door when I came in. My mom's laptop was open and glowing on the table. Neither spoke.

"What's going on?" How could they have heard already that everyone at school knew? Ethan was still in middle school. They weren't close with the parents of my friends.

"Read this." My dad pushed the laptop toward me, turning it so I could see. I sat down to read.

The website belonged to my dad's opponent for the school board seat, Rick Bryant. The banner at the top read "Abstinence for Our Children Now." An article, dated and posted today, followed.

> My fellow concerned citizens. It is with heavy regret that I must inform you that District 3 School Board Member Simon Tremayne is clearly opposed to the essential goal of protecting our

children through abstinence-only education. Sources have told me that Simon Tremayne's daughter, seventeen-year-old Natalie, is herself the secret mother of a one-year-old infant boy, fathered by her classmate during their sophomore year. Natalie was a promising young lady, a talented swimmer and good student, which only makes it all the more regrettable that her future has been ruined in this sad, pointless, and avoidable way. It should come as no surprise, however, given that her parents must have low standards for supervision of their children to allow a fifteen-year-old child access to a male classmate without a chaperone. I understand Simon Tremayne did not insist on a marriage, and that his daughter was abandoned to raise the child alone.

"What kind of bullshit is this?" I shoved the laptop back at him, unable to read further. "I'm the mother of a one-year-old child? That's news to me! Do you see any baby around here? Have you been hiding him? What the hell?"

"We don't know. I sent him an e-mail telling him he's mistaken and asking him to take it down, but he hasn't responded. I'd guess he found out that Campbell has a baby and that you and he were together and assumed the rest."

"But how?"

"Did you tell Marisa?"

A sick feeling spread slowly, like a poison. "Yes." Excuses rose to my lips, but I bottled them up.

The disgusted, disappointed expression I hated even more than anger flashed across his face. "And she's close to her mother. Her mother is friends with Bryant's wife. There's your connection."

"But Mrs. Mercado knows I've never been pregnant. She's seen me practically every week since elementary school."

"I doubt she told Bryant the baby was yours. Like I said, he assumed."

"Can't we sue him for this total lie?"

"No. He was careful to say, 'sources told me.' It will be enough for him to claim he was misinformed."

"How many people read this blog anyway?"

"Probably not many. But he's posted it on his social media pages and tagged me. I took it down, but it's spreading fast. The damage is done."

My mom spoke for the first time. "Your grandmother called. She was horrified. I never really pictured being in the position of having to explain that no, she doesn't have a great-grandson she's never met. I had to remind her she's seen you twice a year, every year. I've gotten Facebook messages from most of my co-workers, and a good chunk of my high school graduating class, congratulating me on being a grandmother. Good God. I'm only forty-four." She picked up her phone and showed it to me. Facebook Messenger alerts replaced each other rapidly on her lock screen. I didn't touch it. She put it down, keeping a cautious watch on it, as if it were a poisonous spider.

"We've spent most of the evening typing furious rebuttals, but we can't keep up. Ethan, as well. A few of his classmates have been surprised. A couple of their mothers got in touch to ask what's going on."

"Oh God, Dad. Mom. I'm sorry." I wrung my hands. I hated how their shoulders slumped like that. They looked old. Every day of forty-four or more. I'd done that to them—me and my stupid relationship that probably didn't even count as a relationship. Tears pricked behind my eyes—I'd never been able to deal with making them unhappy. Shame pressed down on me, tightening my breathing.

It hadn't been even an hour since I'd told Campbell off for letting himself be cowed by shame. Now I'd just apologized because...

Because what?

Because nothing.

"Wait. No. I'm not sorry."

Their worried heads popped up, twin creases appearing on their foreheads. "Pardon?" asked Dad, as if he'd heard me wrong.

"I hate that you have this piece of crap guy trying to unseat you, Dad, but that's not my fault. As I think you're aware, I have no baby and therefore no unprotected sex to apologize for. Even if I did have unprotected sex, I could apologize for one stupid choice I made. The last person at fault for unprotected sex is a baby. It's a person. Someone to love. Campbell's parents and his ex-girlfriend's parents have acted like this is the worst possible thing that could ever happen to anyone anywhere. But you know what? It's not. It's just not."

"Natalie." My dad held up a hand, trying to get in a word.

I ignored him. "I'm not kidding. If his parents think a baby—an adorable, healthy baby that Campbell is raising responsibly and earning money to support while, I might add, maintaining excellent grades and being the star of the play and of the men's swim team—is terrible, then they should talk to parents of teenagers who died in car crashes. Or who stole a car and went to prison. Or who get terminal cancer or get paralyzed or have brain damage. Then they'd know what terrible really is."

My parents exchanged glances. I'd scored a point. Maybe THE point.

"Dad. Here's what you do. You get on Facebook. You quote the ridiculous parts of this blog entry and say how false it is. Point out that during sophomore year, I broke the school record in the backstroke. In a swimsuit. And most definitely not pregnant. Post the link to the school athletic record page. Do it now. If you do it right, you can take him down. He doesn't care about the truth. He only cares about being hateful. Say that. Then you write a letter to the editor of the newspaper that says the same thing. That ought to get the word out to all the old people who haven't heard of the 'inter webs.' He handed you a gift. This blog is a huge, hot-air, grab-bag-of-lies gift. He'll look like a total idiot. Sometimes the thing that seems like the worst is really the best."

"She's right, Simon. That could work." My mom sat up straighter and put a hand on his arm.

"I'll leave you alone. You've got work to do. And by the way, if anyone asks, Campbell and I are apparently done. For real. Forever."

I dashed out of the room before they could ask me any questions. I wouldn't have known the answers to any of them, anyway.

# Nineteen

After that, Dad's opponent kind of subsided. A brief flurry of letters to the editor in support of Dad as the teller of truth had people talking for a few days, but it died out fairly quickly. After all, nobody is really that interested in a local school board race.

My grandma called, hugely amused, and said she was relieved to hear that she wasn't yet a great-grandmother. She hoped I'd clue her in early when that happy day arrived because she very much looked forward to being able to post my ultrasound picture on Twitter. She friended me on Facebook because, she said, "so many interesting things happen there!"

At the next rehearsal, Noah stood and made an impassioned plea to take Campbell's part, on the theory that our play was wholesome and child-friendly, and Campbell's presence would "turn it into a loin-heaving production of *Spring Awakening* in disguise." My heart dropped into my shoes at Campbell's resigned expression and Mrs. M's serious consideration of Noah's suggestion for four whole seconds, but she found a tiny dreg of compassion and let Campbell stay.

The play grew closer and closer. Campbell and I exchanged few words. I stayed away from him, and after the furor died down a couple of weeks later, he went back to virtual silence and invisibility. I'd spent all of high school, except for a two—three if I stretched it—week period this winter entirely boyfriendless and fine with it. Now I knew what I'd been missing. Not sex. Not even the kissing. What I missed was the thrill of arriving at school and seeing him there. Knowing he was happy to see me. Aware that a kind of delicious possibility existed for every odd minute we spent together.

None of the other guys at school held that kind of appeal.

None of them even came close.

March passed into April, and a week before the last results of the college admissions were supposed to arrive, Coach Phillips called me into his office.

His eyes were kind. The kindness scared me more than any other expression I'd ever seen on his face. I sank down into a desk chair, worried my knees wouldn't support me. I dug my fingernails into the mauve vinyl seat and breathed in the regular scent of the office: chlorine, chewing tobacco, and peppermint.

"Natalie. I don't know how to say this the best way, so I'll say it straight out. No scholarships. Not from anyone, except a couple of the smaller schools I don't think you're interested in. It was the state meet that killed it. And that other girl from Portsmouth who was there, the one who swam all the same stuff and kicked your ass. I'm sorry, honey. Coach Moseley at UVA said if you get in, he'd love to talk to you about swimming walk-on for them, but he can't offer you a scholarship."

"Nothing?"

"No Division I. I'm sorry."

Once upon a time, Coach had measured the capacity of my lungs to use oxygen. It turned out my lungs are more than twice as efficient at breathing as most people's, because of the swim training I'd had.

The capacity right now was nowhere near enough.

"If it helps, Moseley said he thought you'd be likely to get in. He wrote a note to the admissions office, which he normally doesn't do except for the scholarship ones."

Breathe. In and out. Saying anything was beyond my ability.

"It means you were on the bubble, Natalie. He really wants you to swim for them."

I took a second, struggling for anything rational to say that wouldn't be a primal howl of anguish.

"Did anybody on our team get anything?"

"Not Division I. A few other schools. Moseley was interested in Campbell, too, but he didn't apply to UVA. He hasn't ruled out talking to him, though."

"Oh." A thin imitation of the anger I felt at Campbell for choosing shame instead of a college education resurfaced. But we were done. It wasn't my place to urge him on anymore.

"I hate to give you news like this, Tremayne. If you're smart, you won't let it screw with your swimming. You're still the same swimmer you were." He smiled at me. "Let me know what you decide."

A week later, I got the news I'd been admitted everywhere I applied: UVA, Berkeley, University of Michigan, Duke, and Northwestern. None of those schools gave academic scholarships. It was an honor just to get in. Without athletic scholarships, choice of a school became more and more about simple, sixth-grade math calculations. I'd need room and board everywhere—I would *not* live at home if I went to UVA. I'd need books and spending money everywhere. At UVA, however, and only at UVA, I'd get in-state tuition. I'd have no travel expenses. All the others would cost twice as much. Did I say sixth-grade math? Even a kindergartner could do this problem.

What kind of crazed egocentric drug had I been on when I did my applications? I hadn't applied to any other in-state schools. I'd been so sure I'd get a scholarship somewhere else. What had been wrong with William and Mary? That would have put me a three-hour drive away. Even Virginia Tech would take me out of my parents' zip code. Given me some hope at independence.

Nothing to do now but pin my hopes on an amazing financial aid package from one of the out-of-state schools. And forget about it for now. The play finally went on stage tonight.

Maybe it was a symptom of how ready I was for graduation to come, but I hadn't had nearly as much fun in this play as I had before. Rehearsals had been tense and not indicative of any particular talent or quality. Various people, Campbell and Noah in particular, had obvious ability, but the production had never gelled into chemistry and magic. I blamed Finney for his hatefulness, and myself for letting memories of the possibility of Campbell intrude now that I'd been returned to the cold light of day.

Mrs. M had gone thin-lipped and silent. Her hair stood permanently on end. At dress rehearsal last night, Finney dropped two lines. Amelia burst into contagious giggles during her song. The backstage crew misplaced the pitchforks. The underclassmen knocked over a piece of scenery during a crowd scene. If we managed to finish tonight without boos, jeers, and an ambulance, I'd call it a win.

I arrived early and did my own makeup, then went to watch the guys get theirs on. Nothing was funnier than watching high school boys clinging desperately to their manhood be forced to have their eyes lined and their lips painted. Makeup for all decreed Mrs. M. We wouldn't want anyone to be washed out under the bright stage lights.

Finney sat at the end of the line of guys waiting their turn. He had to wear much fancier makeup than most, since he was supposed to look like a pudgy clock.

"Mrs. M? Can I help?" I asked, having done makeup for plays for years.

"Sure, dear. Grab one and get started. You know what the make-up plans are, right?"

"I do. Would you like me to do Max's makeup?" I asked sweetly. Finney glowered at me. He strongly suspected me of engineering his trip to the elementary schools in full clock costume, where, it turned out, his two younger sisters went to school along with Joe Carranza's little brother, but he couldn't prove it.

"That would be great. Max? Natalie will do it for you."

I rolled my eyes mentally. Adults had no governor on their ability to say awkward things and not notice.

"Thanks, Mrs. Murchison," Finney said, getting up to follow me. "Though I can think of a thousand girls I'd rather have…"

"Pardon, dear?" Mrs. M paid little attention, engrossed in fighting the frantically fluttering eyelashes of a sophomore who'd never seen an eyeliner before.

"Doing it for me," finished Finney. He must be nervous. That was a halfhearted insult, for Finney. It entirely lacked bite. He sat down for his makeup. I reached into a pot and began smearing white pancake makeup all over his face. I didn't worry about being gentle or careful of his eyes.

"Natalie, do you mind if I talk to you?" Amelia poked her head around the corner.

"No. Talk."

"After you finish doing Max's makeup. Go ahead."

"Whatever, Amelia. Just go ahead."

Her perfect features arranged themselves into surprise as she shook back her hair in her practiced move. Finney sat up straighter, squaring his shoulders and, I swear, flexing a little.

She glanced at him. "Um. No. I'll wait."

"Okay." I dabbed Finney's face, added the clock decorations shown on the drawing for his character, and followed Amelia without a word to him.

She waited for me, adorable in her costume dress. "I didn't want to say this in front of Max. So. You and Campbell are done, right?"

"For over a month, yes." Something tasted funny in my mouth. I swallowed, trying to get it out.

"Anyway. Joe is being awful. He says he's not going to take me to prom. And I need to be at prom. People say they plan to vote for me for queen. I know he's got a baby, but I thought maybe Campbell..."

The taste in my mouth was metallic. Campbell had another supporter, and I hated it. "Sure. He doesn't belong to me. You don't need my permission."

"Well, I know before, you and he were... I wanted to make sure. You've always been nice to me. I'd never ask him if y'all weren't done."

I stared at her in amazement. All these years I'd assumed she took what she wanted whenever she wanted. She wasn't letting the baby bother her. I'd judged a book by its cover. I'd been wrong. "Um. Yeah. It's over."

"Okay. Hey, break a leg, okay? Thanks. Eeeee!" She widened her eyes in excited anticipation and dashed off, presumably to find Campbell. She went the wrong way, though. She'd headed to the thick crowds of underclassmen and stagehands and pit orchestra members lugging their instruments. Campbell wouldn't be there. He'd be wherever people weren't. Too bad. I'd love to be a fly on the wall when she asked him to prom.

If I warned him before she found him, I'd get to see his reaction.

Down the hall, away from the little rooms for changing and make-up tables, I found him sitting on the floor with his back braced against the wall, headphones in, eyes closed. He wore his costume without makeup, because he had a headpiece that covered his face for most of the play. Someone, not me, had the job of putting it on him during the second half of the play before his transformation. It melted under the headpiece if it stayed on long.

I slid down the wall until I sat next to him. He opened his eyes, a wary expression there, and pulled out one earbud.

"Amelia is looking for you. She's going to ask you to prom," I said, without preamble.

His eyes widened in alarm. "You're joking."

"Nope. She asked my permission seconds ago."

He blinked, clearly at a loss as to which part of this new information to address first.

"Relax. I said she didn't need my permission."

"You did? Because…" He turned red, but with more animation than I'd seen on him in a while.

"Because she doesn't, of course. But you're on your own when she finds you."

"Thanks for telling me, I guess."

I chewed my lip, not sure if even my daring was bold enough for the question I wanted to ask. Then it slipped out anyway. "What are you going to say to her?"

Our eyes met. I had to look away before I got lost there. It felt so wrong to sit this close and not be able to touch. He cleared his throat. "I'm not going to prom with Amelia."

"She's pretty persuasive, I hear."

"I can't go with anyone." He pressed his lips together and pulled his knees up to his chest, gripping them tight.

"Right."

We sat there in silence for a while. I tried to think of something fun and careless to say as a parting remark. Nothing came to mind.

Campbell stared at his knees. "Nat. If I could have, I'd have wanted to go with you."

He looked up and met my eyes. A tsunami of longing swept me, leaving wreckage behind. My breathing stuttered, but I caught it and corrected it so he wouldn't see how much what he'd said mattered to me.

*You still could. If you asked.*

He wasn't asking. I waited two more seconds to make sure. It was for the best anyway. He'd only hurt me, and me him. A preview of the pain swept up my spine, hardening my resolve. I plastered a teasing expression on my face.

"Just think. You might miss your chance to be the guy who brought the Prom Queen. I think the formal title of that position is Royal Arm Candy. It's an honor."

He smiled, only a little, maybe employing 22% of his smile muscles. "I'll have to think about it, then. Can't pass up a chance to be Royal Arm Candy."

"Well. Good luck with that weighty decision. And break a leg tonight. You've really been great in this piece of crap play." I hesitated, then patted his arm. Like a sister.

He reached out, towards me, while I willed his hand to move closer, then pulled it back and stuffed it under his costume coat. I jumped up, suddenly wanting to be anywhere else.

AS I STOOD IN THE WINGS, watching the last scene, I breathed a sigh of relief. No missed lines. No flubbed entrances. No inappropriate giggling. Nothing had fallen down, or apart, or off. So there'd been a cracked note sung by Garrett Pannell, who played Gaston. Otherwise, everything had gone well. I'd sung my big song without a hitch. Onstage, the "transformation" took place and Campbell, now prince-like, had taken Amelia in his arms for their kiss.

During rehearsals, the big kiss had been clunky at best. Depending on the ever-changing status of Amelia's relationship with Joe, she either kissed like a dead person, or tried to jump down Campbell's throat. Campbell hadn't shown any aptitude for guessing which it would be on any given day, and usually, this kiss induced snorts and laughter.

Not tonight. I had no idea if Amelia had asked him to prom, or if he'd said yes, but damn. It sure seemed like it from here. Campbell, a good foot taller than Amelia, folded her firmly in his arms, making her look like a delicate flower, and crushed his lips down to hers. Her arms snaked around his neck and clung. I'd seen kisses at weddings and at the end of angsty teen movies with a lot less passion than that.

It hurt. It caused physical pain in my chest. I tried frantically to remind myself that this was a high school play. The two people kissing on stage right now had bashed noses as recently as yesterday. Campbell had surprised everyone with his acting all spring.

Surely I'd been in theater long enough not to be fooled by on-stage emoting.

It hurt anyway.

It hurt too much to be ignored any longer. Oh God. I'd been so stupid. I'd gotten too full of myself and my I-don't-give-a-crap attitude. Who the hell did I think I was, telling Campbell he had to handle his problem the way I said? I knew less than nothing about his family, about what they'd been through, what he'd been through. I'd blamed him for messing up my perfect life, and then had the unbelievable arrogance to tell him how to handle his.

He'd told me I was a child, which burned mainly because it was true. A child fights with her mother and can't control herself. A child expects to live a life without a single wrinkle in her plans. A child expects nothing unexpected ever to happen.

Adults dealt with curveballs and surprise responsibility and… and babies.

Campbell was an adult. I could learn a lot from him. I wanted to learn it.

I watched as the curtain came down. Campbell and Amelia stood, arms around each other, gazing at each other in a blue spotlight of happiness.

AT HOME, my dad went to change clothes and Ethan went off to his room to build naked women out of Minecraft blocks or do whatever it was he did with his phone.

"Would you like some ice cream?" Mom offered, holding the freezer door open long enough to blow visible chill into the kitchen.

"Sure, but last I checked ice cream had calories," I said, cautiously.

"I know," she said, keeping her back to me.

"And?" What was happening here? She hadn't offered me ice cream in a year.

"Have some," she said, getting out the bowls and scooping. "I… I've been wrong. Your dad pointed out that you're built like him, not me. I was comparing you to me at your age. I'm sorry."

Totally willing to look a gift horse in the mouth, I absorbed that and didn't hesitate to press my advantage. "Why does it matter so much? It hurts, Mom, when you say that stuff. You know I'm not unhealthy."

"I know you're not. I was worried if you were heavy, you wouldn't be happy. That kids at school would be unkind. They were when I was…" She shuddered, remembering something I probably didn't want to know. "I wanted to prevent that from happening."

"Jerk kids are jerks no matter what you look like. Marisa gets it for being too skinny. I hear as much about my height as I do my weight."

"I know that. Or I knew that. Once. I'd forgotten. But you're right. I've been wrong. You've been happy all along. You've handled all those jerks like it's nothing." She sat down with the ice cream—big servings with chocolate syrup. "It was me who was unkind."

"I've been mostly happy." It wasn't often she apologized. This was fairly momentous, but somehow I sensed I shouldn't make a huge deal out of it. "Thanks, Mom. I do get it, you know. But it's my body. I've got to take it from here."

We stared at each other for a second or two, feeling our way back.

"I'm so proud of your show. You should be too. You were wonderful."

We dug spoons into the ice cream, still awkwardly glancing at each other. "Thanks. I'm going to be glad tomorrow night when the last show is over. This play hasn't been as much fun as last year."

"Because of Campbell?"

"Yeah."

"He is really a good-looking kid. Good actor, too. Great voice. I can see why you were so interested."

"It was never about his looks. Well, maybe it was his looks a little bit," I admitted, grinning with her. "It was more that he seemed older. More mature. Less involved in the stupid teenage stuff."

"I imagine that's because he is more mature. He has to be more mature. And he hasn't been allowed to be a regular teenager for quite some time, has he?"

"No."

She turned her spoon over and over, staring into space. "It's amazing how a baby turns a regular person into a grown-up overnight. I remember when you were born. I thought I was a grown-up, of course, before that. I was twenty-six. I'd been to college, been married a couple years. I had a responsible job. I didn't know anything, really. All of a sudden they hand you this person who needs you every minute of every single day. Someone you can't leave alone for a second. You can't just go somewhere, even to the store for a quick errand. You have to make arrangements to bring the baby or find someone to watch the baby. Every single time. Even to take a shower. It's exhausting at first, and a change you think you'll never get used to. Your life is never again about you. It's always about someone more important than you."

"Wow, Mom. You make it look easy."

She laughed. "It's never been easy. You've caught plenty of my mistakes. Sometimes I admit to them, like tonight. Most of the time I don't."

"Really?"

"I always think I'm doing it wrong; that someone else could do it better. I can't even imagine combining that feeling with having an unsure future, with having nobody to share it with, with being a teenager. I bet Campbell knows what that's like."

I swallowed past the lump in my throat.

"Oh, honey," she said, licking the back of her spoon like a kid. "I've been too hard on you in too many ways, and all you've ever done is make me proud. Another of my mistakes is letting our fear that you will grow up and away from us get in the way of your amazing kindness to someone who needs it far more than anyone in our family."

"What? But you and Dad said…"

"We said what?" Dad came shuffling into the kitchen, clad in a T-shirt from a 5K he ran before I was born and a pair of shorts made out of sweatpant material that are surely only sold to men over forty.

I considered him, assessing. "You said to stay away from Campbell."

"We were wrong, honey," Mom said with a meaningful look at Dad. "Your dad pointed out how wrong I've been about your weight, and I pointed out to him that he was wrong about

Campbell." She got up to rinse her bowl at the sink and passed an affectionate hand over his upper back.

"I'm sorry for that, Natty," Dad said. "It was a knee jerk reaction. Honestly, I think I'd have found some reason to order you away from any boy. That is my problem and I'm working on it. Not yours."

"For whatever role we played in your breakup," Mom said. "We're sorry. If there's any way to… well, change course, I think you should give it a try."

Dad grunted in grudging agreement. I'd take it.

Something burned in the corners of my eyes. It might be too late with Campbell, but I could give it another try. Even if Campbell was gone, if I couldn't get him back, it felt damn good to sit in a kitchen with my parents and have a conversation that didn't snowball into a brawl.

My phone buzzed with a call. I glanced at it, hoping it would be Campbell. It showed the local area code, 434, but I'd never seen this number before.

"Go get that, honey," Mom said. "I'll get the bowls cleaned up. I loved the play. You were terrific."

"Smashing," Dad said.

"Thanks." I looked at them both, grateful. "Good night."

I took the phone up to my room and listened to the voice mail.

"Natalie. This is Isabelle. I found your number in Campbell's phone. Yes, he knows I look in his phone. He hates it, but whatever. Call me back."

I hit the button to do that, checking the time. 12:22 a.m. What the hell?

"Natalie?"

"Yeah, what's going on, Isabelle? Is something wrong?"

"Was the show good? I wanted to come, but Oliver is fussy. I know Campbell was nervous."

"It was fine. He did well. Listen. What's going on?"

"I figured you'd still be up, and I'm up, because Oliver… right. I said that. Anyway, let me come right out and say it. Campbell hasn't gotten over you. He's upset, and I'm with Tommy now, and anyway, I think you should talk to him."

"What?" Her artless, disorganized way of talking threw me for a loop. It had the whiff of the homeschooled teenager who'd fallen out of the rhythm of teen speech. "He… he said that?"

She laughed self-consciously. "No. He says he's fine, but I know better. Anyway. Um. Don't tell him I called if you do talk to him. He wouldn't like it that I found your number, okay? Or that I called you. And said he wasn't fine. He'd hate it, actually. So."

I didn't know what to make of her. She was telling me to make a try for her baby daddy. At least I thought that's what she was saying. It was admittedly late. I'd been stressed.

But damned if Isabelle didn't keep surprising me.

# Twenty



"**W**here is Campbell?" asked Mrs. M backstage the next night, pre-show, waving underclassmen to the makeup area and to the lighting booth with the multitasking talent of an air-traffic controller. "Last night I saw a little rip in the sleeve of his coat, and I wanted to sew it up. Natalie, can you go get him and tell him to bring it to me? Or tell him to come himself, if he's already wearing it."

"Sure." I glanced at Noah, who skulked around, delaying his candlestick makeup. He rolled his eyes in annoyance but made no overt moves of sabotage.

Saturday in April in Virginia. It had been a beautiful day, and I spent it out at the reservoir, walking. Alone. Marisa had called and asked if I wanted to go shopping with her for shoes to go with her prom dress, but I declined. I needed to think about how, as my mom suggested, to give the Campbell situation another try. Isabelle had handed me permission to call him, but I didn't want to jump the gun and get it wrong.

I hadn't come up with any plan of action except an appreciation for the beauty of spring. If I'd learned nothing else this year, it was that I did better winging it. I was bolder and more daring if I didn't think about things first.

I didn't get more than three steps down the hall when Campbell rushed past me, still wearing his street clothes. Before I could even open my mouth, much less pour out some spontaneous declaration, he demanded, "Where's Mrs. M?"

"She's trying to find you. Over there."

Noah watched, his expression alert.

Mrs. M saw him before I could say anything more and rushed over. "Campbell. Where is your costume—?"

"Mrs. M. I have to go."

A gasp from Noah.

"There's been an accident." Campbell didn't even glance Noah's direction. "The baby…"

Sick fear spread through me.

Mrs. M went pale and bit her lip. "Are you sure?" One glance at his haggard face and anyone would be sure. Oh my God. "Okay. Go. I'll have to do some reshuffling. Noah. This is your lucky day."

Noah gave, in the next second, the best theatrical performance of his life when he managed not to look like he'd just been handed the keys to King Midas's vault.

Mrs. M took no notice. "I can get that sophomore—what's his name? Teddy?—to play Noah's part. I still need your costume. Natalie, could you please get it from Campbell and give it to Noah." She turned to dash away, controlling her panic with admirable effort.

I grabbed Campbell's arm. "What…what happened? Is Oliver okay?"

"I think so," he said, race-walking to his costuming area. "Isabelle got in a car accident. He was in the car seat. He's too little to say if anything hurts. He's at the ER now. The university hospital. Here's the costume." He yanked the hanger off the pole and shoved it at me.

I took it, wavering, hands buried in fabric. I should offer to go with him. He was close to falling apart. His hands were shaking and the skin on his face had gone pale and gray like it had been dead three days. I wasn't sure he should drive even the three or four miles to the university hospital. But Mrs. M would have a nervous breakdown if I left, too. I had an important part. I needed to stay.

"I'll give it to her. Campbell, are you sure you're going to be okay?"

I had a wild fantasy during the two seconds he dug in his backpack for his keys about flinging my arms around him and telling him I'd go with him, but I'd gotten it under control by the time he straightened. Yesterday he'd had an opening to ask me to prom and he hadn't. He probably wouldn't even want me to come with him to the hospital. I couldn't possibly ditch the last night of my senior year musical anyway, could I?

He gave me a look, despair combined with something that I couldn't read. "I'm fine. Thanks. And… break a leg."

I caught myself squeezing the fabric of the Beast's coat so hard I'd made wrinkles. "Oh, Campbell. I should…"

"Nope. You shouldn't. I'll see you."

"Please call me at intermission. Or text. Tell me how he is. Or else I'll worry. Please."

"Okay. I've got to go."

He left. I dragged my feet back to the rush and hurry of a cast of dozens before the last night of a play, uncomfortable with the awareness that I might have made the wrong choice.

That I didn't belong here in this place that meant so much twenty-four hours ago.

At best, what I did on stage during that first half could be referred to as sleepwalking. At worst, zombie-dom. As soon as the curtain fell for intermission, I dashed to my phone. Campbell had texted. It read, "O still being tested. Isabelle in a lot of trouble."

Trouble? She'd had a car accident. Maybe it had been her fault—a single car accident like the time right after I got my license when I scraped a parked car on a narrow residential street. It must have been a worse hit, since it didn't sound like Oliver was in the clear yet.

Mrs. M had followed me out to the dressing rooms. "That was the single worst performance I've ever seen from you, Natalie. I could play that part better." Her face had gone rosy, and determination glinted from her eyes.

I knew she was right, but I hated to do anything badly. "I'm so sorry. I'll—"

"And I think I *will* play that part better. You don't want to be here, and you should go. Go to the hospital. I'll play your part. We're already living on the edge. Hand me that teapot."

Dumbstruck, I lost the power of speech. No doubt she'd memorized all the lines, but I'd never heard her sing. Could she sing?

She laughed, reading my expression. "Yes, dear. I can sing. Believe it or not, in high school, I was in a high school show choir. I sang your song as a solo at the state competition back when it was new."

"Wow. I didn't know that. Are you sure?" I asked, already beginning to strip off the bulky costume.

"Yes. Go. These minutes here, high school activities, they're important, but they're not who you are. Not who you'll be. You're a talented actress. But you don't have any plans to pursue theater as a profession. Thirty years from now, you'll be standing in a hallway telling some teenager you were once in a play. Go. People are far more important than checking boxes on a high school resume you don't even need anymore."

"Okay. I'll go. Everyone is going to die when they see you in that costume."

"You're right," she said, grinning devilishly. "That's part of the fun. Unpredictability is the only weapon we teachers have against the kids. This'll buy me years of that."

I DROVE AS RESPONSIBLY AS I COULD to the hospital, shaking my head over the fact that after all his attempts, Noah had gotten Campbell's part after all. I wished I could see his expression when he realized it was Mrs. M in the teapot costume and not me.

Campbell sat in the ER waiting room with his mom, who talked into her phone. This time she wore a casual blue top and a big blue gemstone on a thin silver pendant. She probably had been planning to go see Campbell in the play. She raised a well-groomed eyebrow, said a polite hello, and returned her attention to her conversation. Campbell stood, shock rearranging his expression, and pulled me away to the corner.

"What the hell are you doing here? The play is still going on."

"I know. Mrs. M has always dreamed of stage stardom, apparently. She took my part." I plopped down into an empty seat. Campbell followed suit.

"What? Mrs. M?"

I smiled at him, wishing I were closer. I'd never taken an active dislike to an armrest before. "She seemed pretty delighted, actually."

"What about your parents? Won't they worry?"

"They came last night. They're at some soccer thing of Ethan's tonight. What's going on? How is Oliver?"

"Still being tested. They think he's okay, but they had to check. I'm hoping that their lack of hurry means he's okay."

I laid a light hand on his forearm. "Are you okay?"

"Yeah," he answered. "I mean, no. I'm not. But I'm glad you came."

I smiled at him as he continued, almost reassuring himself. "Oliver is okay. No scratches, no broken bones. Babies are tough, they said. But he wasn't buckled into the car seat properly. Lucky, they said. That's Isabelle's fault."

"You said she was in trouble."

"It's much worse than a car seat. When I got here, my mom was already here. She said something was wrong with Isabelle, who was in the waiting room with some scratches on her face from the airbag. I went over to ask her what happened and when I sat down, I could smell it. She smelled like she'd gone swimming in a vat of booze."

"Oh no." I gripped the armrest. Drinking. With a baby.

"She said she told her parents she was going to take Oliver to the park. Instead, she went to her boyfriend's house to watch some NBA game and have a cookout. I didn't realize they were so serious: she's wearing an NBA jersey the boyfriend gave her. I guess he had people over. She got drunk. She tried to drive with Oliver."

"So, the accident…"

"She hit a mailbox. Took it all the way out of the ground. One of the rich people ones near the Connaughtons that probably cost $500. She admitted to the officer that she was reading a text."

"Oh God." Texting or reading messages while driving was illegal in Virginia.

"They charged her with a whole list of stuff at the scene. Texting while driving, failure to secure a child, property damage, and DUI. She didn't know what her blood alcohol level was, but it was high enough that she was still stumbling around when the lady came to talk to her." Bloodlust, the kind that dwarfed whatever he'd been prepared to unleash upon Finney, glowed out of the yellow ring around his pupils. I hoped I'd never see that expression there again. "I've been sitting here thinking horrible thoughts about her. How could she? Bad enough by herself, but she had Oliver with her. How could she do it?"

"Who came to talk to her?" I registered pain in my hand where I dug it into the armrest.

"I don't know. Some woman with a badge around her neck on a string. The hospital people knew her. They sent them to a conference room to talk. They've been back there an hour or so."

"Oh, Campbell." Whoever that was couldn't be good. Should Isabelle have a lawyer? I turned to Campbell to suggest that, but the words died on my lips as Isabelle came charging through a door, weeping uncontrollably. She ran straight past us, red-faced and sobbing, and out the automatic doors of the ER. Campbell stood, confused. I stood, too.

The woman with the badge hung around her neck followed her path but stopped at Campbell.

"Are you Campbell Adams? Are you Oliver Barringer's father?" she asked, all business.

"Yes, ma'am. Is he okay?"

"Yes. They're getting ready to release him. I'm Anita Miller. I work for the Department of Social Services. You have visitation with the child?"

"Yes, ma'am."

"Court approved?"

"Yes, ma'am. We agreed on it and the judge signed the paper." Campbell's brows drew together as he tried to keep up.

"We'll be checking on that. Assuming you do have visitation, I'm going to need you to take the child home today and keep him until further notice. We're going to put a safety plan into place for Ms. Barringer, given the circumstances, and she's agreed with our recommendation that Oliver needs to be with you from now on, until she gets her problem under control."

"Her problem?" asked Campbell, pale as a ghost.

Ms. Miller glanced in my direction. Campbell moved closer to me. "Go ahead. This is Natalie Tremayne. She's my friend. My close friend."

"Okay. She blew a .11 on the breathalyzer. Legal limit is .08, and for her, under twenty-one, it's even lower, .02. She was drunk. She told us she took the child to a party at an older male's house, where the guests were all drinking. We ran a background check on the boyfriend, and he's a felon. I smell alcohol on her, and probably marijuana on her clothes, though she was clean for pot. She didn't secure the child properly in the car seat and she's lucky he's not dead, quite frankly. You haven't seen the car."

I sensed Campbell's knees weakening and took his hand. He returned my squeeze, faintly.

"So, are you willing to sign this safety plan that says that you take custody upon Oliver's release?"

"Yes, ma'am. Of course I'll take him."

"You're awfully young. Do you have support? Support is very important for any parent."

Campbell flicked his gaze to his mother, watching but keeping her distance so Campbell could handle it alone.

"Yes, ma'am."

She handed him a clipboard. He read the paper and signed. Ms. Miller gave him her card and wrote down his phone number.

"I'll check the court order before the hospital will release him to you, and I'll be calling you on Monday. Plan for me to visit your home to check on Oliver early next week."

"Yes, ma'am."

"You turned eighteen last week, I see?"

I missed his birthday.

"Yes, ma'am."

"Under the law, you're an adult, but if you have any other family members here, I'd like to speak to them."

"That's my mother over there," Campbell said, pointing. Dr. Adams waved, like she'd been expecting Ms. Miller to develop interest in her. "She's a pediatrician. And that's my dad," he said, indicating a tall brown-haired man in an immaculate button-down and pressed khakis coming through the doors of the ER. "I still live with my parents."

"Oh, I'm familiar with your mother. She's treated some of our other Social Services children. Come on over here." Ms. Miller didn't check behind her to see if Campbell followed.

He held my hand like it was keeping him from slipping into the abyss.

"Come on. Let's go," I said. I didn't let go of his hand even after we made it to the small group of adults.

"Nice to meet you, Mr. Adams," Ms. Miller was saying to Campbell's dad.

"It's Dr. Adams, actually. Call me Mike," he said heartily. I watched his body language. Campbell's dad was the kind of guy used to dominating a room. I didn't know what kind of doctor he was, but I'd guess a surgeon. A brain surgeon or a heart surgeon. Somebody at the top of the hospital food chain.

"Uh huh," Ms. Miller said, giving him a side-eye. "Campbell is eighteen and has the right to make decisions, as is Miss Barringer. Even so, I understand he lives with you, and I want to make sure we're all on the same page."

"Absolutely." Dr. Dad Adams moved to kind of square himself, somehow overpowering his wife with the movement, without even touching her.

"Right," continued Ms. Miller, her nostrils widening so slightly I almost missed it. She'd seen his movement for what it was. "Isabelle and Campbell have agreed that Campbell will have full custody of Oliver for the time being. I pointed out to Isabelle that if she didn't agree, we'd need to take steps in court. We'll get that squared away on the papers this week, if possible, and get the judge to sign off. I've told Campbell I'd like to come out and check out your house early in the week, but I'm sure it's fine."

"Anything you need," murmured Dr. Mom Adams.

"Campbell will need all the support he can get during this time. He's a full-time high school student?"

Dr. Dad opened his mouth, but Campbell beat him to it. "Yes, ma'am. For another month or so."

"Okay. You're willing to help him out with babysitting, relief, that sort of thing, right?" Ms. Miller glanced down at her clipboard, ready to check that box. This time, she missed the flicker of annoyance on Dr. Dad's face.

"No, I'm afraid this is Campbell's problem, and we—his mother and I—feel it's important for him to handle it."

Ms. Miller's eyes widened in shock. "Excuse me?"

Dr. Mom stepped out of her husband's shadow, putting a hand on his arm. "Mike. Of course we'll help him figure something out. It's just that we both work outside the home. Often no one would be home to take care of Oliver when Campbell is at school. It presents a problem."

"I hate to ask this so bluntly, but is there no way you can afford to provide daycare for the child while Campbell finishes high school?"

"We can," Dr. Dad said easily, shutting down his wife with an acid smile, "but we won't. Again, this is Campbell's mess, and he'll have to…"

Ms. Miller clipped her pen to her clipboard and dropped it to her side, drawing herself up to a surprisingly intimidating five foot four or so. She abandoned all pretense of any more polite chitchat. Dr. Mom bit her lip. "Well, then. I can arrange to help him out with daycare if I put him down—erroneously—as indigent and emancipated. Social Services is not generally in the business of making eighteen-year-old kids drop out of school. Especially not when that time is a matter of weeks. To do that, we'll need to take state funds earmarked for some child who is actually indigent, and use them for Oliver, who is most decidedly not. Is that what you want?"

"Oh, Anita, that's not at all what we…" Campbell's mom looked worriedly at his dad, now puffed up like a hateful tomcat. Her hand squeezed his arm hard enough to make him wince when he started to speak. He closed his mouth. "I'm sure we can work out something. We will work out something. It's just, we feel that Campbell needs to understand the weight of his responsibilities and not be given everything on a silver platter, because we happen to have a silver platter. You know what I mean, right?"

"I do," Ms. Miller said, calming slightly. "I'm glad to hear it. I hope you won't mind if I add that none of this is Campbell's fault. He's not the drunk driver—Isabelle was. He's stepped right up, like a man, and offered to take Oliver in. I'm so happy to hear you're willing to help." She smiled at Campbell and me and brandished her clipboard. "Now, if you young people will excuse us, I'm guessing your parents would like to go over the household income without you."

We returned to the seats we'd abandoned. Campbell sat down with the abruptness of a person who couldn't stand much longer.

"Drunk? With Oliver? My God. What was she thinking?" He bent forward and buried his face in his hands. "I should have known. I should have paid more attention to her. She'd been acting funny, like… like a volcano about to blow, or something. I knew she was freaking out, stuck at home. Oh, God. She ruined her entire life in one afternoon. She's never been a drinker. When Oliver was born, she'd never even tasted alcohol. This can't be happening."

I rubbed his arm, cautiously. I was still reeling from the way Campbell's dad had reacted. He'd been so unfeeling I couldn't imagine how Campbell had lived with it for so long. Campbell was so upset he didn't even notice my touch.

"I'm so sorry about Isabelle. I'll help in whatever way I can with Oliver. I can babysit if you need a break. The play is"—I checked my phone for the time—"over now and I'll have more time in the evenings."

He noticed my hand on his arm and reached across to cover it with his. "I can't ask you to do that."

I squeezed his hand. God, he'd been so alone for so long. "You're not asking."

"This is a whole new level of reality. You're not ready for this. I'm not sure I am, either."

I didn't know what to say, so I held his hand as hard as I could.

# Twenty-one

Mrs. Murchison as a teapot had turned what otherwise would have been a lackluster effort—the sophomore Teddy, it turned out, did not know Noah's part and had to be prompted through all his lines from the wings—into a sensation. Everyone still chattered away about it on Monday. It was such a novelty to have a teacher singing in a play that everyone forgot to focus on why Campbell and I had been absent.

Only Marisa asked me. The true story was too big to tell even Marisa.

I told her I went with Campbell to the hospital because the baby had been in a car accident. The truth, but nowhere near all of it.

Campbell missed school Monday. I assumed he was home with Oliver, showing the social worker around his house, though I worried that his father had executed some end run around Ms. Miller and made him drop out.

Tuesday afternoon he appeared at my locker.

"Do you have a few minutes?" he asked.

"Sure. I have literally nothing to do. Swimming and the play are over. Homework is a joke this close to graduation. Let's go out to my car."

In the car, Campbell said, "I wanted to thank you. For coming on Saturday. It was nice… to have the support."

"You're welcome. You would have done it for me. Friends, right?"

He bit the inside of his cheek. "Uh, right. Anyway." He played with the strap of his backpack. "Isabelle's looking at a lot of charges. Supposedly she drank fruit punch with rum in it but had no idea how much rum they'd put in. Not that she's excused. She's miserable without Oliver, but the Social Services lady said I can't let her see him without a caseworker present to supervise. She's been told she has to dump the boyfriend and never see him again if she wants to see Oliver. They'll test her for drugs and alcohol every time. Things are going to have to change. A lot. I didn't know how desperate for a life she was." He examined his hands like they belonged to someone else. "I should have. Why wouldn't she be just as desperate as I was? Or even more?"

I didn't know what to say to that. "How are you handling school? Babysitting, I mean."

"My parents agreed to help me out by either watching Oliver or paying for a sitter until I graduate. Then I have to get a second job to pay for the babysitting. There aren't many of those that pay enough, not with only a high school diploma."

"There's no way you can swing college at all?"

"I didn't apply. I was thinking about community college, but that's only going to work if I can earn enough money to pay for a babysitter while I go. I never expected to have Oliver full-time."

"Coach Phillips said the UVA coach was interested in you."

"I know. He told me. I talked to the guy. He said he'd keep me in mind—waitlisted, I guess—if any of the other scholarship offers didn't pan out."

"Maybe they will. Maybe you can still…"

He met my eyes. So much weariness and hopelessness stared back at me that it took my breath away. "Getting a scholarship would help. A lot. But it wouldn't solve the problem. I'd need a babysitter not only while I work, but also while I was in class. It's too much. I can't afford it."

Somehow I couldn't stop staring back at the green-blue of his eyes. Part of me hoped the despair and resignation would disappear and that I'd get to watch it go. That's what I told myself, anyway.

That wasn't the only reason. Our gaze held and began to burn. The sadness didn't fade, but something else began to show there as well. Our heads moved closer. Campbell's hands stopped playing with the backpack straps and fell still. I became aware of the heat and bulk of his body and my breathing grew jerky. Warmth rushed up to heat my cheeks and I wanted nothing more than to touch him. Any part of him. Oh, God. I wanted him so much.

He moved closer.

I moved to bridge the distance, waiting for the touch of his lips on mine.

It didn't come. I opened my eyes.

Inches away, Campbell closed his, twisting his mouth in misery and leaned sharply back against the window of the car. "We can't do this. It's not fair to you."

"Wh-what?" Dazed, I had trouble forming a thought.

"We broke up. It doesn't even matter now what we broke up over. It's a good thing we did. My life was hard enough when

I only had to earn money and be a father one day a week. Now I have Oliver all the time. It'll take months for Isabelle to get it together, and even longer for the court to agree. When that social worker came to the house yesterday, she was talking about seeing how things go with Isabelle for a year. You'll be a college sophomore by then."

"Stop being noble all the time."

"You don't need this. You don't need to be involved with this. And I'm not being noble. I'm being realistic. I don't have a babysitter to spend any time with you or anyone. Only school, and only until graduation. Besides, my parents sat me down and gave me a very scary lecture on Sunday." He rested his head against the glass of the window as if it were too heavy to hold up.

"And?"

"It's not just you I'm thinking of anymore. My parents are doctors. They work sometimes with Social Services families, and they know about Social Services. Isabelle screwed up. What she did brought a social worker into our lives. Now that Ms. Miller has added us to her caseload, she'll check in regularly. Make sure I'm doing everything exactly right. If I don't, or even if I do but she doesn't think so, she could remove Oliver from me. Then they'd put him in foster care or place him with some family member they think will do a better job than two broke and clueless eighteen-year-olds. It's not good. I have to be perfect." He swallowed. "Because I can never let that happen. Without Oliver, I'd…"

I wanted to say something bracing and helpful. Something encouraging that would take that look out of his eye. I could think of precisely nothing. Nothing I could say would help take the burden of full-time parenting off him, or make his parents inclined to use their money to solve the problem. He'd work, and half of his money would go to pay for the babysitter he needed to work. There'd be no time or money left for school.

With horror, Campbell's future spread out bleakly before me. He'd work a low-paying job—or two—and support his child. That was it. He'd never have money for vacations or huge Christmases or a nice house. He'd never have the chance for the education he'd need to change that. Oliver's childhood wouldn't be like mine, or even like Campbell's. He'd struggle every day to make ends meet, for there to be enough, to pay for Oliver's college.

Suddenly the gulf between what I wanted for a future and what Campbell could reasonably expect opened wide and terrifying, like the time I'd gotten off a ski lift to stare down a slope far too difficult for me. He'd been saying it all along. He knew how incompatible it was, because he'd been raised in a household like mine, like the one I wanted for my own family one day.

For the first time, Campbell did seem impossible. What he said about Social Services watching everything he did made sense. I'd be a distraction and even a disadvantage, maybe. What if the social worker thought Campbell was spending too much time with me and not enough focused on Oliver?

I'd been right about the shame, but any shame still attached to this situation was dwarfed by this new problem. Parenting as a teenager, full-time for the first time ever, while eagle-eyed trained parenting experts watched your every move waiting to pounce on your mistakes had no room at all for error. He didn't have time for me. Not now.

I leaned back, too, the cool glass of the driver's side window against the side of my head. Regret throbbed painfully under my skin.

"I'm sorry, Campbell. I hate that this is happening to you. I want to help any way I can. Just say the word."

"Thanks," he said, his voice dull and stripped of all animation. He opened the car door. "I don't think there's much you can do. Unless you know of a reputable babysitter who works for free."

He unfolded himself stiffly from the passenger seat. "See you."

I DROVE HOME DOING FINE, and then when I got there to find my mom painting her fingernails at the kitchen table. I barely managed to drop my backpack and kick off my flip-flops before the tears ran down my face.

My mom stood immediately to hug me, but stopped short, hamstrung by her wet nails. "What is it?

"It's hopeless. He's just so... so miserable!" I burst into loud, gusty sobs. She blotted her nails with a balled-up paper towel, sacrificing all the work of the manicure, and put her arms around me, guiding me to the sofa in the family room next door.

"Tell me."

And I did.

I gasped to a halt five minutes later. I left out the part at Campbell's house when Oliver interrupted the coitus, but not much else. She sat quietly, rubbing my back like she did when I was little. She let me cry until my sobs slowed and my shoulders stopped heaving.

"You've never been one to quit quickly, honey. You're so stubborn, in the best of ways. I think it says a lot about how personal all this has gotten for you that you're seeing only the negative and not searching for solutions."

"There are no solutions. Campbell has to raise Oliver. His parents won't help, other than to cover it enough that he can graduate, but that's only a few more weeks. After that, it'll be work and more work. No way he can pay child support and for college. Or even for the babysitter if he goes to community college."

"Honey. Stop. Look around you. First of all, if Campbell has custody of the child, the court will remove his child support obligation. Child support is what you pay to support the child when he's with the other parent. The girl—what's her name?—who is the mom would owe the child support now. If that hasn't been straightened out, then Campbell needs to do that right away. If he talks to the social worker, she'll help."

"Really?"

"Really. If she pays child support, that might help ease the financial worries some. It's a start."

Hope flared and then died. "It's not enough. It wouldn't be much money. Not enough for a babysitter that much of the time."

"I think if you work at that, you might be able to solve that one."

I stared at her, wondering what in the hell was going through her mind. "Mom. I can't babysit…"

"Of course you can't. I don't mean you'd do it. You might start by visiting the dean of admissions at UVA."

"Why?"

"I'm sure they have other students who struggle with childcare. Maybe they have some ideas."

I'd call first thing in the morning. I was good at everything that took work and nosy as hell. I'd told Campbell that once. In the morning I'd become an expert on childcare for single parents.

# Twenty-two

Prom seemed out of the question now. It was near the end of April. Most everyone had gotten their dates tied up months before. Marisa and Ron had made plans in October. She'd had the dress since December. Campbell had apparently turned Amelia down, because she announced one day at lunch that Joe had sprung for a limo after all.

I hadn't really expected to go. Before Campbell, I missed most of the dances. Few guys were tall enough for me to dance with, or at least willing to dance with me. It was better for my self-esteem to go on the offense against dances on principle. I did go shopping with Marisa for her dress at Christmas and helped her plan her hairstyle and makeup, but I planned to spend the night watching movies.

For about twelve minutes when Campbell and I were "together," I'd let myself imagine him asking me. I knew better now. In the two weeks since the accident, he'd been at school but had to dash away to his car the second the bell rang at the end of the day. We'd spoken briefly and impersonally. The last

I'd heard, he'd gotten the child support switched with the help of the social worker and had a meeting soon to meet with her to go over his progress. I couldn't remember when that was, however, which said all that's necessary about how close we weren't.

There were times, though, when I caught him staring at me from down the hall or we'd make eye contact at an assembly for a minute.

I hadn't gotten over him. Seeing him every day made it harder. Graduation couldn't come soon enough.

I paid for my lunch and searched for Marisa's dark head. She waved at me, from her seat next to Noah. Across from her sat Amelia and Finney. Joe never ate with Amelia. Everyone in school but Amelia knew he traditionally spent his lunch hour in the library, scamming on freshmen who were too insecure to brave the upperclassman-dominated cafeteria.

I had my doubts about sitting with Finney. He didn't usually join us, but Amelia must have attracted him like chum to a shark. I worried about him. Finney had an axe to grind. He'd gotten in some pretty major trouble when, thinking Mrs. M in my costume was me, he'd told her in the wings it was a good thing the teapot costume was big enough to contain "your lardy ass." Not surprisingly, he blamed me for this.

Noah and I had been friends since our early childhood, but he'd been pretty awful to Campbell throughout the play. I had been none too pleased when Noah convinced Chad Kim, who wrote the features for the school newspaper, to review the performance of the play with Noah as the Beast, and not the one with Campbell. Noah had been reading one line in particular aloud to anyone who'd listen for two weeks now. "Noah Jones, as understudy to a role he clearly should have had all along, emoted with deep personal suffering as the mysterious Beast."

I'd had enough of Noah. He hadn't changed—he still swung wildly between intolerable and endearing, but he spent too much time lately in Intolerable. He still liked me, though. We were down to four more weeks, and I didn't want to deal with the certain drama that would come from telling Noah what I thought of him at this late date.

Sliding in next to Marisa, I tried to catch up on the conversation flinging back and forth.

"I heard she's going to some Christian university. Can you imagine?" asked Noah. "I know at least a dozen guys whose…"

"Thanks, Noah, for that visual," Marisa said.

"Who are you talking about?" I asked.

"Sunny."

"Oh. Should have guessed." Sunny's parents ran a food bank and her dad was a church deacon. She took her rebel responsibility seriously. Her parents had found a way to nip it in the bud. In theory.

"Did you decide where you're going, Amelia?" I asked to change the subject.

"Radford," she said. "It's where Joe is going."

"Really? Are you going there only because Joe is going there?" I should not ask questions I knew the answer to.

"Well, I like the school. It's supposed to be fun. And not too far from home. Joe says it has a good engineering department."

"Yeah, but you're not going to major in engineering, are you?"

"Well, noooo. But I see us getting married someday. It'll make it too hard if we're far apart."

Marisa leaned close to me and muttered, "If she's close by, he'll only be able to sleep with half the girls he otherwise would."

"If that works for you, Amelia, I think it's a great plan." Finney had been stuffing his food in his mouth with great efficiency and speed and only now focused on us. "I'm going to Radford too. We'll have a great time."

"What happened to Duke, Finney?" I asked, remembering his original reason for trying out for the play.

He turned red and purposefully chewed with his mouth open in my direction. "I didn't like it when we visited during spring break. Everybody was deeply uncool. Grade nerds. Not my kind of place at all."

He hadn't gotten in. Obviously.

"And you, Miss Natalie of the Land of Chlorine?" asked Noah. "Where did you decide to go?"

"UVA," I said. I'd come to terms with it. It would be stupid to ignore a world-class university just because it was in my backyard. I could be happy there. There were a lot of ways to be independent that didn't involve moving far away from home. I'd learned that much, at least. "The math didn't work any other way. Little scholarships here and there for out of state couldn't match the in-state tuition."

"You're not going to live at home, are you?" asked Amelia.

"No way. My parents said the dorms are a go. They're just glad I'm not off to California."

"Only losers stay at home to go to college," offered Finney in his infinite wisdom.

"At least I got in everywhere I applied." I ate my pack of crackers with outward calm. Finney had an unerring instinct for getting right at the thing that bothered me most. I'd be damned if I let him see that.

Somehow, I'd managed to do the same to him. He colored and his lips thinned. For a wild second I thought he might pounce on me. Surely not in the cafeteria. He brought himself under control, but barely.

"Doesn't matter where you go," Finney said, rage raising his voice way past normal cafeteria decibel levels. "You'll still be enormous. More whale than person. A lonely fat whale all alone in a dorm room. Tell me, Tree Trunks," he said, his meanness and cruelty so totally unrestrained it scared me, "on prom night are you going to sit on the sofa and eat ice cream and cry, or just pull up a chair in front of the whole refrigerator?"

"Let's go. We don't have to sit here and listen to this shit," Marisa said, pulling on my arm. Amelia turned away, as if from a horror movie murder.

I sat immobile, afraid if I moved, I'd cry and he'd win.

"Campbell didn't ask you? I thought he was going to." Noah leaned forward, not yet committing to which side of this festival of feces he would support.

Finney snorted. "Even that knuckledragger Campbell Adams has better taste than to ask this cow to prom."

A warm hand covered my shoulder while I fought the tears with everything I had. I glanced at Marisa, but she gripped the edge of the table for all she was worth. The hand on my shoulder didn't belong to her.

"I've got very little to lose now," Campbell said, over my head. "You're going to shut up right now, or I'll be happy to take you outside and beat the everlasting shit out of you."

I'd have felt better if Finney had done what he'd done in the auditorium, but he only laughed. "Please. You think I'm going to waste my time and risk my diploma for you? Over her?" he demanded, pointing a scornful finger at me as if I were dung. "You're obviously not too bright, Adams, so I guess I should worry about you dragging me out by my hair. Are you that dim or are you going to take your oversized ass on out of here?"

"Max, stop it," Amelia said. "Leave them alone." For two seconds, Finney hesitated, but he'd gone too far down the road to be halted even by Amelia.

"If you're going to stay, Dad, let's go back to that sex ed class you missed." Finney plucked an uneaten banana off Amelia's tray. "Anybody got a condom?"

Wide-eyed and unable to resist escalating the drama, Noah dug in his back pocket for his wallet. "I have one," he said.

"Let's go," I said, and pushed back my chair. Campbell stayed right behind me, both hands on my shoulders now. Marisa stood too. As horrifying as this whole lunch was, it felt so good to have him near me.

"No, don't go!" barked Finney. "I've got to show you where the condom goes! Especially if you're with her. You wouldn't want to reproduce with Tree Trunks. Look." He stood the banana on end and elbowed Noah, still digging through his wallet for the condom. "You hold your dick like so, and then you unroll…"

"Shut up, Max," begged Marisa, sounding like she was about to cry. Her tortured face and Campbell's hands gripping my shoulders gave me the strength that had deserted me before.

"Yeah, shut up," I said, leaning in to make sure they didn't miss what I was about to say. "That condom's lived in your wallet a long time, Noah. Leave it there. You're so much better than this. Better than him," I said, flicking a hand at Finney. "Choose to be *better* than him."

Noah closed his mouth and looked down at his tray. He let go of his wallet. I caught the expression of guilt I hadn't seen on his face in a couple of years, but I'd gotten rolling and couldn't focus on that right now. All the things I'd wanted to say came flying off my tongue, with Campbell behind me.

"And you, Finney. I notice you're asking to borrow a condom. Not something you have handy? I bet you've never needed one, have you? I don't see a line of girls here, waiting to see your naked glory. Most girls actually expect a guy to speak to them before they strip. They usually expect you to say something nice instead of crude. Every word that comes out of your mouth is misogynistic. That's M-I-S-O-G-Y-N-I-S-T-I-C. Look it up. I know you don't have a damn clue what it means. Wait. Let me help you. It means you are the kind of guy who will spend the rest of your life wondering why no one will date you, let alone sleep with you. You're headed straight for a lifetime as a trollish, basement-dwelling incel."

Finney narrowed his eyes. A muscle twitched at the corner of one, which gave me even greater courage.

"You think it's funny to sit here and make an ass of yourself pretending that you know more than Campbell. You don't know shit, though. None of us do, but we will, soon enough. We all will. Campbell has been at school every day, just like you, except getting better grades, more varsity letters, and bigger parts in plays, while working almost full time and supporting a family. Campbell doesn't need to beat your ass. He's miles ahead of you every day the second he gets out of bed. It'll take you—all of us—ten or fifteen years to figure out what Campbell already knows."

Oh my God. Did I really say all that earnest crap to him? I was just about ready to sink mercifully into the linoleum when I registered Amelia clapping. Marisa joined in. I won't claim the whole cafeteria gave us a standing ovation, in some sort of beautiful end-of-the-movie moment, but two people clapping was pretty damn triumphant.

Or at least I thought it was triumphant before Campbell turned me around and kissed me.

Right there, in the middle of the cafeteria.

It was a good one, too. The kind where there's nothing tentative, nothing fearful, nothing guilty. Proof. Possession. Lips, tongues, even teeth. Nothing at all held back. He pulled me tight against him, full length, and wrapped his arms all the way around me, leaving no room for anyone to mistake what was going on here. Blood shot to my head and a kind of shimmering heat went everywhere. I forgot about Marisa and Amelia and Noah and even Finney, and the audience of hundreds of teenagers whose braces and promises and stupid antics wouldn't keep them from adulthood for very long. I only wanted this moment to last. Just this one. I wrapped my wrists around the back of his neck and held on for dear life.

After a minute or fifteen, I heard Marisa hiss my name as if from underwater. Campbell's grip on the back of my shirt loosened. I let go of his collar with difficulty. Mrs. Molloy, the grimmest of the grim-faced cafeteria workers, approached, her tread making the tables shake. When she saw we'd broken apart, she reversed course without a word.

We pulled apart a little more, but he didn't let go. Our feet stayed planted intertwined. Marisa touched my arm and left, banked glee in her suppressed smile. I didn't care where the others were.

Campbell rubbed the small of my back in little circles, then raised a hand to brush hair away from my face. I ran my hands up and down the sides of his arms. Oh, God. It would take an hour to calm down after that. He looked down into my eyes, rare joy and mischievousness in his blue depths.

"Natalie Tremayne, will you go to prom with me? If I can find a babysitter?"

"Yes."

He searched the food line, made sure Mrs. Molloy's back was turned, and kissed me again.

AFTER SCHOOL, in the few minutes before Campbell had to leave for the Connaughtons, he leaned against Elly Townsend's locker.

"Not that I want to potentially jinx anything," I asked, dying to know, "but why today? Why prom? What happened to all that stuff about not being with me?"

He brushed my collarbone. I touched his hair. We couldn't keep our hands off each other. It was positively zoological.

"I heard that little troll when he started yelling. I was sitting a couple of tables away, and even though I knew you could take care of yourself, and would, I didn't want you to be alone when you did it. I realized I was being stupid."

He traced the whirls of my ear. I ran my hands over the shape of his cheekbones. People passed and a few directed good-natured jeers our way, but I didn't care.

"I wanted you, you know. For a long time," he whispered.

"What? How long?"

"I don't remember when it started. During swim season sometime."

"Ah."

"Swim season last year."

"Last year? You're joking." I stared into his eyes. He wasn't joking.

"You have this... confidence. Like... like a place in the world. Like no matter where you go, whatever you do, things will organize themselves around you to suit you. I sound stupid, but it's attractive, like a magnet. That kind of attraction. And then the way you look in a swimsuit, besides. I wanted to be near you. At first, I wanted to figure out how you did it. Then I just wanted to be near you."

People rushed around us in every direction. Lockers banged and shouts of laughter echoed off the walls. It was like I couldn't even hear them. I reached up and pulled his lips down to mine for the briefest of brushes.

"That's why I tried out for the play," he said, laughing into my mouth.

"Because of me?"

"Because of you. I kind of overstated my interest in theater. I didn't lie; I was in a play at St. Anselms, but only in the crowd scene. The theater teacher wanted the biggest guys to be the Germans in *The Sound of Music*. That was the extent of my experience."

"You had me fooled. You were really good."

"I never imagined I'd get the lead." His face turned serious. "You know what you're getting into if we do this, right?"

"Yes. Lots of nights hanging out at your house watching sports under the watchful eyes of your parents."

"Pretty much."

"As long as it's with you, I don't care. Yes. I know what I'm getting into. We'll take it one step at a time." I smiled at him, teasing. "First I'll watch from the doorway while you change a diaper, then I'll watch from inside the room, then—"

He stopped my words with another kiss. It may have lasted a while, because when we broke apart, Elly Townsend stood there, waiting patiently for us to finish so she could get into her locker.

She smiled at us. "About time." Then she dumped her books, grabbed her phone, and left.

"About prom," Campbell said. "I was serious about that, but I do have to have a babysitter. I'll ask my mom."

"No need. I already found one."

"Who? When did you…?"

"I called before seventh period. They agreed immediately." I couldn't resist a huge grin.

"Who?"

"My mom and dad."

# Epilogue

ampbell and I sat in the middle of a sea of empty folding chairs, discarded or forgotten graduation hats, a half-inflated beach ball no one dared to claim, glitter covering everything. Our parents had gone home half an hour earlier, but we wanted to squeeze a few more minutes together out of graduation day before I left for the school's all-night party and Campbell went home with Oliver. Campbell had insisted I shouldn't miss my last-ever high school event. He'd promised to meet me for breakfast in the morning, with Oliver.

To Oliver, five hundred empty white plastic folding chairs must have seemed like a playground. He grinned and babbled and climbed up them and got down from them and hunted under them. Freed from the restrictive embrace of Campbell's mom he'd suffered during the ceremony, Oliver was happy to roll around in the glitter.

I caught Oliver seconds before he hit the ground after he tangled with a chair leg and lifted him for a quick squeeze before I set him down again. "You should have brought him out long ago: he's a chick magnet. I've never seen anything like it."

Campbell blushed and pushed back his hair reflexively, loosening his tie. "Um. Right."

Right indeed. At least ten of our female classmates had rushed Campbell when he carried Oliver into the ceremony, cooing and squeezing Oliver's little hands until he hid his face in Campbell's chest. That only made it worse. Those puppy commercials had nothing on Campbell with Oliver. I might have dived in and staked my claim. Possibly.

Day after tomorrow, we'd start our summer jobs: Campbell in road construction and me as a lifeguard at one of the country clubs.

After my mom had suggested it, I called the UVA Admissions office. They pointed me to many daycare places with reduced rates for low-income families. Campbell would qualify for that, but only with the help of Social Services. Ms. Miller immediately jumped in and made it happen. Campbell would have a clean, bright, state-approved place to drop Oliver off every morning when he went to work.

We'd carved out something resembling a relationship. I hung out at his house as many evenings as I could manage. When his parents were there, we took Oliver to a playground or out shopping. When they were not, there was time for Netflix and chill. More than once now, Oliver had stayed asleep during those nights. Nothing is risk-free, but Campbell was learning there's such a thing as risk reduction.

I would have fought those classmates of mine tonight if they'd taken even one step closer to Campbell, Oliver or no Oliver.

"Did you talk to Coach Moseley at UVA? I liked him. I decided to try out for the team," I said.

"Yeah. I don't know if it'll work, but I'm going to try. I signed up for online classes, and I'm going to apply to UVA.

Coach Moseley said he'd do what he could. It might not work for the fall, and it might not work ever, but I can't get a college degree if I don't try."

"You'll do it." I leaned in and kissed him. "Nothing will stop you. In time, Isabelle can help."

After some parenting classes and some trips to AA, Social Services had lightened up toward Isabelle. They now allowed Campbell or his parents to supervise her time with him, with an eye toward letting her parent again.

At the mention of her name, Campbell went quiet. Oliver squirmed free from his grasp and set off down the row, drumming on the chair seats and humming some tune only he knew.

"I don't know if I can forgive her," Campbell said.

"You will. Eventually. You'll have to. Without her, there'd be no Oliver."

"You're brave," Campbell said, his tone over-casual. "To take on me plus Oliver plus Isabelle. It's not like most people's exes. She doesn't go away, no matter how I feel about her. We have to get along and we have to be part of each other's lives. Forever, I guess."

"I knew that. Isabelle comes with you like your mom or your dad. And she's a good person underneath. She screwed up, but I think she'll figure out how to move on."

"And Oliver?"

A swell of unexpected emotion dried my throat for a second, taking my breath and speeding my heart. "It's funny. If anyone had asked me a year ago whether I pictured hanging out with my boyfriend's son, I'd have laughed. Once I met him, though, it changed. Oliver makes you… you."

Campbell's smile held relief and joy and burdens and delight. He kissed me, pulling me to my feet. "He's a mess!" he teased, for Oliver's benefit. "A total mess!" Oliver was indeed a mess: the glitter he'd rolled in stuck to his hair and face and arms and the seat of his little pants. His small face shone with glittery joy. He reached up for Campbell, who grabbed one of Oliver's hands.

I took Oliver's other hand and we swung him in the oncoming twilight, over and over, high in the air as he shrieked with laughter and glitter flew off his clothes, making the air sparkle.

# Acknowledgements

I turned in my last published book before this one in January 2021. Since that time, I've lost both my parents and watched both my sons leave the nest. It has been a very, very difficult three years since then, but I could never have gotten back on my feet again without family and my friends. Without them, this book would not be in your hands. Thank you to Frank, Austin, Matthew Wright, and Mary Louise and Frank Wright Sr. Thank you to Geoff, Kari, and Audrey Button. Thank you to Elly Blake, Meghan Crowther, Jennifer Hawkins, Mary Ann Marlowe, Cathy Moore, Dawn Osal, Kelly Siskind, Summer Spence, and Ron Walters. Extra special thanks to the team at Owl Hollow Press: Hannah, Emma, Olivia—take a bow!

I wrote this book after I went to a meet to watch my boys swim. I saw a tall girl with long blonde hair tucked carefully under a swim cap who was carrying more weight than is usual for preteen girls. She jumped in the water and outswam everybody in the place, then got out and accepted her medal, never once holding her hands over her thighs or wrapping a voluminous towel around herself to hide. I swam as a young girl but quit when I stopped being sure about the body I saw in the mirror. I never gave myself a chance to see whether I might be good at it.

This book is for that girl and all the girls who walk confidently, never letting anyone know where your weaknesses are. Go out and swim and sing and take chances.

Kristin Wright lives in Virginia with her husband, two teen-agers, and a beagle named Indiana Jones. She's a native of the Detroit area, a graduate of the University of Michigan Law School and has practiced law in many fields, including big firm litigation, criminal defense, personal injury, local government, and divorce and custody.

She has written many a chapter beside a pool at a swim team practice.

Find Kristin at www.kristinbwright.com

#HeresWhereSheMeetsPrinceCharming